E   E.L.B.   Elsie   F.F.C.

Bobby Bell

PARTNERS

One of Mrs. Hill's most touching romances is a story of a young girl and a young man who find each other after they have first found themselves. Dale Hathaway faced a dreary world when her job with Baker and Company, unpleasant though it was, came to an end. There was little to cheer her at Mrs. Beck's boarding house, but one snowy night after a discouraging day looking for a job, she was startled to awareness when the nice young newspaper man from upstairs knocked frantically on her door. What she saw in his arms was a tiny, half-frozen baby that he had stumbled over on the steps. Partners in the most moving of all enterprises, the saving of a tiny life, Dale Hathaway and George Rand shared many critical experiences, learning how the great truths of life could make for both of them a rich and glowing future. Mrs. Hill's new novel with its inspiring message for today will delight her many readers and add new ones to her audience.

PARTNERS

GRACE
LIVINGSTON
HILL

 This book, while produced under
wartime conditions, in full com-
pliance with government regulations for the conservation of paper
and other essential materials, is
COMPLETE AND UNABRIDGED

GROSSET & DUNLAP
PUBLISHERS   NEW YORK

By arrangement with J. B. Lippincott Company

PRINTED IN THE UNITED STATES OF AMERICA

PARTNERS

Chapter 1

DALE HATHAWAY FINISHED TYPING THE LAST page of the invoicing, snapped the paper out of her machine, and laid it on the top of the pile on her desk with a sigh of relief. She was dog-weary and had eaten nothing all day, hoping to be finished and get out to find a boarding place before dark. But a quick glance at the sombre window across the gloomy room showed her that dusk was already descending.

There had not been anything inviting in the house she had left that morning to tempt her to take even a bite. The woman who did the cleaning there yesterday must have eaten everything worth eating or carried it away with her when she left last night; and Dale, too anxious to get done the work yet remaining to her in the dismal old office, and hoping against hope to be finished before lunch time, had not bothered to stop at a restaurant before she got to the office. There had been a time around noon when she had felt dizzy faintness, but that had passed, and now there was left only weakness and an overwhelming apathy toward all food.

Dale with a sweeping motion gathered up the pages, counted over their numbers, clipped them together, gathered up a few other papers and walked down the hall to another door, tapped, and entered.

"These are the invoices, and all the other papers, Mr. Brower," she said with cool dignity. "And if that is all I'm going now."

The little dried up solemn man at the desk recalled his mind from his own business affairs, accepted the papers, looked them over, and then glanced at the girl, apparently identifying her with a matter that was only remotely within his scope. Then he bowed with due dignity.

"Very good," he said condescendingly. "And do I understand this completes the invoices for the time during which you served Mr. Baker as secretary?"

"Yes. Those are all the invoices with which I have had to do."

"And—did you tell me that you had been paid for the work you have done this week? Is everything clear between yourself and the estate of Baker and Company for which you have been working?"

"No, Mr. Brower," said Dale looking the suave little man bravely in the eyes. "I've had nothing since Mr. Baker was taken ill, three weeks ago yesterday."

"Ah! Yes, I recall now. And the agreement was— yes, here is the paper. You were to receive part of your salary in money and part in board. Is that right?"

"Yes, Mr. Brower."

"And you have been boarding with Mrs. Baker for the past three weeks?"

"I've been staying there nights, and helping about the house before office hours as much as I could during Mr. Baker's illness. Of course since his death Mrs. Baker has been away at the neighbors' most of the time, and the household even before that has been so much upset that the meals have been very irregular. A great deal of the time I have had either to get my own meals or go to a restaurant."

"I see!" Mr. Brower tapped with his long slim fingers on the top of his desk thoughtfully.

He opened a drawer and took out a small sheaf of papers, fluttered them through carefully, studying a paragraph here and there, then set down some neat figures and worried them with his sharp pointed pencil for a minute or two.

"Very well," he said coldly at last, "would seventy-five dollars satisfy you, to cover everything? You know the estate is not large and we want to give Mrs. Baker as much as possible now that she is alone with no one to depend upon. Would you consider seventy-five a fair price for all that you have done?"

Dale drew a sad little sigh.

"I had hoped it would be more than that," she said firmly. "You see there were two weeks when I first came during which I had *no* pay. It was understood that that was a sort of a deposit which would be returned to me if I left at any time. And I really have had to spend quite a little for food at different times when Mrs. Baker was away or ill, and gave me no time to get meals. I had hoped there would be at least a hundred and twenty-five dollars coming to me. I really need it. Mrs. Baker has children who can help her, and I have no one. And now I have no job. I don't know how long it will be before I can secure one. I don't want to beg for more than is due me, but I really feel I have earned more than I have suggested."

Mr. Brower drummed on the desk a little longer.

"Well," he said reluctantly, but with that same colorless tone to his voice, "of course we want you to be satisfied. I'm sorry I do not happen to know of another job for you just now, but we want to do the best we can for you. Suppose I write your check for one hundred dollars. Will that be entirely satisfactory? I really shouldn't feel justified in offering you more than that without consultation with the others who have charge of the estate. I could take it up with some of the family, of course. Possibly Mrs. Baker's son would know more about this matter. If you feel like settling the matter for a hundred dollars and giving me a receipt I can give you your check at once, but if I wait to consult the family there might be some delay. They might not even agree to the hundred dollars. I believe seventy-five was the amount they suggested——"

Great tears were gathering in Dale's eyes, but she

forced them back, and taking a deep breath said sadly:

"Well, I suppose I shall have to accept what you are willing to give me, for I really have immediate need for it, and it would be very hard for me if I had to wait."

The placid look of Mr. Brower's lips showed that he had won an easier victory than he had expected, and Dale almost regretted that she had given in so readily. Yet she dared not risk letting the matter lie over, for she had but a little over three dollars in her worn purse. She was desperately in need of more before she could hope to get settled in new quarters. So she watched her check being written out, and with a bitter feeling in her heart signed the receipt that the man handed over. She reflected as she did so how glad she had been to get that job after the years of hardship while her mother was so ill, and they were going from doctor to doctor seeking for healing, and finding none. And then what a desperate disappointment to have this job turn out so unpleasantly. For she had come to it in high hope of being able to make a little place for herself where she could earn her living. Coming through the recommendation of a dear friend of her dead father, it had been a bitter thing to find that the man for whom she was to work had no kindliness in his make-up, and that his wife was a selfish whining semi-invalid, who demanded service at home from her in addition to the work at her husband's office.

She had served her, yes, as far as she could, hoping constantly to be able to find some better job. But nothing had materialized, and everyone said the times were hard and there seemed to be nothing anywhere.

Having signed the receipt, and received her check, and a wish that she might soon find a good job, Dale Hathaway went down the three long flights of dusty stairs to the street, and started out on her own through the winter's dusk.

There was a place she knew where she could get a good substantial dinner for thirty cents. It was not a particularly attractive place, but they served good palatable food, and she must not spend more than that tonight, for she must find a room before she slept, and she must be sure to have enough to pay for it.

But when she was seated at the counter and the waitress brought the steaming dish of lamb stew that had been the only item on the menu that attracted her, she looked at it with a weary indifference. Somehow it seemed a task to have to eat that, hungry as she had been a little while before. She was so heartsick over the small amount of her check that it scarcely seemed worthwhile to eat. However, one had to eat to live; she couldn't just die at will because she was utterly discouraged. She had been better taught than that. She had grown up believing that God really cared for her, and that all things work together for good to them that love God.

"Of course that doesn't mean all things work out the way we would like them to be," she reflected as she took a casual bite of the stew, and found it didn't taste quite so much like old stewed dishrags as it smelled. "It means He is working out our lives so that His purpose for us shall be fulfilled."

But as she told it over to herself, the lesson that her mother had done her best to impress upon her, somehow the words seemed to have no meaning to her jaded mind. She was so weary and heartsick that even desirable things had lost their zest for her. Why had she ever dreamed that those old skinflints would pay her all they owed her? She had been a fool to stay with them all those awful months. She should have gone out and taken a chance of course, got some kind of a job and been free from them. The fact that she had no money ahead had held her too long a prisoner. In fact she shouldn't ever have agreed to work that first two weeks without being paid at once. Only she had been so much afraid that they would send her drifting if she demurred in any way. And she just couldn't be on her own in a great strange city!

Of course there had been Dinsmore Ramsay, the young man who had grown up working in her father's office, and who had been quite patronizingly

ready to marry her and take her over after her
mother's death. But she couldn't see herself marrying Dinsmore Ramsay, *ever,* even if he hadn't been
patronizing.

And there had been Arliss Webster, a man almost
twenty years older than herself, who had been pite-
ously eager to marry her and take her to a nice smug
house in the best part of the town where she had
grown up.

And there had been Sam Swayne, a nice boy with
whom she had gone to high school. All right in his
way, and smart. Was doing well in business too. He
had been very simple and honest in his proposal.

But she didn't want to marry any of them, and she
was glad she hadn't, even if she was in straits now.

She took another bite of the stew, and tried to
savor it more pleasantly. It wasn't so bad, and it did
feel comforting after it was swallowed. Just the heat
of it in her empty chilly stomach put new heart into
her. Gradually as she coaxed the unappetizing food
down, she began to revive, and to plan ahead. Perhaps if Mrs. Baker happened to be in the house she
would realize that she ought to give her something
extra for the many little personal things she had done
for her, especially during the last few days. That
would be nice. It wouldn't likely be more than five
or ten dollars of course, but even five or ten dollars
would help a little. Still Mrs. Baker wasn't given to
benevolence, and she would never feel that such a

thing would be a natural debt. Well, never mind. She ought to be thankful that she was done with the Bakers now. She had long wished to be out from there, and she should have gone before of course.

She ate a piece of apple pie because it came with the stew and rolls and coffee. There was an infinitesimal scrap of cheese with the pie, the only really tasty bite about the meal, and she dutifully swallowed everything. She could not afford to pay even thirty cents for a meal that she didn't eat. She would need the strength it gave, even if it wasn't appetizing.

Then she began to plan for the next few minutes. She would have to go back to the Baker home of course. Her bags were there, and her trunk, and she would have to say good-by to Mrs. Baker. But all that ought not to take long. She had packed everything before she left to come down to the office that morning. That is everything except her comb and brush and tooth brush and a few things she had left hanging in her closet. But that wouldn't take but a second, just to slip those in her overnight bag. If she only knew where she could get a room she could take a taxi and drive her things right to it, but getting a room she could afford would take time. If they had given her the hundred and twenty-five she would have ventured on that pleasant little room in the new apartment house. It was new and clean, and had a tiny radiator, besides elevator service. It was awfully small, and the price was higher than she ought to pay, but that extra twenty-five would have helped out on the first three or four weeks, and after that she would have time to look around and get something cheaper. Or, it might be she would be able by that time to land a really good job. And it would have been such a comfort to get into a clean new spot where her soul wouldn't have to shrink from everything she hadn't actually cleansed with her own hands. Just to get rested and calm. How blessed that would be!

Then she considered the possibility of being allowed to sleep in the Baker house that night and not start out to hunt a home until morning. Perhaps Mrs. Baker would at least grant that request, in case her conscience did not prompt her to pay her anything more. It was queer she hadn't suggested it. Perhaps she would want her to stay there a few days until the movers came to take her furniture.

Dale was quite accustomed to entering an empty house; during the last few days Mrs. Baker had been out most of the time, staying with the kind neighbors who had invited her.

She mounted the steps of the old brownstone house, the sixth in the row from the corner, and inserted her key into the lock, but even as she swung the door open, and fumbled for the switch of the hall light, the chill of great emptiness came out and smote her with startling keenness.

She stood still for an instant to get used to the strange sensation, and then she snapped on the light in the long hall and then the light for the front room, and stood there staring. The front room, designated by Mrs. Baker as "the parlor" was absolutely empty, and so was the hall. The old hall hatrack was gone, with its mirror and its skewy brass hooks with their three prongs. The parlor table was gone, and the old threadbare Brussels rug that never did quite reach to the dilapidated sofa whose internal works were always protruding. The four chairs of different denominations were gone, and the corner whatnot with its pink china shepherdess, its three pink lined shells with humps on their backs, its hideous red and blue and gilt vases, and the red glass one on top, with its plumes of pampas grass. They were all gone!

Gone was the old-fashioned combination bookcase and secretary that Mrs. Baker used to say belonged to her great grandfather; and all the musty old books that gloomed forth behind the grimy glass doors. Even the two faded photographs of deceased parents, framed in gilded pine cones, were gone. They used to swing on red worsted cords and when the wind blew in at the front window it would waft them around till they made a scratchy sound on the old ugly red wall paper that was faded to a dull magenta in spots. They were all gone, and the rooms were dusty and empty!

In sudden panic Dale started up the stairs.

What had become of her trunk and bags? Where were the few little things she had left hanging in her closet? Her good coat and hat to replace the little jacket and knitted cap she was wearing to her work? Surely, *surely* they wouldn't carry off her things? What would she do if they had? How in the world had the house been cleared of everything so quickly? When she left that morning Mrs. Baker told her that the moving van was not coming for at least two days, and she had planned to get her own things away before they came. What could have happened?

As she flew up the stairs, breathless, she caught a glimpse of the empty dining room, its golden oak table and sideboard, and chairs that were no longer golden, only dirty oak, were gone too, and through the open door into the kitchen she could see that there was nothing left there but the gas range which was built in. No pots and pans hanging about, no old chairs, no gingham apron hanging on the back door.

She dashed into her own room, and found it as empty as all the rest of the house.

"O-hh!" she gasped, and found there were tears falling down her cheeks. Oh, she just couldn't afford to lose *everything* she had! Surely, *surely* Mrs. Baker wouldn't do that to her! Her mother's and father's photographs! The bits of precious family heirlooms, not very valuable perhaps, but wondrously precious. Little things her mother had made for her that it would break her heart to lose!

"Oh, God!" she quavered aloud, "would you let them do that to me? Did I need that, somehow, to make me right for what you want of me?"

Then suddenly the doorbell pealed through the house, and startled her almost out of her senses. It seemed almost like an answering voice to her prayer. Yet God wouldn't ring the doorbell!

Trembling in every fiber she hurried down to answer the ring. Probably only some beggar, or someone selling dishcloths and shoe-strings, she thought.

But when she opened the door, her eyes wide with a kind of fear in them, she saw Mrs. Bartlett, the woman who lived in the house to the right of this one.

"Well, I thought I saw you come in, but I wasn't sure. You see, I've been watching for you more or less all the afternoon, ever since the truck went away. But you must have come while I was out in the kitchen looking at something I had baking in the oven. I guess you were surprised, weren't you, to find everything gone? Or did you know they were going today? Mrs. Baker was surprised herself. She was getting ready to go to Long Island today to say good-by to some old friends over there. But it was a lucky thing she hadn't got started. Her son drove over from Ohio and brought a moving van along with him. He said he could get one cheaper out near where he lives. And they went to work and got it packed up in no time. Then he took his mother in his own car and they went along, back of the truck."

"But—what did they do with *my* things?" asked Dale, wide-eyed, trouble in her voice. "I hadn't got everything packed yet. I meant to finish when I got back tonight, and then they kept me at the office so long today that I didn't even have time to eat until just now."

"Oh! I wondered!" said the unsympathetic voice of the neighbor. "I thought it wasn't very considerate of you not coming back to help poor Mrs. Baker off when she's done so much for you all these months. I don't see what right they had to keep you. You see, your not being here made a lot of trouble. The movers brought down all your things and got them in the van before Mrs. Baker thought to tell them that they weren't hers. They just carried your coat out, dragging the fur collar on the steps, and chucked it in the van. And it would have been there yet if I hadn't seen them carrying it across the sidewalk and dumping it in between the sideboard and table, like it was a cushion. I called right out to them that that was yours, and they brought it back, and then Mrs. Baker spoke to them, and made them bring your best hat back. I recognized it, of course, because I've seen you go out on Sunday wearing it. I guess we got everything. Poor Mrs. Baker wasn't able to go out and climb into the van to see, but I went myself, and I took all your things and brought them in my house to keep for you. Mrs. Baker had the man bring your trunk over too, and she said they only charged fifty cents, and you could pay me if you wanted to."

"Pay! For having my trunk taken into your house when I was coming in a little while to take it away myself in a taxi? That doesn't seem right, Mrs. Bartlett, does it? Mrs. Baker knew I had a key, I don't see why she didn't telephone me. I would have come right back and taken care of my own things."

"Why, the man came the first thing this morning and disconnected the telephone. She couldn't. You see it's the end of the month and she didn't want to pay for next month."

"Oh!" said Dale with a kind of hopeless tone in her voice. "Well, I guess I'd better come in and see if all my things are there. I certainly wouldn't like to lose any of them, and there are some of them that I prize very much."

"Oh, well, I guess you'll find them all there. I'm sure we haven't done anything to them. I certainly went out of my way to keep the mover from carrying them all off to Ohio. But perhaps I should have minded my own business. You never get any thanks when you go out of your way to oblige."

"Oh! I'm sorry, Mrs. Bartlett. I didn't mean to be ungrateful. I am sure I thank you very much for looking after my things. Only you see I was startled when I didn't find them where I left them."

With her chin up offendedly Mrs. Bartlett led the way over to her house and pointed to a chair in her front room on which reposed Dale's best hat with her winter coat dumped on the top of it in a heap, and a small overnight bag dropped on top of that. On another chair nearby was her good dress lying in wrinkles, with a collection of articles from her bureau in a pile atop.

"Oh!" she groaned softly, and then set swiftly to work getting things to rights.

"Well! Are they all there?" asked the offended Mrs. Bartlett.

Dale was just shaking the wrinkles out of her best dress, and brushing off the dust where the dress had trailed across the floor. She didn't answer at once.

"Is anything missing?" hissed the lady impatiently.

"Why, I don't know yet, Mrs. Bartlett. But of course you can't help it if there is. I'm just sorry I didn't know and get home in time to save you from taking so much trouble."

"Oh, I'm always glad to be helpful," said the woman defiantly.

Dale opened her suitcase and put in the garments she had just folded, then slipped the brushes and comb and other toilet articles in place in her overnight bag, every movement she made watched scrupulously by the overseer.

"I wonder—did you happen to see my umbrella, Mrs. Bartlett?" Dale cast a quick look about.

"No, I didn't see any umbrella," said the woman.

"Except Mrs. Baker's umbrella. She brought that over here when she stepped in to say good-by."

"Oh," said Dale with relief in her voice. "There it is, standing in your hall rack."

"*What?*" said Mrs. Bartlett suspiciously. "Why, no, you're mistaken! That's Mrs. Baker's umbrella! She must have stood it there for a minute when she went to shake hands. Now I remember, I saw her set it there!"

"No, Mrs. Bartlett, that's my umbrella. She must have brought it over for me."

The small eyes gleamed at her maliciously.

"That's not your umbrella!" snapped the woman. "It's Mrs. Baker's umbrella."

"Open it, Mrs. Bartlett. You'll find my name on the handle inside," said Dale calmly, taking a deep breath to keep her spirit in leash.

"I don't need to open it!" snapped Mrs. Bartlett. "I guess I know what I'm talking about, and you can't put anything like that over on me!"

Dale gave her a wide-eyed look of astonishment.

"I really don't understand you, Mrs. Bartlett, but if you don't care to open the umbrella I'll open it myself. It is just as well for you to see that I am telling the truth."

And then before the irate woman realized what she was doing, Dale unfurled the umbrella and raised it wide open, pointing to her name in clear round letters painted halfway up the rod.

"There!" she said, turning so that the woman could see it.

But Mrs. Bartlett suddenly screamed out.

"Put that umbrella down at once!" she yelled. "Don't you know it's terribly bad luck to open an umbrella in the house? Don't you know it's a sign somebody in that house will die before the year is up, if you open an umbrella in the house?"

Dale looked at her in amazement, and then burst into a ripple of laughter.

"How could a lifted umbrella in a house possibly have anything to do with death?" she asked, looking at Mrs. Bartlett with wonder.

"Put it *down*, I tell you!" screamed the woman. "Shut it this *instant!*" Mrs. Bartlett was fairly frantic. "Shut it *quick!* You've no right to come in here and bring death on my house!"

Dale closed the umbrella abruptly.

"But my dear, what in the world do you mean? I haven't brought anything on your house. How could an umbrella have anything to do with death?"

The woman was almost in tears from fright.

"I don't know!" she cried, wringing her hands, "but I know it's true! Everybody knows it. I've heard it ever since I was a little child. My uncle opened his wet umbrella and stood it to dry in the kitchen the day my Aunt Gabrielle died, and when my mother found it she shut it down quick, and she said, 'Oh,

John, what have you done! Now Gabrielle's going ta die!' She shut it down quick, but that night my Aunt Gabrielle *died!* And I've always known it. It's an old saying. You mustn't ever open an umbrella in the house, nor break a looking glass, because somebody's sure to die."

"Oh, Mrs. Bartlett!" said Dale aghast. "Why, that's nothing but superstition! None of that *could* be true. It's against reason! I've opened umbrellas plenty of times in the house, and we've had broken mirrors too."

"Well, *your* mother's dead, isn't she? And your father too, I suppose!"

"But Mrs. Bartlett, you don't suppose God has to wait till somebody opens an umbrella in the house, or breaks a looking glass, before He can send for one of His children to come home to Heaven, do you?"

"I don't know anything about that, but I think you're awfully presumptive to be so sure your parents were God's children, and got to *Heaven* when they died! I don't suppose they were any better than the general run of folks even if they were your parents. However, I wish you'd take your things and get out before you do any more damage in my house! Now I shan't have a bit of peace till this year is out! I'm glad it's so near Christmas. I shan't sleep a wink tonight thinking of that raised umbrella."

"I'm sorry, Mrs. Bartlett. I'll be going at once. Could you please tell me where my trunk is?"

"It's out there at the back end of the hall," said the indignant woman. "But I don't see how you're going to carry that! It took a man to carry it in. And you needn't go off and think you can come back again in a little while to get it, for *I'm* going out, and I don't know *when* I'm coming back. If my friend invites me to stay to dinner I may stay. I can't come running home just to wait on you! I've wasted half my day on you as it is, watching for you to come home."

"I'm sorry!" said Dale with gentle dignity. "Well, then, could I telephone for a taxi?"

"I s'pose you can!" said the woman grudgingly.

Dale turned to the telephone and called for a taxi at once, and then carefully laid a fifty cent piece and a nickel on the telephone table.

"There's the money for the trunk, and for the phone call," she said quietly. "Thank you. Now, I'll put these things in the trunk!"

She took out her little bunch of keys and they jingled as she walked into the back hall, her arms full of garments.

She put them all carefully into her trunk, including the jacket and cap she had been wearing, and then came back and put on her coat and hat from Mrs. Bartlett's big chair. By that time the taxi driver was outside.

"Good-by, Mrs. Bartlett," said Dale as she stepped to the door. "I'm sorry I've troubled you so much.

Thank you for what you've done for me!" and then she summoned the taxi driver to get her trunk, and gathering up her bags she followed him out to the cab, thankful in her heart to be out and away from it all.

But as she climbed into the taxi it came to her that she had nowhere to go, and the driver would want to know where to take her. What was she going to do next?

Chapter 2

"WHERE TO, LADY?" ASKED THE TAXI MAN, AS HE swung himself into his seat and turned back to get his direction.

"Just a minute," said Dale, frantically searching through her hand bag for a clipping she had taken from the paper that morning. There had been two or three likely advertisements. She would just have to go and try one or two of them. She gave the address of the first one that had attracted her, and wondered what it would be like. She knew very little about the streets of this great city in which she had been living for nearly eight months. The Bakers hadn't given her time to go anywhere except back and forth from their house to the office. Every spare minute had been occupied. They had certainly got their money's worth out of Dale Hathaway.

But when she drew up at the address given and noted the fine old brownstone fronts, and the neat appearance of the whole street, her heart sank. This would be a lovely neighborhood in which to live, but it would be far beyond her purse. She had set her limit and she must not go over it.

They tried several others, but found they had all been rented.

The last in the newspaper list was a sordid gloomy house in a dirty street, with hoards of children screaming on the doorsteps, and a drunken man leering at one corner.

"No!" said Dale. "No, I couldn't come here! It looks dreadful!"

She hadn't intended to speak aloud, nor to call the attention of her driver to her troubles, but she had spoken and he could not help hearing.

"No, lady, this ain't no place for the likes of yous! What ya huntin', lady? Mebbe I cud he'p ya. Is it a house yer wantin'?"

"Oh, no, just a room in a plain rooming house where it would be quiet and respectable, and not cost too much. That first house was wonderful but the price was away more than I could afford."

"Well, thur ain't sa many!" mused the driver, "but I might know of one. I took a party ta the station from back here in the twenty-three hundreds. Her room might do. It might be too small for ye, though, but it was only up one flight. I went up ta get her trunk, an' I give it the once-over as I passed out. It ain't so fancy, but I shouldn't think it would come so high as some others. I cud take ya ta see it, though o' course it might be rented by now. It was 'leven o'clock this mornin' when she left it."

"Oh," said Dale, "that sounds good. I'd like to see it. Is it a respectable neighborhood? I wouldn't want to go anywhere where I would be afraid to come home at night."

"Course ya wouldn't, lady. An' I ain't takin' ya ta any such a place as that. Sure, it's respectable. There's a church next door, an' that usually makes a neighborhood a little tastier, ya know. Right down this way. It ain't sa fur! I'll show ya!"

He turned the taxi down a quiet street. Rows and rows of what used to be fine old houses, in a neighborhood that wasn't fashionable now. It wasn't far from the business section. That would be all the more desirable for Dale.

But her heart sank as she got out and went in. Likely it would be too much. Oh, if it only would be a place where she could afford to stay! If she could just have her things brought in and lock her door and lie down and sleep a little while, before she had to get up and go on hunting for a job. She was so tired and bewildered!

As she went up the steps the door opened and a young man came out and hurried down the street. She wondered if he was a roomer there. He had a nice pleasant face, though preoccupied. He wasn't noticing her, and that made her feel more comfortable. She wouldn't like to be in a house where the people were unpleasantly friendly. However, in a rooming house one couldn't select all the fellow-

lodgers. Also it might be this man was only a sales-
man, or just stopping at the door on business. But he
looked sensible, and furnished a bit of background
to build a faint hope upon. If this only turned out to
be the right kind of a place!

But the room, when she had climbed the steep
stair, which was really the height of two flights,
wasn't so grand as she had hoped. It was at the back
of the house overlooking a dreary alley of ash bar-
rels, with a view of a multiplicity of untidy back
doors from the next street. However, what was a
view? A curtain would shut it out. And she would
mostly be asleep when she stayed in her room. A
more serious difficulty developed when she discovered that there was no radiator. But there was an
oil stove which the landlady declared "het up the
room real well" and "didn't smoke." She suggested
also that she wouldn't say anything if the young lady
wanted to make coffee "of a morning" on it. As the
price was within her means, that settled it. If she
could get her own breakfasts it would save quite a
little.

So she hurried down to her taxi driver and presently saw her steamer trunk traveling up on his stout
shoulder.

When the taxi had rattled away down the street,
Dale felt as if she had parted with her last friend. He
had been such a cheerful, friendly soul, and he really
had helped her out of a predicament. She looked

down at the soiled card he had left in her hand as he grinned farewell saying:

"Any time ya need me just call that number, an' I'll be comin' as fast as I can ta serve ya."

An investigating glance out the window showed that her cheap room was a recent addition built out over the back kitchen of an old house. Further inspection revealed no closet in the room, only a shelf with a calico curtain nailed around it, and some hooks driven into the wall upon which to hang her garments. The only light was a single electric bulb, bald and unshaded, hanging on a cord from the ceiling. Well, that didn't matter. She could easily manage a cheap little lamp shade.

There was no running water in the room, only a frail old-fashioned washstand with rods across the arms for towel racks. The landlady had pointed to the bathroom down the hall. There was a tin basin and water pitcher on the washstand. It was all more primitive than one would expect in a city house, but hence the cheapness, and she looked about the bleak place and tried to tell herself that she was fortunate to get it. There were two chairs, cane-seated, rather shackly, a cot bed, a small table known in former days as a "stand," and an old chest of drawers with a crazy mirror hanging over them. Dale looked into the mirror, shrugged her shoulders at the image of herself she saw there, laughed a weak little tired laugh and turned away. Well, at least she was placed somewhere in probable safety and comparative decency for the night. If she didn't like it by morning she would have a whole day to find some other place, even if she had to forfeit the small deposit she had made on the room.

Perhaps she had better go out and purchase a coffee pot before it got dark, and some coffee and bread, or something for her breakfast.

The entrance of a shiftless looking maid carrying a coal-oil stove that reeked of kerosene gave her pause until the stove was placed and lighted and she was inducted into its mysteries; for she never had met a kerosene stove before.

She asked the woman a few questions about the neighborhood, where she could purchase a coffee pot and a few eatables, and discovered that the maid was not a maid at all, only a cleaning woman who came in by the day as needed.

When the woman, who said her name was Ida, had departed, Dale locked her door and went out in search of what she needed. She discovered a restaurant about a block and a half away, although it didn't look inviting.

She came back with her coffee pot, bread, butter, some cereal, a tin box of crackers, half a dozen oranges, and a bottle of milk. She felt that she would rather get her own breakfasts than to be always going out for them.

She examined the bedding on the cot, found it

fairly clean, decided she would have to ask for more blankets if the weather grew any colder, drew out the shackly little stand and sat down to write a letter and looked about her in the dim light with some satisfaction that she was out of the Baker house at last. Perhaps some day she would be glad to get out of this house too, but tonight she was amazingly glad to have found it, and to be able after she had hung up a few of the things from her trunk, to get into her hard little bed and drop off to sleep, knowing that for this one time at least she needn't get up in the morning until she felt like it.

So at last she turned out the stranger-stove, which *did* smoke in spite of what the landlady had said, snapped off her light, and got into bed.

Yet tired as she was she found it wasn't so easy to fall asleep in this strange new room, in a hard shivery bed, with the odor of kerosene smoke lingering on the air. Even the sharp winter wind that came in from that back alley when the window was open did not clear the air.

It wasn't easy to forget the noises that were coming in continually from the street, voices, sometimes in strange languages, clamoring, occasional yells, drunken outcries, screaming babies, and neighborhood radios. What a world she had come to, and must stay in, until she could find a way to work herself into one that would be more pleasant!

Later on that night when she had just drifted off

into sleep she heard the front door open. Heard
footsteps up the stairs, other doors down the hall
opening and closing, a babel of voices calling good
night to one another. Heard some voices high and
shrill, and others thick, illucid. What kind of a home
had she found for herself? But she must stay here until she had found a real job. She *must,* if she *possibly*
could stand it.

Then there came the sound of a fire siren, and fire
engines clattering down the street, a red light showing through the window at the foot of her bed. She
recalled that the room was a wooden affair, but tried
to comfort herself with the fact that it wasn't any
higher than the second story, and so went off to sleep
again.

It was late when she woke in the morning, woke
with a sense that she was all wrong and would be re-
proved for being late. Then she came to herself and
realized that there was nobody just at present who
had a right to reprove her. She was free of the Bakers, free from the office, and out on her own. There
might be others soon, she hoped there would be, who
would have a right to find fault with her if she did
not do their work on time, but just this morning
there was no one, and her heart breathed a little
thankful sigh.

All the noises were going on outside, the sounds
from the other houses. All but the radios. They were
silent for the time being. But there were footsteps,

many, on the sidewalk. Loud conversation, dogs barking, hucksters calling. A noisy world! She would have to learn to detach her mind from all sound to hope for any rest in a place like this. Well, she would probably get used to it.

She got up and closed her window, lighted her wicked little stove and shivered through her morning dressing. By the time she was ready for her breakfast the worst of the chill was off the room, but there was the distinct smell of kerosene. Was that going to be the price of warmth? Perhaps if she stopped at a place where they sold such stoves she might find out the secret of how to take care of it. It wasn't an ideal heat, of course, but if there was a way to keep it from smoking, at least it was heat she could control and have when she needed it.

By the time she had finished her orange and cereal, and the cup of coffee she allowed herself, she felt a little more cheerful. She decided that as soon as she had cleared away her breakfast things and washed her dishes—a cup and saucer, plate and spoon from home that she treasured in her trunk—she would go out to walk. She wouldn't even pretend to hunt for a job, not till tomorrow. She wanted just one day free. Oh, of course if she saw a notice in a shop window, "Help Wanted" she might go in and enquire about it.

But just as she was ready to put on her hat and coat and go out the landlady tapped at the door and came in. She ensconced herself in the other chair and sat down to get acquainted with her new roomer. She introduced herself as Mrs. Beck, widow, and said she had run a rooming house for a good many years.

"You'll find this is a real pleasant neighborhood," she vouchsafed. "Got an undertaker's place just down across the street, and a church almost next door. They got a good bell in their steeple, and it sounds real cheerful-like on Sundays and holidays, unless you might wantta sleep late, an' then it ain't sa handy, till you get useta it. But it gives respectability ta the neighborhood, ya know, so I don't mind. Who sent ya here? How'd ya know I had a room vacant? I hadn't got around ta put up the vacancy sign in the winda yet."

Dale smiled.

"Why, nobody sent me exactly," she said. "I was out hunting up two or three places that were advertised, and I didn't like any of them, and then the taxi man told me he had taken a lady away from here to the station and maybe the room wasn't taken yet."

"Oh," said Mrs. Beck interestedly. "Ya never know how ya'll get advertised, do ya? A taxi man! Just ta think it! Well, I'm glad I didn't spend the money ta advertise again. That girl that left was going out west to her mother. I figured from what I saw of her that her ma didn't want her ta come here in the first place, and she didn't get on as well as she ex-

pected, so when her ma telegraphed her some money
she beat it home. But 'tisn't every girl has a mother
with money to telegraph. Well, I say a girl is fortunate if she has her mother. A girl has no friend like
her mother. I always say a girl's best friend is her
mother. Mine, she's dead a good many years ago, but
my grandmother's livin'. She's just like a mother ta
me. She really brought me up. That's why I keep her
here with me, though she's a good deal of trouble.
She's gettin' old, and has the rheumatiz something
awful. But other times she's real handy to tend the
door, when she ain't sa lame. Seen her yet? Most
of the roomers is real fond of her. They call her
'gramma.' But my! I often think, ef I'd had a mother
alive she'd a ben some use ta me now. She'd be
younger, ya know, and not sa crippled up as gramma.
But then, what can ya do? They will die, and mostly
it's just the handy ones that are taken off.''

Dale suppressed a desire to laugh and tried to say
"Yes?" with an accent that would sound like cordial
interest.

"Well, the reason I ast ya who sent ya here, I
thought mebbe it was one of our roomers. You
'quainted with any of the roomers?"

"No," said Dale. "I don't know this part of the
city very well."

"Well, we've got some real classy roomers," said
Mrs. Beck with satisfaction. "The three girls along
this hall are actresses. They're in the Follies now!

They're all good lookers, an' smart dressers. I've often took notice how people watch 'em when they come in the door. There's one called Lily that has real what they call ash-blond hair, and light blue eyes. She looks sweet when she has her make-up on. She dances, and one time when we had a Halloween party here she give us a sample of her tap dancing before she went over to the night club where she worked. The other two girls, Rosine and Arletta haven't quite sa much style, but they make up pretty. Not a man comes ta this house but he admires those three girls! He can't tell which he likes the best. All except the roomer on the third floor front. He don't pay any attention ta nobody, not any women. He's awful quiet, never stops ta have a little conversation, just goes on his way, busy all day long, and sometimes all night too. He's something on a newspaper. I haven't been able to find out just which one, nor what he is. Mebbe a reporter, though he ain't quite so flip as some o' them. I've had newspaper men before, and they're generally pretty flip. This man is named Rand. George Rand. He's so awful kind of dignified he isn't much of an ad for my house. The only thing is he's very prompt pay, and that's something. I like people that pay on time. You know I can't keep my house going if people don't pay me on time."

"Of course not," said Dale drearily.

"And by the way," said Mrs. Beck, "I was goin' ta

ask you if you were suited. You know you wanted to take it only for the night last night and try it out. Didn't you find it a nice comfortable place?" She smirked at Dale with a sickening glare, perhaps trying to intimidate her.

"Why, fairly so, Mrs. Beck," said Dale unenthusiastically. "There are a few things I shall want to talk to you about some time later in the day when I have had a chance to look about me and see what I shall need."

"Oh!" said Mrs. Beck malignantly. "What's wrong! People don't generally find fault with this room. Not at the price you're getting it for!"

"I'm not finding fault, Mrs. Beck. I'm merely trying to decide whether this is going to be the right place for me. For one thing I should need more blankets of course, especially with no heat but the oil stove. Also, it does smoke. But perhaps that can be remedied."

"Well, I don't understand that," said the woman indignantly. "Nobody has ever made a complaint about *that* before. But of course if you've done something to it, you'll have to have it repaired."

"I haven't done anything to it," said Dale quietly. "It may be that the wick needs a good cleaning and trimming. I guess it's up to you to have that done, as you are supposed to be furnishing heat by that means. A person who is working doesn't have time to do that sort of work too."

"Oh, we expect to keep the stove in order of course," said the landlady with a toss of her head. "By the way, where are you working? You've got a job, have you? I should think you would have been up early and gone to it."

"I'm just changing," said Dale with dignity.

"*H'm!* I've heard *that* tale before. What did you get fired for? I think I'd better ask you for references. I've always had respectable people in my house. I can't run the risk of losing such people as my newspaper man. Mr. Rand is particular about his fellow lodgers."

"It was not a question of being fired, Mrs. Beck! The man for whom I have been working for sometime died last week, and the business has been closed up. I am getting a new position, and it will depend upon which job I take, whether I shall want to stay in this part of the city or not."

"Oh, I see!" Mrs. Beck's voice was very cold and suspicious. "I don't know about taking on a lodger that has no means of paying me. I'm not a benevolent society. I think I shall have to have a week in advance. That's the way I always do with newcomers."

Dale considered that a moment.

"That will be quite all right with me, Mrs. Beck if I decide to stay," she said, and her voice was steady and firm. "I am going out for a little while and I'll be back sometime during the afternoon, perhaps very soon. Then I'll let you know my decision at once, and I'll be glad to pay a week in advance of course."

"Oh!" said the woman, somewhat mollified. "Well, of course that'll be all right then, and if you pay that way I think I can find another blanket for you, and a new wick for the stove. Was you going to look for a special job somewhere?" she asked curiously. "Because if you aren't maybe I could suggest one. The girls told me about it last night. It's in the Follies. They need a couple more girls in the chorus, an' they pay real well. You're right pretty, an' you look athaletic. I wouldn't doubt but they'd be glad to get you. When you're made up I think you'll look swell! If you'd like to try for it I might call up Lily and ask her to be on the lookout for you, and introduce you to her manager. I'm sure she'd do that. She's an awful kind-hearted girl."

"Thank you, Mrs. Beck, but that kind of work would be out of my line. It's very kind of you to suggest it, but I just wouldn't be interested."

"Oh! What is your line?"

The woman's eyes were curiously, superciliously upon her.

"Why, I've been a private secretary, typing, book keeping, that sort of thing," said Dale pleasantly.

"H'm!" said the woman contemptuously. "There isn't much money in a thing like that. A lotta hard work, and no pay!"

"It's what I'm fitted for," Dale said decidedly. "And now," she glanced at her watch, "I have one or two things in mind that I must attend to this morning, so if you will excuse me I'll see you later in the afternoon and tell you definitely yes or no."

Mrs. Beck arose with heightened color. Was she going to lose this lodger? One who had come right out of the blue as it were, through the instrumentality of a mere taxi driver?

"Well," she said uncertainly, glancing around the room, "I'll be here most of the afternoon. And if you decide to stay I think I can let you have a pair of blankets, nice new ones that haven't been used scarcely at all. And perhaps you'd like a shade on your light. I don't know but I've got a white glass globe you could use."

"Thank you," said Dale, "that would be nice. But there's one thing I would like to have, and that is a firm table. I do a good deal of writing sometimes, and that table over there is very shaky, so if you can find a firmer one it would help."

"I'll look around and see what I can find that I can spare you," promised Mrs. Beck as she sailed away.

Dale put on her hat and coat and hurried away. It was good to get out into the sunshine and breathe the air again. When she reached the corner she looked back on her house. It was respectable on the outside, and bearable on the inside, and of course cheap. She must not dare to get dissatisfied with it until she had an assured job.

Now, the first thing she must do was to go and put her hundred dollars in the bank, and draw out enough of it to pay Mrs. Beck as soon as she got back. *If* she went back. Of course if a miracle should happen, and she should land a marvelous job she would just go and take that room with the tiny kitchenette that she had read about in one of the advertisements. But that was wholly unlikely. Miracles did not happen for such as she. She wondered why. They used to happen sometimes for her mother. But mother was a wonderful woman, a saintly woman, who lived so near to God that He was always real to her, and she was sure of His love. Would she ever get to be like that, perhaps, when she grew old? Did God grow on people, she wondered, or did they have to do something about it themselves?

Fortunately her connection with the Baker office had made her known at the bank where they had done business, and so when she carried her check from the Baker estate and deposited it she had no trouble in cashing a small check, enough to carry her through the next week at least. But as she received the cash and turned to put it away in her handbag, it came to her what a hole even a very little check made in her hundred dollars. She fairly trembled as she walked out of the bank. In how very short a time her hundred dollars would melt away and leave her nothing, unless she could get a job that would bring her in at least a little every week.

Suddenly instead of opening the door she turned back to the teller who had been waiting upon her and smiled at him wistfully.

"I wonder if you would know where would be the best place for me to go to apply for a new job?" She asked it shyly. "I've been so busy helping the Baker people get settled up that I haven't had any time to go out and hunt a new job, and I'm sort of a stranger in the city. I just don't know what to do first."

The teller shook his head.

"I'm sorry," he said, "I don't know of any place open just now. There are agencies of course, but I really don't know which is most likely. Everybody of course is hunting jobs. Couldn't you get some of the Baker family to recommend you to someone?"

"No, they're gone to Ohio, all of them. The lawyer of course wouldn't know me, except as I've done some of the typing for the settlement. And he said he knew of nothing. I thought perhaps you would know a likely place for me to start hunting."

"Well, I don't, not just now. Over at the city hall they might have odd jobs of typing. You're a stenographer? Well, copying might help while you're hunting a real job. Have you a typewriter?"

"Yes, an old one. I hadn't thought of getting copying to take home."

"Well, try it, and in three or four days, that is, when you happen to be back this way, drop in, and if I've heard of anything I'll tell you. What's your address?"

Dale hesitated, then gave the Beck address. She could leave a forwarding address in case she moved.

She thanked the teller and went out. Then she bought a paper, and sat down in a park to look through the advertisements. Not much that was intriguing, but still she'd better try them all.

So she started on her weary pilgrim way, forgetting entirely that she had promised herself a whole day of rest before she began to hunt a job.

Wearily she plodded on from one advertised "Want" to another, until she had covered all that had sounded in the least hopeful.

Some of the most interesting wants had already been filled when she got there and she would turn sadly away and go on to the next.

She was thoroughly discouraged when the day was at an end and she had found no trace of anything hopeful. And then she remembered that she hadn't intended hunting today anyway.

She sat down on a park bench in the dusk and shivered. The sky was still luminous with a hint of sunset, but darkness was creeping fast into the shadows near the earth, and when she looked up again there was a single star smiling out from the night sky gaily and winking at her till she almost felt like smiling back.

With her eyes on the star she continued looking up.

"Oh God," she said in her heart, but looking at
the star as if she could almost see the Most High up
there in that point of brightness. "Mother used to
believe You cared. She used to tell me You loved me,
and that when she was gone You would care for me.
I suppose I believe that. Yes, I think I do. But oh,
God, I'm so tired and so discouraged, and so alone!
If that's true won't You do something for me just to
make me realize that it's true! If You'd only send me
a little more money. Oh, if You'd only send me a
place to work, and someone to be friendly with. Dear
Father in Heaven, won't You comfort me?" And two
great tears stole out and rolled down her cheeks in
the dusk.

There were people going by her, hurrying home
to warmth and light and pleasant loving voices, nice
suppers. But they were happy, going home, and she
had no home to go to.

"Dear God, if You really love me as mother said,
won't You send me some sign, just a little money
from somewhere, even if it's only a little bit, or some
kind of a job, even a very humble job, or *some*body
to be a friend, so I won't feel so very lonely? Just so I
know You have heard me and are taking account
of me?"

After a little she got up and went to a cheap res-

taurant for a very cheap dinner. She mustn't spend
what she had in a hurry. But as she went she kept
breathing softly under her breath: "Dear God, I'm
trusting You to take care of me. I can't feel it's true,
but I'm going to trust You, and I want to try to do
what You want me to do."

That night she went to bed at once when she got
back to the house. She would have paid her landlady
for the week in advance but Mrs. Beck had gone to
the movies, and "gramma" had the door locked, and
didn't want to get up to unlock it, so Dale went to
bed too, and went sound asleep before the roomers
got back from their various evening occupations.
Her mind for the time being at least had found a
place to rest.

Chapter 3

WHEN DALE AWOKE IN THE MORNING SHE HAD forgotten all about her prayer, and half wondered at herself that she seemed to have lost that sense of heaviness and worry. Things were just as they were the night before, and she supposed she ought to fret and try to think a way out of her difficulties, but somehow the day seemed more hopeful than any day yet, and there wasn't any reason for it to be so either. Not a reason that seemed sensible.

She got up, put on her cereal to cook, and made the coffee. Her breakfast tasted good to her.

When she had finished she cleared away everything, and then hurried down to pay her landlady and prevent another visit from her if possible.

Mrs. Beck was honey itself when she saw the money, and produced a pair of blankets that looked as if they hadn't seen really very hard wear yet. Though Dale resolved that she would hang them out the window after dark and let them get a good airing before she used them. Mrs. Beck tried to make Dale sit down and have a little chat, did her best to find out where she had been hunting for a job and whether she had succeeded in getting one yet, but Dale only lingered by the door a minute and evaded her questions very cleverly.

"I must hurry," she said, "I have things to do this morning. And Mrs. Beck, that stove still smokes. Did you do anything about it yet?"

"Well, no," said Mrs. Beck, "I hadta go out last night, but I'll see to it right away this morning."

But Dale had got only halfway up the stairs before she heard the telephone ring in Mrs. Beck's part of the house, and just a moment later came Mrs. Beck's voice calling:

"Miss Hathaway, oh, Miss Hathaway! Somebody wants ya on the phone! I think he's in a hurry!"

Breathless, Dale turned and sped downstairs. What could that mean? Who could possibly be calling her? There wasn't anyone in the city who would be likely to call her, and no one in her old home that knew where she was! It was very strange. It was almost as if God Himself was calling her in answer to her queer little prayer of the night before. Her hand trembled as she took up the receiver, and her voice was shaky as she answered: "Yes?"

The telephone was in the middle room. Mrs. Beck was lingering close to the kitchen door, her ear to the crack, listening, and "gramma" was in the front room with her ear to another crack, and one eye also. They had taken the precaution to open the door half an inch before Dale got down there, and they were pretty well versed in translating the rumble of the phone into real words when their roomers were called to the telephone.

"This is John Ward, teller in the First National Bank," said the voice on the wire.

"Yes, Mr. Ward?" said Dale, and guarded the sudden enthusiasm in her voice so that it sounded almost matter-of-fact.

"Well, if you aren't satisfied yet I think I have heard of something you might like. Are you going to be down this way this morning?"

"Yes, Mr. Ward, I am."

"Could you make it about eleven?"

"Yes, Mr. Ward, I'll be there. It's very kind of you to let me know."

"That's all right, Miss Hathaway. I hope it proves to be what you want."

The soft click announced the end of the conversation, and the two listeners turned away disappointed.

Mrs. Beck was on hand in the hall as Dale hurried away.

"Thank you, Mrs. Beck," she said as she fairly flew up the stairs.

"Oh, that's all right," said Mrs. Beck raising her voice to suit the tempo of Dale's footsteps, "I hope it wasn't any unpleasant message?" she added hopefully.

"Oh, no, just a matter of business," said Dale, and

closed her door on the disappointed voice.

Five minutes later Dale hurried downstairs and out the door, and both Beck ladies hurried to the front room windows and took account of her apparel.

"She's got on another dress and hat," said Mrs. Beck. "It isn't the one she wore when she came here."

"Oh, yes, it is," said the old grandmother. "You can't fool me. I don't suppose she's got more than one hat anyway. She didn't show any hat boxes or any signs of another hat when she come. I was watching behind the curtain, and I know."

"Well, anyhow, she's all spruced up. She looks ta me as if she's going out fer a new job. I hope she gets it. She's a right nice looker. I shouldn't liketa havta turn her away, not as hard as jobs is ta find taday."

"Well, you can't afford to keep folks that don't pay, Molly."

"No, I know I can't," sighed the woman. "But she is right nice lookin'. Seems like she was what they call sophisticated, an' that allus gives tone to a house. It brings a good class of roomers."

"Yes," said the old lady in a tone that could whine as easily as not on the very slightest provocation.

Dale walked briskly into the sunshine of the morning and recalled the tone of the teller's voice as he spoke to her. He hadn't said much but somehow it cheered her. And a sudden thought came to her. Was

it possible that God had done this? Was He trying
to show her that He really cared? Oh, if this should
turn out to be something good she would always be
sure that God had heard and God really cared, and
that He had spoken to her through this. But she
mustn't think too much about it yet. It might turn
out to be something impossible.

So she entered the bank with a gentle poise about
her that made a nice impression on the business man
who stood at one side waiting for her.

It wasn't a permanent job. The man wanted someone to fill the place of his own private secretary who
had been taken ill and must go away for a rest for an
indefinite time, several weeks, or even months. He
could not tell how long he would need her. But he
would be glad to recommend her afterwards to someone else if she had done her work well. It was on the
whole a better thing than she could have hoped for.
The pay was not large but it was enough to meet her
expenses, and perhaps she could save a little if she
tried. And she might begin at once!

She went to her new job walking as if on winged
feet.

The work was not difficult because of her experience in the Baker office, and moreover this new job
was better organized. The office and filing cabinets
and other arrangements were much more complete
and convenient. She sat down to her work with great
relief and joy, and now and again it would come to

her that God really cared.

Late in the afternoon Mr. Ward, the teller from the bank, called on the telephone asking her to stop at the bank on her way home and get a letter that had been sent in the care of the bank.

Wondering greatly Dale went around by way of the bank and found Mr. Ward waiting for her at the door to hand her the letter. She stopped in the little park to read it.

It was from a firm of lawyers in the far west, and it appeared that a half brother of Dale's father who had died a few years ago had at the time of her birth put a small sum of money at interest in her name, and from time to time had added small sums. It was to be handed over to her when she came of age. They knew that her twenty-first birthday would occur very soon, and they were anxious to get in touch with her now that they might put it in her charge as soon as the day came. Her old home address of course had not reached her, and when they wrote to the Baker address their letter had been returned.

This was the first realization Dale had that she was practically isolated in the world, with not even any old acquaintances knowing her address. She must write to the old home town post office and give them her present address, that is, as soon as she was sure she was going to stay here.

The lawyers had had no little trouble in discovering what had become of her, until they had been able to find out what bank the Bakers had dealt with, and so now they were asking Dale to send them identification papers from someone in that bank who knew her.

Breathlessly she gathered up her papers. Why, here was another answer to her prayers of the night before! Money! Of course it might not be much, but she had not asked for much. But if this half uncle had only put in ten dollars every year it would be over a hundred dollars now, with the interest, and that would be wonderful. If she had even that much to fall back on it would ease her mind greatly.

But more wonderful than the material good was the assurance in her soul that God had really heard her sorrowful weary plea and that He *did care*. With that belief an established fact she could go forward and trust.

Or would the job have come anyway whether she prayed or not? As if her little prayer could have brought the job! Or the letter about a little money! That was what reason clamored into her ears as she started down the street to her rooming house.

But no, there was a new understanding between her heart and God now. Perhaps God had indeed been meaning to do these things for her, even before she prayed, but by answering her definitely this way He had established a contact with her soul to make her sure that He was thinking of her! That was it. Maybe He really wanted her fellowship, really cared

what an unknown, unloved young girl felt about
Him! Oh, that was a *wonderful* idea! God caring
about her, wanting to be her Friend!

And now, there was only one other thing she had
asked for, a friend! Just someone to speak to, and
smile to across the hard days. But, maybe that would
come later!

As she passed a fruit store she remembered that
she would soon be almost out of oranges and there
were some lovely ones that seemed to be cheap. She
would celebrate by getting a whole dozen. She had
to work hard now, and must be well fed to keep herself in good condition to do her best.

So she bought her oranges and started on, a happy
smile on her face. Life wasn't going to be so terrible
after all if God was caring, and little nice things
could happen to her.

But the oranges were heavy and the package was
awkward to carry. The bag seemed to be made of
very flimsy paper. Twice the package almost slipped
from her arms, and she had to walk steadily to keep
the oranges from brimming over the top and careen-
ing along the sidewalk. Well it was only a half a
block more! She would soon be there!

She eased one weary arm as she reached the steps,
and the top edge of the bag ripped down five inches.
Oh! She paused, and tried to readjust the package.
Someone was coming out of the house, but she could
not look up. She had to walk very carefully lest that

bag would give way and send her oranges all abroad. Then suddenly like a petulant child who wasn't getting its own way the bag tore relentlessly in three or four places and ripped half way down one side. The oranges went catapulting out, bouncing on the steps and everywhere; one rolled out and down across the sidewalk to the gutter!

In horror she clutched the rest of them in one arm, and tried to reach for a couple that were on the step just before her, for that someone, whoever it was, was coming down the steps. A man. She must clear them out of his way!

But then the rest of the oranges like naughty children who had got the upper hand, leaped out and went abroad in every direction, and Dale was left clutching a limp empty paper bag and looking foolishly up at the young man above her.

It was the young man who occupied the third story front, the one Mrs. Beck had called George Rand, and he had a nice grin on his face. His eyes were kind.

"Hold everything!" he cried, and stooping over began to pick up oranges and stow them in the newspaper he had been carrying under his arm, spreading it handily on the second step.

"Oh! Thank you!" said Dale breathlessly, "but please don't trouble. It was my awkwardness."

"Oh, no!" said the young man with more grin. "It was the thinness of the paper bag. Too bad! I'm afraid some of these will need a bath after this," and he turned and picked two out of the gutter.

She reached to take them from him but he evaded her.

"Oh no," he said pleasantly. "I'm carrying them up for you. You can't be trusted with them, they're too wet and dirty. Besides they are full of mischief and will run away at the slightest provocation. Lead the way, will you?"

"Oh, that's very kind of you," said Dale, "but really that's not necessary. Just lend me your newspaper till I dump them in my room and I'll bring it right down to you."

"Don't worry about the paper," he said, "I was through with it anyway. But I'm carrying these oranges home, see? I claim it as my right."

He held the door open for her, smiling, with a determined expression on his pleasant lips, and there was nothing for her to do but walk in.

She made a decided stand on the top landing, but he only stepped up beside her, slipped one hand under her elbow to help her, and her pale cheeks flushed rosily.

Downstairs she was suddenly aware of the front room door opening a crack, and a watching eye applied to the crack, so she hastened her steps and arrived a bit breathless at her own door, making as if to take the oranges, but he still held them.

"Open your door," he said. "They'll go all abroad again if you don't."

She was glad to remember that she had left everything in perfect order. But he wasn't looking at the room. He stooped and laid the paper of oranges down on the little table beside her pile of paper and envelopes, and then backing out he lifted his hat, smiled again, and said:

"I guess they can't get away again now, but mind you wash them before you eat them! I wouldn't trust the germs around this street!"

And then he was gone, evading utterly the eager thanks with which her voice endeavored to follow him.

A moment later she heard slow footsteps coming determinedly up the stairs. Mrs. Beck was on her way to inspection.

Dale hurriedly slipped the paper, oranges and all, under the curtain of her wardrobe corner and was washing her hands composedly when the tap came at her door. She waited to wipe her face and hands before she went to open it, and to give just a brush to her soft hair, trying to gather her composure. How terrible it was going to be to have an espionage like this over her!

"Yes?" she said pleasantly, as she opened the door part way. "Did you want something, Mrs. Beck? I was just freshening up a little after my day in town."

But Mrs. Beck did not take the hint that Dale was not anxious to receive callers just then, and her glance was searching hurriedly through the room as she stood firmly waiting to be invited in.

A kind of cunning came into the hard eyes as she faced her young roomer.

"Oh, I won't hinder you. I'll just set down and talk a little while you dress. How d'you make out?"

Mrs. Beck took firm hold of the door and opened it enough to admit her skinny frame, entered and sat down on the nearest chair, her eyes searching every corner of the room again to find out where the oranges were that had required the assistance of the third-story-front unapproachable young man.

"Make out?" said Dale sinking wearily into the other chair, but she made no move to go on with her dressing. "Make out with what, Mrs. Beck?"

"Why, get on with the man you went to meet? The man that telephoned you?"

"Oh," smiled Dale, "that was only a business appointment." She spoke lightly. "Thank you for calling me. I'm sorry you had the trouble."

The woman looked at her vexedly.

"Yes, but how'd ya make out?"

"Make out? Oh, I got there in time, thank you, and got the information I needed. It was all right."

"Oh, was that all!" said Mrs. Beck disappointedly. "I thought perhaps you had found a good job. A good paying job, ya know. That's what I'm always interested in. Ya know I don't run this house for benevolence, and this is a good room. I can always find a tenant for this at more than you are payin' me."

"Well, now that's kind of you to take an interest in me, Mrs. Beck. But if at any time you find a tenant that you think would be a better prospect than I am be sure you come right and tell me. I wouldn't want to stand in the way of your getting a good paying tenant who can give more than I can."

"Oh, I wasn't hintin' that I want ya to get out," said Mrs. Beck retracting her severe manner somewhat. "Of course I haven't known ya very long, and I don't know so much about ya. I just wanted to make sure that ya are going to be able ta go along all right."

"Yes?" said Dale, with a flavor of the question "Oh, yeah?" in her tone. Then she smiled. "Of course I know you have to look out for your roomers, Mrs. Beck. But don't worry about me. I'm all right for the present, and if there comes a time when I think I can't pay my rent I'll be sure to let you know in plenty of time. And thank you for the table. It's going to be quite convenient I know."

"Well, of course I like to do all I can for my roomers," said Mrs. Beck. "It was one that I always used in my own room, but I don't mind makin' a few sacrifices for folks that pays on time."

Dale considered this and decided to accept the

sacrifice without any words about it, and the pause gave space for Mrs. Beck to come to the real point of her visit.

"Didn't I see Mr. Rand comin' back up the stairs with ya? I thought I'd find him up in his room, but I listened and he don't seem to be there."

"Oh, was that Mr. Rand? I didn't know," said Dale indifferently. "He was coming out just as I was coming in, and I was having a little trouble with some of my packages. The bag broke on some fruit I was carrying, and he very kindly helped me to gather it up, and insisted on carrying it the rest of the way up. But I think he went right down again. I didn't notice. I came into my room. It was very kind of him."

"Then you'd met him?"

"Met him? Oh, no. I didn't even know who he was. But he certainly was very polite."

"Well, I've noticed you girls all have your clever tricks of gettin' acquainted," said Mrs. Beck with an unpleasant grin that sat unkindly upon her shrewd bony countenance.

An angry flash came into Dale's eyes, but she turned away and lifted her chin haughtily.

"There's going to be a gorgeous sunset," she said irrelevantly. "I'm wondering if that stove is going to be enough to keep this room comfortable when really cold weather begins."

Mrs. Beck bristled at once.

"Nobody's ever complained that this room wasn't comfortable, even in really zero weather," she said sharply.

"Oh, is that so? That sounds hopeful. I shouldn't wonder if we're due for some pretty cold weather the next few weeks. The sky tonight, though it's beautiful, looks almost threatening. I wouldn't be surprised to see snow before morning."

"Oh, no," said Mrs. Beck decidedly. "No snow this month. We always have such lovely falls in this region. Say, why don't ya go down and visit those girls along your hall? They was speakin' of you this mornin'. Lily said they was havin' a good game of cards down in the parlor and she said they wouldn't feel bad if you wanted ta get in on it. You can consider that an invitation. I know they'll be glad ta see ya."

"Well, thank you. That is kind of them, but you see I have some work that I must do tonight. And besides I don't play cards. I'm afraid I wouldn't be very welcome even if they did invite me."

"Oh, they'd teach ya. They've taught several young men. I know ya'd have a good time. They always go out for a beer, or ice cream or somethin' at the end. Dutch treat, ya know. They're an awful jolly lot, and I'm sure ya'd fit in with 'em real good if ya'd only come and try it."

"Well, I do appreciate their interest, Mrs. Beck, but I really haven't time for such things, and I'm sure you would find I didn't fit. You see I'm a very busy person, and can't take time for play very often. Not that kind of play. I have a great deal of reading I want to do, and I must get to sleep early. Please tell them thank you for me, and say I can't spare the time."

"Well, ya're makin' a great mistake, that's all I've got ta say," said Mrs. Beck with a sniff. "It don't pay to be all work an' no play. Ya'd oughtta learn ta play cards, and drink beer, and be a jolly good fella. Ya can't expect to get jobs and keep 'em if ya can't get on with other girls in your class and age. It ain't natural."

"Well, I'm sorry, Mrs. Beck, but I guess it's up to me to plan my own life. There are certain things I know I must do, and I haven't time for the others."

"Well, don't blame me if ya break down an' get sick, an' hafta be took off ta the hospital."

"Oh, no, Mrs. Beck. I won't blame you!" laughed Dale, as Mrs. Beck arose haughtily and left the room, slamming the roomer's door just the least little bit.

But then almost immediately she opened it again a narrow crack and added:

"An' don't flatter yerself that yer gonna curry favor with that stuck up newspaper man, breakin' yer fruit bags all over the place till he has ta take pity on ya and carry 'em up fer ya! That don't mean a thing with him. He don't take ta no ladies at all. He's all fer hisself an' no mistake!"

This time the door was shut finally and firmly, and presently Dale ventured to lock it, and sit down for a good hearty laugh.

Chapter 4

THE NEW JOB WENT WELL, AND DALE WAS CONtented in it. Only that from the first it was evident that the former secretary was the real one who owned that job, and Dale was considered only a substitute. For Miss Alice Carhart was beloved by all, and everything that was done was done on the pattern that "Miss Alice" had left behind her. Dale had no quarrel with her ways, for they seemed to be excellent ones in every line. But the constant feeling that everyone was waiting for Miss Alice to return, and she was nothing here, and never would be, made her lose heart sometimes. There was no incentive to work, feeling that the day might very soon come when she would again be without a job.

Oh, they were kind to her at the office, always ready to help if her work was heavy, always cheerful and smiling. But she felt an outsider, and it seemed to be kept continually before her mind that she was nothing else.

Sometimes she would try to tell herself that perhaps this would go on longer than they all seemed to think. Only that would mean that the other girl

Alice would be disappointed in not getting her strength back as soon as she had hoped, and Dale didn't want disappointment for any girl. This other girl needed it as much as she did probably, and had evidently worked for her promotions and this place in the office as hard as ever she was willing to work. She was not jealous, and would not for anything take aught away from another. Only she wanted so much to have a place of her own, where she was wanted and needed.

So when she would come to this time of an evening, and lie in the dim light of the oil stove trying to get the better of her loneliness her heart would almost break. There was only the sound of the hilarious laughter from downstairs where they were playing cards, or where the radio was rolling out a lot of jazz music.

Then she would get up, turn on her light, now shrouded under a soft pretty shade, and sit down with her Bible for a little while.

It wasn't often she gave way to discouragement, because as the days went by she grew more and more interested in her work, and, whether it was counting for her personal advancement or not, she liked to do it well. She liked to feel that each day's work had been done for the Lord Christ, for He was growing more and more a clear Presence in her life, to Whom she was accountable, and to Whom she turned for approval.

And she was not without approval from those for whom she worked. They recognized her worth, and often gave commendation, which made a warm pleasant feeling around her heart.

There were a few other girls in the office who were uniformly friendly, and three or four young men, but they all had their own little circles and Dale was not one to push herself in. So for the most part she went her own way alone, and had a feeling that the world was a very large lonely place.

She hadn't even found a church in which she felt at home, though she knew that was largely her own fault. Those she had encountered had either been too far away for regular attendance, or had been so formal and almost worldly in their tone, that they did not draw her. Also she was very tired on Sunday, and sometimes slept late, too late to go a distance, and she knew she must not spend money in carfare. She must save every penny possible, and be ready for a long and perhaps a desperate time in the middle of winter without a job.

If she could have had a tiny radio it would have helped her greatly, but there again she was stopped by the cost of buying one. Even books from the library and magazines must be seldom indulged in. Her work was close and strenuous, and she must save her eyes. Some of the other girls were wearing glasses, and they talked in the office now and then of the cost of having eyes examined. She must just take care of her eyes and prevent the need of glasses.

Dale had met the three girls of whom Mrs. Beck discoursed so frequently, and they had mutually disliked and scorned each other and kept apart.

But she had not met the young man again who had helped her pick up her oranges, except briefly as they passed one another in the hall and nodded good morning. For mindful of Mrs. Beck's insinuations Dale had been most careful not to be around when she knew he would be likely to be there. She wanted that fine old gossip to have as little to hang her gossip on as possible. She wanted her to see that she was not the kind of girl who would go out and tear open a bag of oranges at the feet of a desirable young man in order to get acquainted. Why she cared what Mrs. Beck thought of her, she didn't know, but she kept out of sight as much as possible. And considering the fact that George Rand was a most reticent young man himself, it was not strange that they had not met often, and that the vision of his pleasant grin gradually faded from Dale's thoughts.

Also George Rand was away a good deal, covering conventions of importance, political and otherwise, for his paper. Sometimes he was sent far west, and again to New York, and then to Chicago or Texas. Sometimes down to Washington for a day or a week. Always he came back to his third story front room between each migration, but often it was late at night when he returned, and he would be away again early in the morning. At last even Mrs. Beck ceased to speak of him to Dale, as if he were of no particular moment to her. She had about decided that Dale was hopelessly uninteresting. She couldn't fathom her at all. Why did a girl want to be like that? Why didn't she want to have good times with other girls? Why didn't she make herself up a little, and get a "boy friend"? Dale seemed to her almost as grown up and far away from ordinary living as a middle-aged business man, and yet she was a pretty girl if she only would fix herself up.

But whenever Dale did think of the young man whom she had met so pleasantly that one time, she found she was glad he belonged in the house. He seemed a bit of respectable atmosphere, in the midst of so much that was impossible.

And then one day there began to be talk of the return of "Miss Alice." She was better, it appeared, and longing to get back to her work.

It was the young foreman from the printing department who told Dale.

"They say Miss Alice is coming back before Christmas," he said cheerily, and Dale felt as if he had struck her across the heart. Did that then mean she was out of a job?

She scarcely slept that night for thinking of it. True the manager had promised to let her know in due time, and had said he would do his best to get something else for her, but she had been working for other people long enough to realize that they did not always remember what they had promised to do, or often were unable to do what they wished. It would therefore likely be entirely up to her to find a new job, and so she set to work making quiet enquiries. She couldn't leave, of course, until the former secretary returned, but if she had something definite to go to it would make the way much easier.

She thought about going to the manager to find out if the report was true about Miss Alice, but she decided against it. It was better to go on doing the best that she could, just hoping that a place would be made for her somewhere. But she cut short each lunch hour and systematically set to work to discover any vacant places near by. None however were forthcoming that she felt were right for her, and the days which had been fairly bright and interesting now went slowly dragging under a heavy burden of worry. And now, more and more the rumors kept coming. Different ones of her fellow laborers had received letters from Miss Alice rather confirming the report the young foreman had told her. And one night when she had come home after a fruitless search and cast herself down on her bed letting the tears have their way, it came to her that this was no way to trust God. She had told Him she would trust Him and let Him have His way with her, even if it seemed for a time as if she would starve. Well, she was a long way from starving yet. She still had money enough to pay for her room for few weeks yet, enough if she was very careful to feed her also the same length of time. And of course there would be at least a week's pay coming to her if they discharged her. She wasn't down to the limit yet. She must learn to trust. Perhaps that was the reason why God was bringing her so low, that she might learn to trust Him. As for the money from the fabulous uncle, she discounted it entirely.

So she got up and washed her face, dashing the cold water over it refreshingly, combed her hair, and changed her dress as if she were going out somewhere. Then she made a game of getting an interesting supper out of the odds and ends she had in her little tin box out the window, which she called her refrigerator. A stalk of celery, too tough to enjoy raw, nearly a cup of stewed tomatoes left over from yesterday, a lump of baked beans, the last of a can she had opened a week ago, a scrap of hamburg.

She put them all in her little tin saucepan, and watched over them carefully, till there came out a very tasty dish of soup—was it bean or beef? At any rate, it had a delicious flavor.

There was also a lettuce leaf, two leaves of spinach, one radish, and half a tiny onion, besides the little white leaf top of the celery stalk. Minced fine they made a very attractive salad, with the last cracker from the box and a tiny wedge of cheese. It was a good dinner, and she really enjoyed it. And then as she nibbled at a single chocolate peppermint left over from some that had been passed around in the office that day, and now serving as dessert, she got to thinking that she really ought to go out somewhere and get a brighter outlook on life. She must not let herself slump this way. It was spoiling her morale. She wasn't even going to church. Perhaps that was what she needed to help her keep her trust in God.

All these days she had been like one groping, as if everything was dark about her. If only she could get to a place where it was light! She could walk with confidence again if it were only light about her! What did that remind her of? Suddenly from somewhere back in the dear happy days of her girlhood, came words that she had often heard her mother read.

Impulsively she got out her mother's Bible. Those words were somewhere in the little Johns, first or second, she was sure.

Scattered here and there over the pages were precious pencilings from her mother's own hand, and there all at once the verses stood out underlined:

"This then is the message . . . that God is light, and in Him is no darkness at all.

If we say that we have fellowship with Him and walk

in darkness, we lie, and do not the truth:

But if we walk in the light, as He is in the light, we have fellowship one with another—"

Fellowship! She paused and read the verses over again. Fellowship. She hadn't been having fellowship with anyone for this long time. She hadn't even tried to have fellowship with any other Christians. She could almost hear the troubled words her dear mother would have spoken about it.

And suddenly there came to her a desire to change that. She would go to church! She would go this very night! This was Wednesday night and some church would likely be having prayer meeting. She would just start out and find a prayer meeting!

So she put on her hat and coat and gloves and started.

There were loud voices from the front room where the noisy roomers were gathered playing cards. Their raucous voices rang out to the hall and made Dale's sensitive nerves cringe.

"What am I? A frail flower?" she said to herself angrily, "that I can't stand the unpleasant things of earth. Fellowship!" she repeated. "How could one have fellowship with people like that?"

She gave a little shudder as an oath ripped out through the hall, and then one of the girls screeched "Give me another glass of beer, can'tcha? I'm perishing fer a drink!"

She hurried out into the evening, glad to get away

from the atmosphere.

"Am I wrong," she asked herself, "that I can't fellowship with such people?"

Then to her soul came a clear quick answer, from more words stored away in her memory, hardly comprehended until now.

"Come ye out from among them, and be ye separate, saith the Lord." That must mean come out from people who are not His own. The fellowship must be with those who know and love the Lord, else there can be no true fellowship for a believer. That's why she was going to church tonight, to try and find some people who love the Lord; to get strength and assurance from being with them.

It was marvelous the way the things she had learned in the past were coming back to her now. How she had wandered away from the path in which her father and mother had trained her young feet from babyhood! How many things she knew that she had not put to use in these hard days! What a fool she had been to let them slip away from her when these were just the times for which they had been given, to save her from drifting into doubt and despair. She had allowed a kind of belligerence to get into her mind, as if her troubles and fears were God's fault, and she had been going on in her hard way, half pitying herself for being treated like this!

Then all at once she came to a little chapel where she had been twice before, and where she had heard great truths uttered in a sweet simplicity.

They were singing as she entered.

> "God's way is the right way,
>   God's way is the best way,
> I'll trust in Him alway,
>   He knoweth the best."

It seemed extraordinary that they should have sung that just then, as she was entering. She could not get away from the thought that God was speaking to her through the whole service.

The young minister began to read the eighth chapter of Romans, and presently he came to the verse:

"And we know that all things work together for good to them that love God, to them who are the called according to His purpose."

The minister lifted his eyes a moment and in a quiet voice asked, "And what *is* that purpose to which He has called us?"

He read the next verse:

"For whom he did foreknow, he also did predestinate *to be conformed to the image of His Son!*"

He lifted his eyes again and looked steadily at them, speaking in a quiet impressive conversational tone.

"Then God's whole purpose in whatever He is doing to you, whatever He is allowing in your life, is that you may be transformed into the image of God's Son. That you may be *like Him*. Remember

God first made man in his own image, but through sin man lost that glorious image. No man today would ever be recognized as being from God's family, would he? But God loved us so much that He sent His dear Son to be crucified for our sins, to purchase our pardon with His precious blood, and to restore us to His image. All that He allows to come to us is for that purpose, that we may resemble God again, that we may be as younger brethren to His dear Son. It is only so that we can really represent our Lord and witness for Him."

Dale sat startled, fascinated by his words. It seemed as if they had been spoken just for her, and as if God Himself had sent them to her. She felt arraigned there in the presence of God for having doubted Him, for having grieved and worried about her small trials, when all the time it was just God, doing needful things for her, that the presence of His glory might be restored to her marred and sinful self!

She wanted to bow her head and weep, but she sat there quietly enough, the color soft in her pale cheeks, the glint of earnestness in her sweet eyes. She did not know it herself of course, but she was very sweet and attractive as she sat there listening, and more than one noted the lovely girl who seemed to be drinking in what was said.

Afterwards they came and spoke to her, welcomed her to their midst. Some of them asked her where she lived, and begged her to come again.

"I'm not sure I shall be there very long," she said as she gave her address, with sudden remembrance of her vanishing job. "It's a long way off, but I'll come again when I can, and if I move I'll try to get near here. I like your church. I'll surely come again if I can. I've been helped tonight." She said it shyly, very quietly, and they watched her and really hoped she would come again. She had come out here to this little church in search of fellowship. Fellowship of those who knew and loved her Lord. She had been trying to walk in the light, and now she had found fellowship, and it was sweet to her. They were strangers, yes, but they spoke as brothers and sisters. They spoke the dear old family language of those who were God's children, born-again ones. How the old accustomed phrases came back and slipped into place. She was among God's family again, and it was good to be here.

And then the very next morning the blow fell!

Chapter 5

THE SUN HAD A VERY UNCERTAIN LOOK AS SHE glanced out of the window while she was hurrying to get her dressing and breakfast out of the way. There were many anxious-looking little bluish gray clouds scurrying around as if uncertain of directions. And when she went out the door a bitter wind caught her, and pulled at her garments, and flung cold down her neck and into her face; a wild wicked wind that set her shivering, and gave her a miserable inadequate feeling as if the way to the office was too hard, too long.

"But I am trusting in the Lord," she told herself. "I must not forget that all day. He is setting the pace for me, and there is nothing for me to do but follow where He leads me."

She took a deep breath of the sharp cold and lifted her head and shoulders to go forward. This was a day that made her remember the promise of a nice warm squirrel coat that her father had made to her just before Christmas, the year he died. He wasn't there when Christmas came, and she hadn't had the fur coat. Mother couldn't get it for her, though she would gladly have done so. There wasn't money enough, and mother had to have doctors and operations; there never had been money enough. But just the thought of that promise in the long ago was pleasant. How good it would have felt to snuggle into the deep fur collar this morning, and how glad both her father and mother would have been to have left it behind them to keep their child warm! And God cared just as much as they did, only He saw that there was something that Dale Hathaway needed more than fur coats, to help her to conform to the image of His Son. That was the important thing.

Of course, for the time being, and down here in the cold, Dale couldn't quite understand how important it was for her to conform to the image of God's Son, but He did, and she had just come to realize that He did, therefore she must not worry, nor fret for a fur coat.

So she started to hum the tune of the song they had sung in meeting last night, and her spirits rose in spite of the fierce wind.

As she turned the corner into the broad avenue where her office was located a wicked little bitter snowflake stung her face. Snow? Was it going to snow? She cast an imploring look up at those scurrying, turbulent, multicolored clouds. They might snow, or they might clear away into brightness by and by, but somehow they had an ominous look.

She was glad when she was safe at the office and seated at her desk, getting a few odds and ends from yesterday out of the way before the mail and dictation time came.

It was mid-morning when Miss Alice arrived, blowing in with stars in her eyes and flowers on her cheeks and snowflakes in her hair.

Dale looked up as the door opened, perhaps because her heart had been waiting for just this, expecting. She knew at once who she was, and her heart almost skipped a beat and then hobbled painfully on.

She wasn't a young girl, she was older than Dale, with experience written all over her plain pleasant face, and joy and sunshine in her eyes. It was incredible that she could have retained so much joy and sunshine when she was just emerging from such a desperate illness as they said she had been experiencing.

She had gray eyes, and long heavy hair coiled graciously and easily about her head in smooth braids. She had pleasant lips devoid of make-up, and a faint color whipped into her cheeks by the wind. She was glad to get back. You could see that in her eyes. Those stars in her eyes were gladness, and Dale liked her at once, and felt a sudden pride that she had been able to substitute for such a woman.

The office came clamoring joyously about her, welcoming her. There hadn't been such a hubbub in that office since Dale had been there. And she must sit quietly and do her work until it was taken from her!

So her fingers went skillfully forward accomplishing wonders in a short time. She didn't want to leave scraps of work behind for the other secretary to finish up.

They introduced her to Miss Alice, and strangely she felt as if she was a friend, at least one whom she would like to have for a friend, even if her coming did mean that her job was gone.

But she went on and finished the typing of the dictation she had taken. And then when she took the letters to her chief for his signature, he asked her to sit down.

"Perhaps you know that the one whose place you have been taking has returned," he said pleasantly. He was trying to let her down easily. It choked her all up so that she couldn't make her voice sound natural as she tried to answer.

"Yes," she managed, trying to look as if she were cheery about it.

The manager was eyeing her keenly.

"Well, I've done what I promised," he said. "I've been looking around to find something else for you, for you see we do appreciate it that you were willing to come in for an uncertain time, and you've done well! We've no fault to find with your work. You understand if we had need for another secretary you would undoubtedly be our choice, and we can recommend you most heartily to anyone who is in need of such work. I'm just sorry that we have no place for you here. But I think I have found something even better for you."

He paused and Dale drew another long breath, and looked at him wistfully, with just a shade of hope in her eyes.

"Oh, that's very kind of you," she murmured, too tense really to take in what he was saying. Something better! That wouldn't be likely.

"Yes," he said with a satisfied smile. "It's a better salary. I suppose that will please you, won't it?"

"Better salary?" said Dale half dazed. She hadn't dared to dream of anything like that. "What is it? Where is it?"

"Well, that's it. It isn't exactly what you're doing now. And it wouldn't be daytime work. It would be evening work."

"Evening work?" Dale looked at him startled.

The manager was appraising her.

"Yes," he said pleasantly. "I thought I was rather fortunate in finding it for you. Of course you may never have done anything of the sort, but I'm banking on you being able to work into it."

"But—where is it? What could I do at night?"

"Why, it's with a very high grade night club," he said calmly. "They want you for a hostess. An acquaintance of mine is at the head of it, and I found he was looking for somebody, and I suggested you.

From what I told him of you he was so interested
that he came in here yesterday to look you over, and
was quite pleased with your appearance. You know
appearance goes a long way in such work. He said he
felt that you might work into the business wonder-
fully well if you were adaptable. I told him I had
found you so, and I could recommend you heartily.
Your salary will be satisfactory, I am quite sure."

He mentioned a sum that the man had suggested,
and it was so breath-taking that Dale didn't even
take it in.

"Oh!" she said in dismay. She felt as if she were
sinking, sinking down, down, through unfathomable
depths, and she wasn't at all sure she would be able
to keep her head and answer him.

"Oh, but Mr. Fletcher! I couldn't work at a night
club!"

"Why not?" said the man sharply. He thought he
had done well for her, and now she was beginning
an argument.

She looked at him steadily for an instant, and then
in a firm little voice she answered with her head
held up.

"It isn't my world," she said clearly. "I don't belong in a place like that."

"Why not?" came the question sharply again.
"Make it your world, then. That's all nonsense. It's
all a matter of clothes, I suppose, and they will look
after those for you. They will pay you enough to

cover any amount of garments they want you to wear. And they'll send you to the best beauty parlor you can find and when you get your hair done the way they want it, and your face made up to bring out your type you won't know yourself, my dear girl! They would brush you up on your dancing and teach you exactly what to do. You wouldn't need to be embarrassed."

"No!" said Dale definitely. "No! I could not possibly do that!"

"Well, I still say, why not?" said the man with almost contempt in his voice. "It is a perfectly respectable night club! Everybody in the best society goes there. I go there sometimes myself. You'd go there yourself if you had the time and money!"

"No!" said Dale quietly. "I would never go to night clubs! Not if I had all the money in the world. They are not the kind of place I would think it was right to go!"

"Why not? What's the matter with night clubs? And what has *right* got to do with it anyhow when you have your living to earn?"

Dale was still for a minute, and then she lifted her head and looked at him steadily with a strange new sweetness in her eyes.

"It is because I am a child of God," she said clearly, "and I don't want to do anything that I know my Lord would not like me to do, even if I can't earn my living. I would rather starve!"

The man looked at her brave young face with
astonishment, and almost a kind of shame. He had
never had a girl, much less an employee, talk to him
like that. He had never seen a girl who was willing
even to suggest starving for the sake of doing right.
This was a strange new thing to him. But he rallied
and was back to normal after a brief moment of be-
wilderment.

"That is pure nonsense, of course. Pure fanatical
nonsense! Anybody who takes up with a standard
like that ought to try a mild form of starving, and
see how quickly they would turn around and walk
the other way. There just aren't any sensible people
who act like that. Well, I'm sorry," he added in a
hostile voice. "If that is your unalterable decision I
guess that's about all I can do for you. If you're so
choosey you'll have to get your own job, and I'd hate
to say I hope you starve a little just to take some of
the cockiness out of you. But of course, if by tomorrow morning you have changed your mind and
come to see this matter in a more reasonable manner
you might drop in and see me, and I think I can still
turn things your way. That'll be about all, Miss
Hathaway! Here's your order. Just stop down at the
desk and take your pay."

He handed out a card such as she usually received
on pay days, and turned away toward the papers on
his desk.

Dale accepted the card, hesitated a second with a

glance at the manager. Then she said in a little controlled voice:

"Good-by, Mr. Fletcher. I thank you for your kind intentions," and walked quietly out of the room, and the man sat and watched her in amazement. It could not be that she meant to let it go like this! Surely she would come back tomorrow!

But Dale had walked as definitely out of his life as if she had stepped into another country.

Chapter 6

Somehow Dale felt strangely stronger as she put on her things and walked down the street, away from that place that had seemed so good to her when she first came.

The others had gone out to their lunch and so there was no opportunity to explain that she was leaving them. Well, perhaps she would meet them somewhere again. She was too much excited and almost frightened at the words she had dared to speak to Mr. Fletcher to be able to talk intelligently with anyone else.

She went to a restaurant at some distance from the office where she had been working. Just now she did not want to meet anyone.

It was not until she settled down and had ordered a comforting hot meal that would not require much determination to eat, that she discovered that Mr. Fletcher had ordered an extra fifteen dollars put into her envelope to cover the other three days of the week. Well, that would help. She was glad, and she gave a bit of thanksgiving for it as she closed her eyes for an instant and bowed her head before eating.

And while she ate her meal in a leisurely way she was trying to think out the course ahead of her.

If possible she must keep Mrs. Beck from finding out that she had no more job. To that end it would be a good idea to leave the house at her usual time in the morning and not return to it until her usual time at night. The interval of the day could be filled with hunting for a job again. It was near to Christmas, and surely she could get some kind of a job now.

After she had finished her meal she went to the great railroad station. It was big and warm there, and she could even get a meal there in the restaurant if necessary. A railroad station could be a refuge for her if the days continued to multiply without a place to work. There was even a big rest room with rocking chairs, and a couch upon which one could lie to rest if the day got too strenuous. There were other places, too. She wouldn't need to occupy a conspicuous place in the station too often. There were libraries and museums. One could kill time in several places.

She went and bought a paper and studied the advertisements. Then with a choice list in hand she started out, for it was still early in the afternoon. But none of the advertisements proved of any use. They were either already filled, or trained workers of some sort were wanted. Some of the openings were utterly impossible.

She went home that night at her usual time, made some milk toast on her little oil stove, and went to bed, for she found herself greatly shaken by the occurrences of the day, and she didn't want to sit and think them over. She would just commit them all to her Lord and go to sleep.

For the three succeeding days she had much the same experience, tramping the city over in search of work with no result.

The fourth day she found a place in the toy section of a small department store, selling picture puzzles and blocks. They took her on, only waiting to telephone to Mr. Fletcher for his character endorsement, and she went to work at once. But the work was not to last beyond Christmas, and perhaps not all that time. It depended on how well the picture puzzles sold. She was an extra, and must be content to work from day to day. And the salary was a mere pittance compared with what she had been getting. Still, every cent would help, and she could not hope to get anything steady until after Christmas now, unless a miracle happened in her behalf.

The toy store kept open evenings, and her day was long. She was on her feet continually, and too weary to get her supper and eat it when she went home at night. She would generally stop somewhere and get a cup of coffee or a glass of milk, and find no appetite for anything more. She was too weary to read, or do anything but go to bed, and some days she found it

almost impossible to waken in the morning in time
to get a bite to eat and get to the store in time.

She had begun to count the days until Christmas,
and wonder if she would be able to get something
better after the holidays were passed. Her faith was
often at the breaking point, and night after night the
tears would come. Could she hold out till Christmas?

And then one night in the night the fire sirens
screamed and the sky grew lurid with raging flames.
When she reached the toy store in the morning, it
was gone, root and branch! Only charred walls and
ghastly ghosts of blackened toys scattered grotesquely
about showed what had been the merchandise. And
her job was gone! Gone in a breath of smoke and
flame!

Stunned she crept away to try and find another,
but there was nothing, apparently, now. Everybody
was in a fever getting ready for Christmas. There
were no more vacant places. Soon the Christmas rush
would be over, and merchants did not want to take
on any more salespeople just to dismiss them in a few
days, so Dale crept back that night and lay down in
despair. She didn't even stop to undress she was so
worn out. And it was so cold. She felt her clothes
were all needed to keep her warm. For even the
double blankets that Mrs. Beck had grudgingly
meted out to her did not seem sufficient this night.
Besides she had a strange obsession upon her that any
house might burn up in the night, and it would be

better to be dressed and be ready for anything. At least that was the way she felt when she lay down, though really in the back of her mind she intended to get up by and by and undress regularly. She knew that only so could she get a real rest, and if she was to go on hunting a job, and of course she must, it was only through sleeping and eating regularly that she could keep fit.

It had begun to snow fitfully through the day, little hard grains of snow, that increased toward night and pelted against her window panes with loud ominous clicks, like shot. She shuddered as she lit her oil stove. The slatternly maid had had it downstairs all day supposedly cleaning it and filling it. It was to be hoped that she had improved it. For in these days when she was gone so long, even into the evening, her room did not get much chance to heat up. So she shivered as she lay down, glad that she had stopped down town to get a little supper and hadn't depended on cooking anything tonight.

The wicked little stove was well fed that night, and didn't smell of kerosene quite as much as usual. It gave forth a bright cheery light and comforted her. So she tried to rest.

Christmas! What was Christmas going to be? And she had always loved Christmas so much!

Well, never mind. Though she couldn't understand just what all this dread and loneliness was doing for her, she intended to trust to the end.

Gradually the little pellets of snow that bounded on the window pane so chirkly grew less pronounced, softer and plushier, and changed into big soft flakes that were making a lacy cover for the windows. Their plush blanket on the city wiped out the sharpness of the earlier snow, and softened the city everywhere into a beautiful white world of wonder.

Dale, as she lay there listening, hearing the sounds of the house die away to silence, was thinking about it all, the world around her. The tap dancing girls gone to their theatre, coming home long afterwards to babble silly nothings and drop into a drunken sleep. Mrs. Beck gone to the movies as usual. The two school teachers on the second story front who had recently come to the house, sitting in their big chilly room with sweaters around them, or even blankets, correcting school papers. The newspaper young man of the third story front, where? Off reporting some happening of the night, perhaps. She hadn't seen or heard of him in several weeks. He might have moved, though Mrs. Beck had implied that he had been sent away on what she said he called "a consignment" covering some political gathering. She wondered idly where he was. Likely he had friends, or he had gone to some entertainment, if he wasn't working. How she wished, even tired as she was, that she had to work tonight. It was desolate, desolate, lying here, waiting to be conformed into His image.

Now and again she would drift off into a doze, and

come awake again at a sound from the world outside.

Once she got up and went to her window to see if she dared open it a crack. But the wind swept in with a drift of snow so quietly and damply that she closed it at once, and breathing on the pane to clear a place where she could look through she stood there a moment and gazed down at the city in this wild whirl of snow. There came to her memory a poem she had read during that first year of college before her mother had been taken sick. It spoke of the dim lovely vision of a city, in the early morning with the mists upon it, just waking to the work of the world. And then there was another, about that same city at night, and the throngs that filled its streets, the darkness and the trouble that creeps in hidden places, the gaudy glitter and the folly sought by men trying to forget the agony and shame and woe that is theirs.

That poem haunted her now as she looked out on the city spread before her through a mist of snow, made visible by gleaming garish brilliant lights that seemed out of place amid the soft whiteness now filling the world. She tried to repeat the words of the poem to herself:

> "The stars of God that seemed to rest us so
> Are shut in outer darkness by the light
> That flares down on the life which fills the city
> With what we love or loathe, but ever pity."

But there were no stars now. One could not see the darkness above, for everything was deep whiteness.

Even that darkness above was white and dense. And if it had not been for the city lights, those brilliant man-made garish lights, she could not have seen the city, not even the high domes and spires, snow capped. But yet the evil and the agony and the shame and sorrow were all there in that wide white city, its only thought of God one of blame for the unhappiness.

She thought of the movies where all the poor Mrs. Becks were sitting, enjoying the sorrows of poor imaginary people, to get away from their own sorrow. She thought of the gay stage where the girls from down the hall were dancing now to solace other sad ones searching for forgetfulness. She thought of "gramma" locked into her front room downstairs, taking her sleep alone and trying to forget that she was no longer young. Dale was filled with sadness.

Then she looked about her own little chilly room, lit now only by the dismal light from the oil stove, and was thankful that she still had this. Even this might not be hers for long, if she found no other job, but it was hers tonight, and she must be thankful for that. She wasn't wandering the streets tonight with no refuge from the storm. She was safe, and she was warm, and not even hungry.

So she went and lay down again.

She must have dropped asleep, for a little later she was suddenly roused by voices downstairs, a man tramping heavily in the hall below, calling out, knocking! Perhaps she ought to get up and open her door and listen. Maybe someone had been hurt or sick and had been brought home. The voice was excited, and now it seemed to be coming up the stairs, heavy footsteps, rubbered ones, tramping toward her door! And then that voice again!

Chapter 7

GEORGE RAND WAS DOG-WEARY AND COLD AND hungry, but he was too worn out to go in search of something to eat. He wanted to get to his bed and rest.

He had been out all day in the storm, covering the great fire that had been raging in one part of the city, a fire in which not only part of the shopping district, but a fine residential section was threatened. It was late when he had handed in his copy and started for his dreary lodging. He had been the last one in the office to finish. He had been distracted by their conversation as they got ready to go! They had talked cheerily of home, or some night club they were to visit that evening. One man told how he was making a doll house for his little girl for Christmas, and how tonight after he was sure she was asleep he was going to finish the little staircase. Landings it had, real landings, and he described them. He was as eager over it as if he had been a child himself. He told how his wife came and sat near with the dolls she was dressing for the house, and talked to him. Home,

that was what that man had. But there was no such
thing for George Rand. He had nothing but a dreary
room in a cheap lodging house.

One after another finished their copy, donned
their overcoats and plunged whistling out into the
storm. They were all happy because Christmas was
coming, but there was no hint of Christmas coming
George's way. Oh, perhaps some of them might invite him over for a turkey dinner, but he wasn't going. Not he! He didn't believe in spoiling other
people's Christmas. Christmas was for families, not
for lonely bachelors who had no family. He would
get through the day somehow, he supposed. He always did. Though this would be the loneliest Christmas he had ever known, because now his mother was
gone and there was no hope that he could ever give
her the happy holiday time he had been hoping for.
His interest in his work seemed to be gone, too. He
had hoped so to be a success and take care of her the
way he had planned to do when he first left home on
his career. But last spring she had slipped away out
of the world, and left him stranded, and since that
time he had just been plodding along, covering all
the jobs they had given him without a let-up. He
hadn't realized till now how desperately tired and
discouraged he was. Christmas! That had been the
goal that he had set to have his mother in a little
home, some kind of a home with him. You couldn't
have Christmas without a home. Ever since his father

died when he was only sixteen that had been his aim, to make a real home for his mother; and now the reason for it was gone, and he was stranded.

The desolate look was on his face as he handed in his copy. He had found a letter in his box which usually held assignments. He read it idly. It was a scribbled line of commendation from his chief praising his work and assuring him of a long coveted promotion for which he had almost ceased to hope. It meant a big rise in salary, but he was too tired and too blue to feel much elated. What was the good of more money? It was too late to get the things for his mother that he knew she had needed a long time.

If he had been almost any other young man he would by this time have established a social circle for himself, but he had been so determined to carry out his life ambition, and keep his promise to his dead father to look after his mother, that he had made it paramount. He had not been interested in girls, simply because he didn't have time to go to their shindigs as he called them, nor money to spend on their fancies. Oh, there were some nice girls on the paper, regular girls, who had courage and talent and a lot of initiative. He admired them, but he had never gone beyond a certain point in intimacy. He met them in his work, talked to them as if they were other fellows, but so far his mind had been set on getting his mother into comfort and having a home. After that there would be time enough for girls.

And now his mother was gone, and his thought of a home was gone too. Sometime, maybe, things would be brighter, but he hadn't reached the point where he could think so yet.

As Rand turned the corner into his own street a terrific gust of wind seized him and almost took his breath away. Merciless sleet lashed out at him like a rank of drawn sabers. As he got his breath again he felt how easily one could drop and let the storm put an icy end to things. Futile life! Why did one have to live? He felt as if his great reason for living was gone now. Money? What was money when he had no one to help him enjoy it?

The snow came hurtling in long slant lines straight from the side of the sky now. It was thick and white and breath-taking, with a pitiless sting in the tail of each lovely flake.

The city lights only made weirdly luminous the menacing white gloom in which he moved.

The clang of an ambulance ahead cut sharply into the awesome loneliness with a sudden shut-in nearness, then the sound seemed to go silent, into the snow, like plush. A great white light blurred out uncertainly ahead, and two burly figures stooped and lifted a huddled form from the snow. The sleet stung into his eyes so viciously he could scarcely see. Scattered words came strangely through the intimate silence. He caught the phrase "passed out" and then the gong clanged harshly staccato, and the lights of the ambulance were snuffed out in the whiteness again.

As Rand went up the steps of his lodging house, his keys in his hand, he noticed that the outer door of the vestibule was open a crack. The pale ghastly stab of light from the low-powered electric bulb swinging from the ceiling of the vestibule slashed a queer yellow gash in the storm. A drift of snow had filtered in and was holding the door. It would neither open nor shut. He put his shoulder to it and almost fell across a dark bundle, lying just inside on the floor.

He gave it a shove out of the way with his foot and applied his latch key to the inner door, but a strange sound like the mew of a sick kitten arrested his attention, and looking down he saw the bundle begin to move!

Startled he dropped his bunch of keys and stared at the thing. Was he going out of his mind? The bundle seemed to be wrapped in an old ragged coat, and it was distinctly agitated, emitting weird terrifying little sounds. Had somebody left a cat in the vestibule?

Suddenly the coat flapped apart and a tiny baby hand and arm clawed out futilely, feebly!

Rand watched it with growing horror. A baby! Abandoned! And on a night like this!

As the coat slowly dropped away the scrawny little body was revealed, naked except for a huddle of dirty rags about the loins.

The thin little arms beat vaguely at the freezing air, the pinched baby face was blue with cold, the whole tiny body was trembling and shaking with the rigors of terrible cold. The pitiful quivering lips and chin, the grieved look in the frightened eyes, the feeble hoarse little wail, cut him to the heart.

A baby! Like that! *More* life! And he used to believe in a God!

Rand knew nothing whatever about babies, but just ordinary common sense told him that it would not take long for the cold to snuff out this little life. It might already be too late to save it! Was that ambulance too far gone out of hailing distance?

With a wild idea of calling it Rand jerked open the door again. But the icy blast swooped in and lashed at the baby, silencing it in the midst of a pathetic squeak, slithering down upon the unclad little body, like a cruel thing that was glad to hurt.

The baby gasped and choked and turned bluer in the face, and then puckered its pitiful lips in a long terrified wail, and Rand was horrified at what he had done. With all his might he pushed, and shut that door. Obviously this unclad child could not go out again into the storm.

Awkwardly he stooped and pulled the filthy coat about the little naked shaking body. He had had to pull off his glove to find his keys that had fallen on the floor, and his hand came in contact with the small icy claw of the baby as it beat impotently at bitter emptiness and shivered violently. He had never seen a baby shiver before. Its tiny waxen eyelids fluttered open and two bright anguished eyes searched this strange cold world.

Double panic seized Rand. He must do something!

Frantically he unlocked the inner door. Reluctantly, fearfully, he picked up the old coat by its ragged fringes, and lifted it as if it were a basket, the baby in imminent peril of sliding out, and so carrying it he strode down the hall to the landlady's door and gave a thunderous knock. Slow unwilling steps came presently, and "gramma" poked her head irritably out of the door.

"Where is Mrs. Beck?" Rand demanded.

"Gone ta the movies!" answered the old woman in a sharp querulous voice.

"Well, somebody has left a baby in the vestibule," explained Rand excitedly, "and I don't know what to do with it."

"Well, you better call the p'lice," answered the crone indifferently. "I've got the rheumatiz'. I can't be bothered!" and she made as if to close the door.

"But it's freezing!" roared Rand.

"Put it outside and call the p'lice!" reiterated the old woman stolidly. "There's the pay phone in the hall. It isn't my baby. It isn't yours, is it?"

"No, but I'm not a murderer, if you are!" shouted Rand as the door closed in his face.

He heard the grinding of the key in the lock, and the old woman's whine:

"I can't be bothered! I've got the rheumatiz'!"

Fiercely Rand grappled the child in his arms with a half caressing motion to still the ghastly little wails. He went to the telephone and fumbled with his free hand for a nickel, but could find none. The baby was kicking out of its covers again and wailing heart-brokenly.

With an exclamation of impatience Rand grasped the old coat tighter around the baby and tore up the stairs two steps at a time. Those two school-teacher-women on the second floor front! They would likely know what to do. Perhaps they would help. But his several knocks brought no response.

He turned wildly, dazedly, not knowing what to do next, and felt the quiver of the shivering little creature in his arms. He had not known how small and helpless a baby would feel in his arms. He was frightened at the responsibility thrust upon him. Angry, too, at the whole situation, and most of all at the old woman who ought to know what to do and ought to try to help, and wouldn't.

Then as he turned from that second story front room he caught the line of dim light in the little back bedroom at the extreme end of the hall. Ah! The small pale girl lodged there, whose oranges he had once picked up for her. Perhaps she would help. He didn't know her name. He doubted if he had ever heard it, but he strode down the hall, gripping the little dirty bundle and frantically trying to still the wails that came from it.

He knocked imperatively, and then called out in a clear voice that could easily be heard down on the first floor if the kind old hag down there happened to be listening.

"Can you help me, quick? I've found a baby in the vestibule freezing to death!"

He heard a step and the door was opened almost instantly, though the girl inside looked as if she had been interrupted in crying. There were tears on her white cheeks and dark circles under her eyes.

So, here was another in some kind of trouble! Some more of the thing they called Life! He and she, and the filthy little freezing baby, and that huddled form in the storm being shoved into an ambulance! What was it all about anyway?

There was no light in the second story back save what came from a small oil stove in the middle of the room, but even in the shadows he could not fail to see the drawn tired look on the sweet young face of the girl as she put out instant arms to take the baby.

"The poor little beggar is frightfully dirty!" he warned, suddenly aware of the girl's delicate refinement. "Perhaps you'd better not touch him. Couldn't I lay him on the floor somewhere till I can call for help?"

The baby wailed feebly and flopped its arms till

the old coat fell away from the little shivering body again.

"The poor little lamb!" crooned Dale suddenly, gathering the little waif into her arms tenderly. "Dirt doesn't matter. Poor little darling mite! I wonder what we ought to do first?"

"The sweet old saint down on the first floor suggested putting him out on the doorstep and phoning for the police," said Rand contemptuously, "but I couldn't locate a nickel and hold him too, so I came to find a place to park him."

"She would talk that way!" said Dale bitterly. "Would it hurt him, do you suppose, to put him right into warm water? I have some here on the stove. Or should it be cold first? I don't know."

"Search me!" said Rand shrugging his shoulders helplessly. "What I don't know about babies would fill several books. But since you ask I shouldn't suppose anything one would do could really injure the little beggar if he can weather lying naked in that vestibule with a drift of snow close beside him."

"Oh, poor little soul!" said Dale sorrowfully, and then took the initiative.

"Turn on the light, please, won't you? I have a little tin tub in the closet over there, under that curtain. Could you get it, and pour some cold water in from the pitcher on the washstand, and then temper it with some hot water from the pan on the stove. It mustn't be too hot, you know, at first, just warm and comfortable, and we can pour in more as he gets used to the warmish temperature."

Deftly Dale got rid of the rags, leaving them in a heap on a newspaper in the hall. Tenderly she lifted the trembling bit of humanity, crooning to it as the quivering baby mouthed the air, and wailed hoarsely.

George Rand went anxiously around, preparing the bath, following Dale's directions, finding a clean towel and washcloth and a cake of soap.

He stood by wonderingly as Dale lowered the baby gently into the warm water, keeping her arm about the little quivering shoulders, passing the water over his face and chest with her warm hand.

It was amazing how surprised even a young baby like that could look, as the warmth began to penetrate the cold cold flesh, and comfort began gradually to steal into the little body. The baby relaxed a little and rested against Dale's arm. Then he suddenly seized hold of Dale's wrist with his eager weak chilly lips and began to suck frantically.

"Why, he's *hungry!*" said Dale with quick motherly instinct.

"I have a bag of crackers in my room," suggested Rand anxiously.

"But babies can't eat crackers!" said Dale wisely.

"Oh, can't they?" said Rand in a troubled tone. "I thought perhaps—in an emergency—!"

"No, they can't. They haven't any teeth, you know." There was a gentleness about her voice that suggested tender amusement at his ignorance. "Babies need milk! I wonder if the drug store is open yet. They always have milk."

"I'll go and see," said Rand eagerly. "Is there anything else I could get?"

"Yes, you might get a bottle and a nipple," said Dale, just as if she had always been looking after starved babies.

She put more warm water into the tub now, and the baby relaxed a little more and let his small head rest against her arm again. She lowered him down a little farther so the warmth would come around his shoulders which were still very cold to the touch, but the baby started in fear, struggling weakly, and clutched at Dale's arm, blinking and gasping like a drowning kitten.

"There! There! There! Darling!" crooned Dale. "Don't be frightened! You'll soon be warm now! There, isn't that nice?"

Dale bent a madonna smile upon the baby, and Rand, watching in the doorway felt something turn over in his heart. He bolted down the stairs in a hurry, the croon of Dale's voice following him like an unexpected joy.

As the heat began to penetrate the frozen little body the shivering gradually ceased, the tiny limbs relaxed, and the baby blinked up at her with a small bleat like a wee lamb.

The storm raged without, the snow growing

deeper inch by inch, the wind rioting outside the snow-draped windows. Dale's troubles were all there, slunk behind her chair waiting for her attention again, but Dale and the baby were having a lovely time with the soft rag and the sweet smelling soap, and the nice warm water. The little body was slowly taking on a less ghastly color.

She drew him presently from the water and cuddled him in the big towel, patting him dry, and then wrapped him in an old flannelette nightgown, soft and warm, and tucked a blanket close about him. The baby nestled in her arms for a moment with a comforted look, but suddenly the little mouth like a baby-bird's beak, was wide open again, snuffing and mouthing for deeper satisfaction.

When George came back Dale had the baby in her lap, and was feeding him hot water with a bit of sugar in it, from a teaspoon, a drop at a time.

"Now," she said looking up brightly, "you hold him and give him more hot water, while I fix his bottle."

So George, greatly fearful, but nevertheless eager, took off his wet coat and hung it on the stair rail out in the hall, and then sat down and took the baby gingerly into his arms. It seemed to him a daring thing for him to handle that frail bit of humanity.

Dale watched him furtively as she went about washing the bottle and heating the milk, filling the bottle with her unaccustomed hands. How kind the young man was as he looked down at the wizened little protesting face. His eyes were tender, and there were gentle lines around his mouth that made her feel he was a man one could trust. But the baby had set up a fierce wail once more with the cessation of the hot water.

"He wants more water," said Dale. "Give him a few drops at a time with the spoon until the milk is ready," and she put the glass and spoon on a chair beside him.

So George fed the baby hot water and sugar, and was filled with delight when he swallowed it.

"Why, the little beggar likes it!" he exclaimed, and Dale smiled assent.

They were like two children when the bottle was finally ready and Dale took the baby again to feed him. They hung over that meal, both of them, as if they were hungry themselves, and they laughed aloud as the baby seized the nipple in his hungry lips, and went to work, smacking and choking and gurgling over the first few mouthfuls.

"Why, the little beggar!" said George grinning. "That was what he wanted! Look out there, you little pig! Don't get your feet in the trough! That bottle isn't going to run away. There's more where that came from!"

The baby settled down finally to long pulls and little grunts of satisfaction, rolling his eyes with ecstasy, and George and Dale, their heads close together watching him were no less happy.

The delicate blue-veined lids began to droop before the bottle was quite finished, and they enjoyed watching the process of going to sleep. They hadn't known before how interesting a baby was. They began to hope just a little that they had really saved the baby's life, although it seemed almost incredible that so young a child could survive such exposure.

But George saw more than the baby as he sat there watching. He saw again the madonna look in Dale's eyes when she lifted them to give a whispered direction about getting the bed ready for her to lay the baby down. He saw the lovely droop of her head over the baby, the sweet curve of her shoulders, the little brown curl at the nape of her white neck, and he had a foolish desire to stoop and kiss it, although he'd never felt that way about any girl in his life before.

He turned away half shamedly and let his cheeks go hot in the shadowed room. Dale's small electric bulb could not compete with the darkness of the whole room very successfully, and the oil stove only helped out a tiny bit. But then he turned back, not willing to miss the lovely sight of her sitting there with bent head holding the bottle to the baby's lips, his little fuzzy head nestled in the hollow of her arm.

"Why, the little beggar has hair!" he exclaimed

suddenly as if it were a great discovery. "Yellow hair. I guess he was so filthy it didn't show before that bath!"

He watched the girl and the baby wistfully, almost hungrily.

"Yes, and it's curly, too!" murmured Dale happily. Then with sudden dread in her voice:

"Did you call the police?"

"No," said George. "I thought it was more important to get him warmed and fed first. He couldn't go anywhere on a night like this anyway. Do you think I ought to call them tonight?"

"I don't see why morning won't do," said Dale. "Anybody who left him here likely knows where he is."

"He might be stolen of course," hazarded George anxiously. "I wouldn't like to think anybody was worrying about him. Poor little chipmunk!"

"I don't think they are," said Dale thoughtfully. "He looks too undernourished to belong to anybody who would worry about him. Though maybe that's the reason they had to give him up. But if he was stolen it would have been sometime ago. Nobody would steal a poor child like that. He certainly was not attired in the garments of the rich."

"I should say not!" said George with satisfaction. Then after a pause, "He looks too awfully young to be stolen. People don't steal babies that young as a rule. It's too risky. They can't get their money out of the transaction. The kid might die on them, and they couldn't realize soon enough."

"Yes, I guess you're right," said Dale.

They were silent for a little, standing there beside the bed watching the child sleep.

"Then you know," said George after a minute, "his mother might have been taken sick, and just slipped him in this doorway because she couldn't navigate any longer. It was bitter cold outside, and I seem to remember hearing an ambulance. Saw them pick up somebody before I came in. I thought then it was some drunk, but it might have been a woman."

"Oh!" said Dale pitifully. "Then perhaps you ought to telephone tonight. We might be able to do something for the mother if we could find her!"

"I hadn't thought of that!" said George. "But I'd hate like the dickens to have the little sucker taken to the orphanage of the poor farm. I suppose that's what the police would do with him. And he oughtn't to go out in this storm."

"Oh!" said Dale. "The poor little darling!" Her eyes filled with sudden yearning. "How I wish I had a home!"

"Here too!" said George fervently, his eyes devouring the picture Dale made as she bent over and tucked the hot water bottle under the blanket close beside the sleeping baby.

"The little chap looks better already, I believe,"

exclaimed George, standing close beside her. "He's not so blue as he was. I'd like to see the little sucker have a chance after he's weathered all this. But I suppose I ought to do something about him. What time do you have to leave in the morning?"

A sudden gray look swept over Dale's face.

"I don't!" she said in a sad little voice.

"You *don't?*" chirruped George in glad surprise. "You mean you could look after him for a little while in the morning till I can rustle around and do something about it. Aren't you—employed?"

"Not any more," said Dale looking up with a brave little smile. "The company I was working for burned down last night."

"Say, now, that's tough luck!" said George sympathetically. "That must have been the fire I was covering."

"Yes, I suppose it was," said Dale with downcast eyes. "I was feeling pretty badly about it till you brought in this dear baby, who was so much worse off than I was. But I guess we'll weather it. The worst of it is there isn't any chance to get a new job until after Christmas now, anyway, so I can easily look after the baby tomorrow. I'd be so glad to keep the baby myself if I had any home, or money enough to make one for him without having to leave him to go to work. But I can easily look after the baby tomorrow."

"Good!" said George brightening. "That'll be a

help. Can you beat that to have things work out and fit in so neatly? But say, I've just got a raise. A big one! Been hoping for it a long time now and had given up expecting it. And now it's come I haven't a soul in the world to spend it on. So if you don't get something good right away you'll accept a loan from me for a while till things brighten up for you. There's no need in the world for you to get worried. Take it easy till you can really better yourself. That's all right. You helped me out, and now I'll help you out."

"Oh, I couldn't possibly do that," said Dale firmly. "I *couldn't*, you know. But you are very kind."

"Now look here—" began George eagerly, "in a way this is *my* baby. *I* found him. You might let me pay for his care—"

"Did I understand you to say it was *your* baby, Mr. Rand?" challenged the hard voice of Mrs. Beck from the doorway.

Chapter 8

THE TWO YOUNG PEOPLE SWUNG AROUND STAR-
tled, for even though the door had been wide open
into the hall they had not heard the approach of their
landlady. Her rubber-shod feet had acquired a habit
of silence. She liked to come upon her roomers unawares. There she stood in the doorway and fixed
them with a steely glance.

"Gosh!" said George, under his breath.

Then the woman spoke:

"Miss Hathaway, I *am* surprised at you, letting a
man come into your room! And at this time of night!
I *thought* you were *respectable!* I remember men-
tioning that to you, that I had always had a respectable class of roomers. This house has always had a
good name. If I think there is any doubt about people I always ask for recommends. And Mr. Rand, I
wouldn't have thought it of *you!* You was always a
nice quiet appearing young man! But I suppose men
are all alike, they'll go anywhere when a girl has a
"come-hither" in her eye. And now after what I've
just heard you say! My! I never would have thought

it! You never can tell about anybody! As for this girl! Miss Hathaway, you can get *right out!* It was probably all your fault. I can't have any young woman of questionable character in *my* house. I've always kept *respectable!* I ought to have sent you away long ago. I've been worried ever since I found out how you tore that bag on purpose and flung all those oranges out on the sidewalk right in front of him to make him pick them up for you and carry them upstairs."

She turned to Rand.

"She just did that of course to get acquainted with you. And now see what it's led to! But this settles the matter. I can't have a girl like that around, not a girl that lets strange men come into her room. It isn't *decent!*"

Dale gasped at the appalling words.

"Mrs. Beck," she said in a clear voice, "you can't talk that way! Neither Mr. Rand nor I had one thought of ourselves or of what room we were in. We were trying to save that little baby's life. It was starving and freezing and nothing else was of any importance then."

"Well, you'll find it *is* of importance *now*," said the furious woman grimly. "You've got *me* to reckon with. I guess you knew good and well where you were, too! You can't pull the wool over my eyes! And as for Mr. Rand, men always know what they're doing, and if he hadn't he was told. Gramma says she advised him to put the baby on the doorstep and call the police! That's what he should have done of course, instead of making it an excuse to go and hobnob in a girl's room. But of course—if it's *his baby,* that explains—"

Rand was white with fury now. He strode forward and seized the irate Beck's arm in a firm grip.

"Look here!" he roared. "You old whited sepulchre you! You can't get away with saying things like that. I never saw nor even heard of that baby till I fell over it in your vestibule. It was practically naked, with snow blowing in over it, and it was the most pitiful sight I ever saw, shivering like a leaf and giving hoarse weak little cries. I don't know who put it in your house and I don't care. I only know it would have been murder to leave it there. Your tenderhearted grandmother wouldn't do a thing to help me, and I couldn't find anybody else at home, so I saw a light in the crack under this door and I asked Miss Hathaway to help me. Now, if you dare to say a word against her you've got me to deal with, see?"

"Leave me alone, young man!" said the invincible Mrs. Beck, glaring at George and pulling away from his firm grip. "If you don't take your hand off me this instant I'll have you arrested for assault! And as for your sob-story, there must have been some reason why that brat was left in *this* house instead of some other! If you expect me to believe your story, let's see you do something about it. If that ain't your baby

take it down ta the p'lice station this minute! I don't
harbor any foundling brats in my respectable home,
not even over night! *Go!*" and she pointed dramati-
cally toward the blanketed baby sleeping sweetly on
Dale's pillow.

"On a night like this, at an hour like this?" blazed
Rand contemptuously. "You old hypocrite you!"

"Yes, on a night like this!" mimicked the hard old
voice. "Go!"

"Not on your life!" said Rand firmly. "We'll get
out in the morning and no sooner! I can't answer for
Miss Hathaway, but I rather think she won't care to
stay here any longer after the insulting things you've
said to her!"

"Certainly not!" said Dale quietly, giving George
a grateful look. She suddenly felt a thrill of thank-
fulness as she realized the sympathy and understanding that seemed to have sprung up between herself
and this young man with the tender eyes and the
trustworthy mouth.

"Oh no, of course not!" mocked the angry woman
looking contemptuously at Dale, "I don't suppose
you'd care to stay after *he* left!"

Dale's face flamed but she spoke calmly:

"No, I shouldn't, Mrs. Beck. I've never addressed
more than half a dozen sentences to Mr. Rand before
tonight, nor he to me. We've barely nodded as we
passed each other on the stairs occasionally, but he
seems to be the only honorable person in the house,

and I certainly would not want to remain here after he was gone. If you'll wait just a minute, Mrs. Beck, I'll give you that fifty cents you paid for my laundry this morning while I was away."

Mrs. Beck received the money grimly, looked down at the fifty-cent piece doubtfully, then glanced toward the bed where the sleeping baby lay.

"Two in a room is extra!" she announced vindictively. "A dollar a night for transients!"

Indignantly Dale took out a dollar from her worn little purse, and was about to give it to Mrs. Beck, but a hand intervened.

"That'll be on the baby, Mrs. Beck!" said George Rand with flashing eyes. "Try and collect!"

The old Pharisee gave him a vengeful look and met one from the young man that made her quail. Presently without another word she turned and stamped down the stairs, and the two young people were left alone with the baby.

"I'm sorry!" said Rand penitently when they heard the click of the lock in the downstairs door. "I had no idea what I was getting you into. I didn't know that there were people in the world so inhuman!"

Dale held her head high and there was almost a smile on her lips.

"I'm *glad!*" she said with a glint of pride in her eye. "You were wonderful!"

Rand looked at her in wonder. What a girl she

was! Somehow he had a desire to put his arms about her and comfort her, but he only said gently:

"You ought to go to bed! You're getting all blue under the eyes like the baby!"

Dale laughed softly. She wanted to cry but she put on a brave front and laughed.

"Oh, I'm all right," she said, taking a deep breath. "Only I do wish there was some way to keep that baby! He's such a darling, and I'm afraid somebody else won't care and will let him die. I hate to think of his going to an institution. Institutions are all right, I suppose, only he seems something special. He's very sweet, even sick and thin the way he is. I haven't anybody in the world, and it's likely he hasn't either. I'd like to have him if I had a way to keep him. It seems a pity there isn't a way."

"Well, I'm in the same boat myself. I haven't anybody in the world any more. I'm all alone!"

Rand sighed wistfully.

"He certainly is a cute little beggar," he went on. "I wish—" He hesitated and then abruptly stepped to the door.

"Well, good night. You get some sleep. Call me if you need me. There may be a solution in the morning, who knows?"

He stamped noisily up the stairs to the third story front and slammed his door, locking it with a decided rattle of the key.

Dale smiled to herself as she closed her own with

a bit of a slam too, and equal clattering of her key. She felt morally certain a pharisaical ear was down in the hall listening.

It was getting on toward morning before the dawn had really come, that she heard a soft tapping of finger tips on her door, though she had heard no step.

She slipped softly from the bed, drew her kimono about her closer and opened the door.

There stood Rand under the weak bulb that illumined that end of the hall. He looked anxiously at her, his rumpled hair giving him an endearing boyish look.

"Are you all right?" he whispered. "I thought I heard the little chap cry. I'll bet you haven't slept a wink all night!"

Dale smiled.

"Well, I didn't sleep so much, but I'm all right. I'm fine. I had the baby on my mind, you see. But I loved it. He was as good as gold."

"Well, he better be!" growled Rand tenderly. "All you've done for him! Can't I take him now and let you get some sleep?"

Dale giggled softly.

"He's sound asleep and mustn't be disturbed," she whispered. "But you don't look as if you'd slept a wink yourself," she challenged.

Rand grinned.

"I had you on my mind," he countered. "You were good as gold but I had to worry about you."

Their eyes met and something flashed between them, something deep and sweet and tender.

Dale's eyes lit with a sudden gladness. She drooped their fringes to hide her soul that came up to look out, and her delicate face grew suddenly rosy with embarrassment.

He gave her a lovely smile with an admonition to go back to bed, and was gone, as silently as he had come.

It was in the rose and gray of a new day that the baby stirred from its deep sleep and began to whimper, turning its little fuzzy head from side to side and vainly striving to extract nourishment from the blanket that enveloped it.

Dale came awake startled. She had been crouched uncomfortably by the baby's side on the narrow bed, and now she heard the hoarseness in his small outcry. Was he going to have croup or something terrible? Of course it was to be quite expected after the exposure he had been through. She put out an anxious hand and touched his forehead. It was hot and dry and his thin little cheeks were flushed. Oh, if he had a fever how would that affect his being moved today? For she couldn't think of staying in that house with a sick baby. Mrs. Beck would make it intolerable.

With anxiety in her heart she went about warming the bottle and got the baby as comfortable as she could, glad that he dropped off to sleep again while he was feeding. Then she tiptoed around the room gathering up her things. She must be packed and ready for whatever came.

There wasn't much to pack of course. She hadn't a very large wardrobe, and many of her summer things were laid neatly in her trunk already, to be out of the way.

She had been burning the oil stove all night to keep the room tolerably warm for the baby, and now she began to realize that the oil would soon be spent and the stove would go out. She wouldn't dare go down and ask for more oil. If she did Mrs. Beck would not give it to her, she was sure, even if she offered to pay more than the regular price for it.

She cast an anxious glance at the flame to see if it was as bright as usual, and felt of the pan of water on the top. The water was pretty hot so she took the precaution to fill the hot water bottle which was now only lukewarm after the long night of service. Then she wrapped the bottle with thick covers to save its heat, and laid the bundle close to the baby.

Her own toilet had to be brief for the baby might wake at any minute. She laid her hat and coat and purse on a chair and set her door a little ajar so that Rand could signal to her without calling the attention of the first floor to the fact.

She had no fear that the other girls on the hall would disturb her for they had come in very late, and by the few words of their maudlin conversation she had overheard she judged it would be later in the morning before they came on the scene. She hoped she and the baby could get off before that.

She sat waiting, glancing out the window at the lovely scene. The storm was over and the sun had arisen. The world looked like fairy-land. The city's grime and dirt were covered with fleecy white, and the rose of the sky was reflected in its whiteness. The lovely poem about a city lying like a world newborn came and hovered on the edge of her memory again, but she was too anxious to try to think out the words. The baby was breathing hoarsely, and crying out now and then like a wee protest. She was sure he was going to be sick. And the fire was blinking low. She turned down the wick to preserve the oil as long as possible, and began to feel cold herself. What ought she to do? It wouldn't do to let the baby get cold. He had given one or two hoarse little coughs already. Should she go to the front hall and call up the stairs for Mr. Rand? Of course that would bring more scorn down upon her head, but she couldn't stop for that if there was more danger for the baby.

She bowed her head and asked for quick guidance, and then she heard the front door open and close, and feet in the lower hall stamping off the snow. Then quiet footsteps stole up the stairs and she saw Rand coming toward her door. Ah! He must have got up early and gone out! Perhaps he had gone to the police. But would they care for a sick baby clothed mostly in blankets? Her heart sank.

She was standing by her door with her eyes wide when he came up to her, and the baby chose that second to cry out, and give a wild little hoarse croupy cough.

She saw that Rand was on the alert at once.

"Is he sick?" he asked in a low whisper.

"I'm afraid so," said Dale. "His head is hot and he keeps giving those sharp tight little coughs."

Rand looked troubled.

"Well, we're getting out of here! I've been to the police station, and I'm taking the baby at once. Can you fix him up so he won't get much cold air?"

Dale's heart sank.

"I'll do my best," she said sadly, "but I'm afraid for him. Are you going to hand him over to the police?"

"Supposedly." George Rand grinned briefly. "But don't you worry. Now, *I'm* taking the baby, understand, *not* you! You will stay here and finish picking up things, and be ready when your taxi comes in fifteen minutes. Is that too soon?"

"Oh, no," said Dale struggling for self-control. "I'm all ready now."

"That's good. Now! What's this? The hot water bag? Well, all right. Yes, I'll hold it carefully. I won't let it get away from him. And I'll watch out for that veil thing you have over his face. No, I won't let him smother, and I won't let the cold air get to him. By the way, is this the old Pharisee's blanket you have around him? I ought to pay her for it."

"No, thank goodness," said Dale. "It's an old one of my own."

"Okay. That's fine. Now is he ready?"

"Yes! *Oh!*" said Dale, and the tears welled to her eyes. George Rand turned, holding the baby cautiously, and looked deep into her eyes.

"Can't you trust me?" he asked in a very low voice. "Here! Don't read this till you get in the taxi," and he slid a letter into her hand and hurried away down the stairs.

Dale stood at the head of the stairs and looked after him. The baby was gone, and she didn't know whether she would ever see it again! Perhaps the police would not understand and would let it die! Well, probably Mrs. Beck would think that was a good thing for everybody concerned, but somehow it broke her heart to think of it.

Then the feel of the letter in her hand recalled her to the present, and she backed into her room and concealed the letter in her handbag. Mrs. Beck was liable to appear at any minute, and she did not wish to be questioned about that letter.

There had been a furtive opening of the door of the downstairs front room into the hall as Rand went out noisily, and Dale had no doubt but that two women were curiously looking out their front window. Mrs. Beck would be sure to come up very soon now and she felt she would like to forestall her. So she turned out the little blinking stove that was giving final gasps of light in a hectic way. She went carefully through the four drawers of the pine chest to make sure she had left nothing, and she turned the bedclothes back and left them neatly airing. Then she hurried downstairs, and none too soon for Mrs. Beck was just opening her door to come out and presumably go up.

"I brought you my key, Mrs. Beck," said Dale in a cold young voice. "I turned out the stove and left the bed to air. I guess that's about all. There goes the doorbell. I think that's my taxi. I'll just go up and show him the way."

"No, you won't either, I'll go myself," said Mrs. Beck disagreeably. "I never let strangers go out of the house without inspecting my room before they leave!"

"Oh, of course, Mrs. Beck. That's quite all right!"

"Well it had better be all right!" said Mrs. Beck irately, tramping up the stairs, leaving Dale to open the door and escort her taxi driver up after her trunk.

She had her bags piled together on the trunk in the middle of the floor, and the man gathered them up and said he would come back for the trunk. While he was gone Mrs. Beck nosed around and counted the sheets and pillow case and towels, and looked scornfully at the small portion of scented soap that

Dale had left in the soap dish, and finally said, with a withering glance about, "Where's the baby?"

"Mr. Rand took it away," said Dale quietly.

"Did he take it to the police?" The voice was very sharp. "Because if he didn't I'm going to call them up myself."

"I really don't know, Mrs. Beck," said Dale haughtily. "He told me he had been to police headquarters, and I suppose that is where he was taking the baby."

"Oh! You don't know! You *say* you don't know!"

The taxi man returned and gathered up the trunk, and Dale with a lifting of her head proudly walked down the stairs after him and made no reply.

But Mrs. Beck followed after.

"You'd better leave me your address," she called after her in a raucous voice. "There might be some mail."

Dale turned and answered:

"There will be no mail, I am sure, but if there should be you can tell the postman to put it in General Delivery." And Dale went down the steps and got into the taxi.

As soon as they had turned the corner out of sight of the house Dale opened her letter.

It was not long. Only a single sheet, written in haste.

Dear Partner: Your driver will take you to 728 Carroll Building, South Seventeenth Street. I'll meet you at the desk. Don't worry. For your protection I am doing it this way.

That was all, and it was unsigned. Her heart beat rather wildly as she folded the paper and put it back in her bag. Sudden tears sprang to her eyes. For her "protection," the note said. That must mean so that it would be impossible for her to tell Mrs. Beck anything. Well, she hadn't told anything to Mrs. Beck and now presently this anxiety would be over. Seventeenth Street wasn't so very far away. But oh, if he had only told her what he had done with the baby!

Chapter 9

As the taxi rolled along through the streets that were so clogged with snow that traffic was very much impeded, Dale sat there trying to be calm, and praying in her heart:

"Oh, God, help me to trust You in this. Help me to be willing to have this as You want it. I don't know why I care so awfully about it, but it does seem as if that poor little baby had taken right hold of my heart strings. Of course I know I couldn't have him, but Lord, do give him to somebody who will care, and love him, and help him to get well and strong. Lord, please take care of him, and help me to trust it all with You."

The apartment house before which the taxi stopped was unpretentious, but pleasant-looking, and there was a tiny park across from it. At another time Dale would have enjoyed looking about and wishing such a place could be her destination. But now her mind was full of what had become of the baby, and what she was going to do next.

"You want yoh baggage carried upta seventh flo'?"

questioned the driver. "The gentleman said 728."

Dale caught her breath and tried to answer as if she knew all about it. Where in the world was she going, anyway? Should she go blindly any farther? But of course she could trust Mr. Rand. His eyes had been so honest as he looked into hers just as he was leaving, and had said "Can't you trust me?" Of course she had to trust him.

True, she had not known him long, but even Mrs. Beck's words about him were a recommendation, although her standards were low. But if there had been anything very wrong about him she surely would have made it known.

Then again she lifted her heart:

"Dear Father, don't let me go wrong. Guide me!"

She got out of the cab, and went in to the building, and there stepping out of the elevator and coming toward her was Rand, smiling and quiet.

"So glad you came through all right," he said. "Is the man bringing your things in? Yes, porter," to the doorman, "those are the bags. Take them right up."

Rand did not talk on the way as they shot up to the seventh floor, and Dale tried to keep the question out of her eyes, but he knew she was imploring him to tell her where the baby was.

"He's all right," he assured her gravely with a comforting smile.

And then the elevator door opened and they were walking down the hall, with her trunk and bags miraculously appearing from the opposite end of the hall.

Rand opened a door and let Dale into what seemed like a heaven below in contrast to her little back hall bedroom.

And there was the baby still in his chrysalis of blanket, veil and all, lying in a cunning willow crib, and yelling his little head off in a fair frenzy, getting all tangled up in the fine knit white shoulder shawl that Dale had put over his face to protect him from the cold.

Dale flung off her hat and coat and flew to his assistance. The stolid chambermaid who had been put on duty while Rand went down to meet Dale, looked at her curiously, but Rand dismissed her, and closed the door.

"A doctor, a child specialist, will be here in half an hour, and he is bringing a nurse with him," Rand said. "I thought perhaps you would like to put some warm suitable garments on the baby before they get here. I had a lot of things sent up for you to pick out what you thought would be best."

He pointed to a big white box lying on a table. He lifted the cover and Dale recognized a dainty little layette.

"Oh, that's nice!" she said in relief. "I was going to try to make him some, only there wasn't time last night."

"Well, I didn't know just what to get of course, so

I told the woman he was about so long, and she sent up what she thought would do." He measured solemnly the approximate length of the little foundling, and Dale smiled in her heart over the scene of this purchase. It would be something she could laugh about later perhaps, but just now there was too much to be done.

The baby was crying fiercely, mouthing at the blanket, and struggling with his entanglements, and every time he drew in his breath there was a tight hoarse cough. Whooooo-*ough!* Whoooooo-ough! It was nerve racking. It seemed as if the little throat and lungs were being torn apart with each spasm.

Dale untangled the big soft cobweb of veil and flung it aside and Rand stood gravely by and gathered it up, folding it awkwardly and laying it on a chair.

"If these things aren't right the shop is just around the corner and I can go and get whatever you want," Rand said meekly.

Dale turned an abstracted smile upon him.

"How nice!" she said, and worked deftly on.

The room was heavenly warm, and that was good. Dale got off the wrappings as fast as she could, and with one hand reached for some garments, putting them on hurriedly, taking the struggling mite unawares as it were. Perhaps she would have been more awkward herself, doing this unaccustomed work with Rand gravely watching her, if she had not realized that at any minute now a strange doctor and a critical trained nurse might enter, and see her little charge in lowly attire. She must get him into some shape where he could be handled decently, and kept warm.

"Poor baby! Poor little fellow!" she crooned, as Rand handed her out the garments.

There was a little wool shirt with long sleeves, and the tiny form was almost lost in its generous folds. There was a little wool slip or petticoat of finest weave. Even in her haste Dale recognized how fine and dainty the garments were, and she rejoiced that Rand had done this. Little fine wool stockings that came above the spindling skinny knees in a comforting way, and a little flannel dressing gown of palest blue all scalloped round about with hand embroidered buttonholing. Oh, he could have gotten plainer cheaper things at that little shop around the corner, Dale was sure, but he had picked out fine sweet attire for the little stray waif, and Dale was glad!

"Are they all right?" he asked meekly. "Will they do?"

"They are wonderful!" said Dale. "Lovely as any baby could desire. It was wonderful of you to get them! And now I wonder if we ought not to give him a little hot water? I'm a bit afraid to try milk till the doctor gets here. And he is so hoarse! Oh, I wish he would come!"

Dale sat down beside the crib and fed the baby drops of hot water, and the little fellow looked up pitifully at her, protesting, but swallowed the water, though he spilled a great part of it on the towel that was under his chin.

Rand had opened another package, and there were a pair of lovely white blankets with blue satin ribbon bindings. He spread one out over the child's feet.

"He doesn't look so bad now, does he?" said George, looking proudly down on his protégé. "Looks like a regular guy, doesn't he?"

Dale looked up and smiled, and then amazingly found she was weeping!

The telephone announced that the doctor and nurse had arrived and were coming up, and Dale gave the last touches to the child's outfit, brushed the tears away from her eyes, and bent her energies upon soothing the baby.

Rand had already, it appeared, given a brief outline of the baby's history to date, so far as he knew it, and after he had introduced Dale as the young woman who had helped get the child warmed and fed, he proceeded to describe it again, most briefly.

"Yes. Well, old man, you've been through a lot in a short time, haven't you?" said Dr. Mackenzie, putting on some earphones and stooping to listen to the baby's lungs and heart.

The room was very still while the doctor looked the baby over carefully, asked a few keen questions, some of which Rand and Dale could answer and some they could not.

The nurse stood by the radiator warming her

hands. She had stepped into one of the side rooms, and returned in full array of uniform. Now she was capable and ready for the next act when the doctor should give the word.

At last the doctor straightened up and looked at them.

"Well, I guess we've got a good rousing case of pneumonia. I don't see how we're going to get by without it."

Then he called for glasses and a spoon, and gave quick directions to the nurse.

Dale listened to every word carefully and took mental note for her own use when she should be taking care of the baby—if she did. For as yet they had not talked over any plans, and Dale had not been able to think connectedly about what she herself was going to do. Her whole mind was taken up by this little sick child. It was foolish of course, but she couldn't possibly continue to care for him while she was working for her living, and she must have a job as soon as possible. There was no other way. She could not think of taking a loan from Mr. Rand. That was out of the question. Even a few dollars would be a load upon her mind until she got it repaid.

She still had her hundred dollars of course, for she had put it in the bank at once before she left the lawyer's office, and she had been able to add just a little to it now and then, but not much. Experience

had taught her that it would not take long for even
a hundred dollars to melt away under daily use. Especially in a lovely apartment like this one. She could
not afford to stay. Not after the stress of the illness
was over.

Of course she would not desert the baby while she
was needed here, at least till after the crisis. She knew
what pneumonia was, and her heart sank as she saw
the look on the doctor's face. It was serious all right,
and perhaps the poor little flower of a life would not
last but a few hours. It would not be strange if that
was the case, a poor little bit of humanity out in the
bitter cold unclad!

She looked around on the pleasant room, large,
with two long windows looking toward that snow-
clad park; a soft velvet carpet on the floor, good
furniture; a luxurious couch, several easy chairs, a
combined desk and bookcase, though there were no
books in it. There were two bedrooms connecting,
and a bath, and later she discovered there was a small
kitchenette, though scarcely more than a boxed-in
stove and cabinet and sink. It was quite possible to
get simple meals there.

She discovered that Rand had taken a room on a
lower floor of the same house, and there was a telephone in each room so he could be called at any
time in the night if he should be needed.

Rand had gone out with the doctor, but when he
came back and she had a chance to talk with him she

remonstrated with him.

"You shouldn't have got such a fine apartment," she said. "This must be awfully expensive. You couldn't afford it."

He smiled gravely, almost sadly.

"Yes, I could afford it," he said. "You know I had been saving up to get such an apartment for my mother. But now she is gone I have no more need to go on starvation rations. I think she would like me to do this. The little chap needed it, and we couldn't really hope to save his life at Mrs. Beck's. Besides, we hadn't time to shop around. I had to be spry to get all done I had to do this morning. Then there was the doctor and the nurse to be considered, to say nothing of my partner."

He gave her a warm look and a flush stole into her cheeks.

"Well, of course the nurse," she agreed. "They are used to pretty fine places, I imagine. She seems to be a wonderful nurse. But you didn't need to bother about me. I could have gone anywhere."

"Yes?" he said with an amused lifting of his brows. "I know you *would*, but I felt you shouldn't. You have done wonders in that little hole of a back room with that outrageous smelling oil stove, and nothing to work with. But you deserve the best that can be found, and I meant you should have it, at least while you are interested enough in this kid to help me. So please don't let's have any more protests on that score. I knew we had to have a nurse, and she had to have her room, and you needed another. The nurse is about the best that can be had for pneumonia, the doctor tells me, and the two of you together ought to pull the little fellow through if it can be done. What I want to find out is just how soon you absolutely must go to a job. I hope you'll let me make up to you anything you may be losing through this activity in which we are engaged?"

"I don't see why you should," said Dale a little proudly. "Aren't I a partner? You called me that!"

She looked up at him shyly and smiled.

"And if I'm a partner I have a right to at least a share in the expenses, even if I can't afford to pay half. I have a little money saved up, not much, but it may help out some, and I can stay and help through the crisis, and not suffer. It wouldn't be of the least use for me to try to hunt a job just now. It's too near Christmas for people to be hiring new helpers, and I'd be too worried about the child."

A tender beautiful light came into his eyes as she said that, and she flushed a little at the look he gave her.

"Okay, partner! If that's the way you want it, so it shall be! And perhaps after this is straightened out I may be able to help a little at getting that job you are anxious about. They do have secretaries and stenographers in newspaper offices, you know. I'll keep it in mind, and you needn't worry."

Suddenly he reached out and laid his hand gently on hers.

"I appreciate you!" he said looking deeply into her eyes. And then with a warm grasp of her hand he pulled her to her feet. "Come on," he said, "you and I are going down to the house restaurant to lunch! I've got some things to tell you. And the nurse said she wouldn't be needing us for an hour. Then you can come back and spell her while she goes to lunch."

They went down to a quiet table in the far end of a large dining room, and as soon as they had ordered he began to talk in a low tone.

"You know I haven't been idle this morning," he said.

"I didn't think you had," said Dale. "You've accomplished wonders in so short a time. Getting us all moved to such a delightful place, contacting the doctor and nurse, and even buying a layette! That was two or three days' hard work. And you said you went to the police headquarters. I don't see when you did it all."

"Oh, I did that last night before I slept. It was only a couple of blocks away, and I felt uneasy till it was accomplished."

"Well, what did they say? Did you find out anything?"

"Yes, I did. I found the baby's mother!"

"You did?" said Dale, her eyes full of mingling

delight and anxiety. "What was she like?"

"Like a little dead white lily!"

"Dead?" Dale's eyes were wide with sorrow. "Oh, poor little thing. Then she didn't just throw her baby away."

"No, I think not! She gave evidence of having been half starved herself. She must have dropped in the snow just after she laid the baby in the doorway. The ambulance took her to the hospital but she was gone, they say, by the time she reached there."

"Do they know who she was? Was there anything about her to identify her?"

"No, not really. She was wearing a thin little gold ring, a wedding ring, but there were only initials in it. It might be traced somehow, I don't know. We'll do our best. But there were no marks on her clothing, which was of the plainest and much worn."

"But how can you be sure she was the baby's mother?"

"Well, it's a curious thing. She was wearing a man's vest underneath her tattered dress, either for the slight warmth it would give her, or because she wished to save it. It looks very much to me like the same cloth that is in the old coat the baby was wearing! I'm having the coat thoroughly cleaned now and compared with the vest. I thought it might be a clue to trace who the child was. He might sometime be glad we had done it."

Her eyes met his with deep sympathy in them.

"Oh, yes," she said. "That was right."

"I brought the ring with me," he said, and taking out a tiny fold of tissue paper he handed it over to her.

She unwrapped it tenderly. Some poor little girl away from everybody who loved her. Her husband gone! Or was he? Would he leave her wantonly, a woman with a tiny baby? No, for she wouldn't have cherished his old clothes. There was so little warmth in just a vest. Dale felt sure the woman would have left it behind if she hadn't loved it. But she said nothing about it then, just turned the pitiful little ring in her fingers and studied the inscription carefully.

"This should be kept for him," she said softly.

"Yes," said Rand. "It shall be."

"Where—was she? In the hospital?"

"No, in the morgue," said Rand sadly. "I had the body moved to an undertaker's. I'd like to arrange for a little service, just for the sake of leaving the record of it for the kid. It might mean something to him—if he lives."

Dale's face softened.

"Yes," she said. "Of course. We can write an account of it for him. It is bound to mean something to him."

"I was thinking," said Rand after a pause during which their order was brought, "I was wondering if you would mind, if you can be spared a few minutes, just running out and trying to find something—a dress and things for the woman. It would be nice, wouldn't it?"

"Of course," said Dale understandingly. "I'll be glad to go. White, I think would be good, wouldn't you? Like the snow on the night she died. White like one of God's angels. It would be nice to tell the child it was white. How does she look? What kind of hair?"

"Rather lovely if she weren't so worn and thin. Her hair is gold, and curly. She might have been beautiful once when she was in health."

"Poor little girl," said Dale. "I wish we could have told her that we were caring for the little child. But perhaps—the angels may tell her. God may tell her!"

Rand gave her a quick appreciative look. He liked her tender faraway gaze. He felt she really believed what she was saying. He had never met any girls who would have said a thing like that, or who would have believed it.

"Perhaps!" he said thoughtfully. "There are probably a lot of things like that that we don't understand, and don't know about. I wish I knew more about such things. I've rather got away from what my mother taught me, but I find a longing now and then to get back to them. I wonder, now, where I could find a preacher who wouldn't mind coming out of his way to hold a little service for a poor little unknown? Would you know any? Of course I know who the great preachers are, the eloquent and renowned. Somehow I wouldn't want to ask them, even if I paid them something pretty nice. I would rather have a plain one who understood and would be in sympathy."

"Yes," said Dale unexpectedly, "I do know one. He preaches at a little chapel where the people are real. I haven't been but a few times, but always there has been something good to remember."

"That sounds like it," said Rand. "I wanted somebody like that. Of course there'll be nobody there but—myself perhaps. Would you go?"

"Of course," said Dale, "unless I'm needed here."

"I think we could fix it at a right time. Now, suppose I call up that preacher. What is his number?"

"I have it upstairs in my bag. I'll get it for you before you go."

They planned the brief service as thoughtfully as though it had been for one of their own, and then when they had finished eating Rand took her out and showed her where the dress shop was, and together they selected a soft white frock that the angels might look on with content, a little boy might grow up to be happy about, and a mother long gone to glory might be glad and thankful about.

"There must be flowers," said Dale sweetly. "She won't have had many flowers in these latter days, I'm sure. Of course there will be flowers in Heaven where she's gone, but there must be flowers in the picture for the little boy to think about. I will send white roses. I'll put a white rose in her hand."

"I'll send flowers too," said Rand. "Bright flowers to make it cheerful. Crimson perhaps."

"Crimson for the blood of Christ that washes white as snow and saves from sin," said Dale very softly, and looked up shyly. She did not know what the young man would think of that. They hadn't ever spoken about such things. "Perhaps she was saved," she murmured.

Rand looked at her almost embarrassed.

"My mother used to talk that way," he said after a minute. "I'm glad you're like that."

She flashed a little tender smile at him.

"And I think," she said after a minute, "that we should send some flowers from the baby. She would like that, and he will like to be told that he sent them. Forget-me-nots would be nice if we can find them."

"Yes, forget-me-nots," said Rand. "We'll find them! Perhaps as you say she will be watching."

"Yes, and the angels will be there to see. It will be quite a gathering. I never thought of that before."

"You make everything rather wonderful, you know," said Rand in quiet admiration. "That's a beautiful thought. It makes it all worth while."

"Yes," said Dale, "I suppose everything is worth while if we can only see God and the angels in it."

Rand looked at her and marveled. This was a girl

in a thousand. He hadn't even known there was one
in the whole world like this one. And he had happened on her! He knew girls in the office. Plenty of
them. Hard working girls, with tired eyes and be-
draggled hair. Sometimes they got a permanent or
a wave, and even then it looked as if it were made
out of cloth, cut in scallops, and one knew it wouldn't
stay looking dressed up. He knew other girls with
hard eyes, and highly illuminated countenances, and
hair that was precise in regular waves, or rolls or
whatever fashion ordained, well done, and often
becoming. Some of them were even brave and clever
and would go into fire or danger or in the vicinity of
crime, with a daring that would befit a man, but he
knew not one who even thought about God, or angels, or would dare voice such a thought if they had
ever had it. But this girl had a sweet face, with great
brown eyes that had a real tenderness in them, eyes
that hadn't been used to flirting. They were tired
eyes, and yet they could twinkle. There was a shadow
of sadness about the sweet droop to her mouth, but
those lips could smile, and they could frame lovely
comfort for a little helpless cherub of the street.
Something happened to his heart as he watched her,
getting a glimpse of a world invisible that might be
all around him at that moment.

"Perhaps it is!" he said thoughtfully. "My mother
used to talk that way sometimes. That is, she used to

seem as if God was very near to her. I don't know whether she had got so far as to take the angels into her scheme of things or not. But Heaven was pretty real to her I know, and they must have been somewhere in the background, I'm sure."

Dale gave him a quick appreciative look.

"Oh, you *would* have had a mother like that of course!" she said earnestly. "And how glad she must be for what you are doing now."

"I guess she is," he said, giving her a wistful look that grew into a tender smile.

Then he glanced at his watch.

"Well, say, partner, we'll have to be hurrying if we're going to get back and relieve the nurse. We might just stop on the way and give the order for the flowers."

So they went on their way together, partners in a blessed mission for an unknown woman whose body was waiting to be laid away with unexpected ceremony and dignity.

It was lovely the way they chose the flowers, all with the thought of the little baby who was lying so desperately sick not far away, trying to think what he would want some far day if he lived to grow up and know about the little dead mother who had perhaps done the best she could for him.

But when they got back to the apartment, even their inexperienced eyes could see that the baby was no better, and that the nurse wore her gravest professional look.

"I've sent for the doctor!" she said crisply, as if she were giving an order. "You'd better both stay by till he comes."

Chapter 10

WHEN THE DOCTOR ARRIVED HIS FACE WAS GRAVE indeed.

"I don't know how it is going to come out," he said quietly to Rand. "We'll do our best to save the little life, but it looks exceedingly doubtful. This thing has taken a form that is always hard to combat, and what you have told me of the child and the experience he went through, makes his background of the worst. Still he may pull through. Be assured that the best we have we'll be giving you."

And when he went away, and the nurse went out for a brief walk and her lunch, Rand and Dale settled down near the little willow crib to wait and watch.

There wasn't much that they could do, just a little matter of giving medicine, a few spoonfuls of feeding, certain directions to be followed in case of emergency which might or might not come.

They did not talk, except now and then in whispers when it was necessary.

Rand sat in a big chair with his eyes closed for the

most part, and Dale, a little closer to the crib, sat with bowed head. And then finally she slipped down on her knees, her head bent, her eyes closed. Once when Rand opened his eyes he saw her lips were moving. She was praying! He wasn't used to girls who prayed—at least not before anyone, even quietly.

Very gravely he sat there thinking about it. He hadn't prayed himself in a long time. His life in the city away from his home influences had not helped him to feel near to God. But he began then to pray in his heart.

But the baby began to start and cry out and they were on the alert again, doing what they had been told to do, their hearts failing them as they touched the little hot hands, so feeble and helpless. The poor little lamb who had no one of his own to do for him. The more they worked the more their own hearts went out to the child, and looking at her once as he laid the baby softly down on its pillow, Rand saw that there were tears on Dale's cheeks, though perhaps she did not know it.

The nurse came in presently, gave a quick glance at the child, another at the clock, asked a crisp question or two, and then took charge.

Rand took his coat and hat and stepped to the door, and Dale followed him into the hall for a moment.

"Does he look worse to you?" she asked anxiously.

"Why, I'm afraid my judgment wouldn't be worth

much," he said. "I've never been around sickness much, and especially with children. He looks sick enough, but they say children can be very sick and get well quickly. I wouldn't grieve. He isn't our baby. He belongs to God, I guess. If God wants him to live I think he will, don't you?"

She smiled tenderly.

"Yes, I guess that's right," said Dale with a tremble of her lip, "but somehow I guess I've been thinking—he belonged—to us—to *you*, I mean. You found him."

"To *us*." He said it with a grave smile, and he reached out and laid his hand on hers. "If I found him you saved his life. How you have worked to save him! I'll never forget that of you!"

"Well," she said smiling in the midst of her tears, "you can't help loving a little scrap of helplessness like that. He's sweet! I don't see how he can be so sweet when he's been through so much."

"I know," said Rand, and he brushed a mist from his own eyes. "It gets you, doesn't it? Well, I've got to go along. I'm going to find that preacher if I can, and arrange for that service. It will have to be adjustable, because we might be needed here, you know. Would you feel like going to it?"

"Oh, yes, I *must!*" said Dale. "I would want to see that everything was right to remember—to tell the baby if he lives. Oh—anyway, I'd want to be there.

I feel as if she belonged to us. She hasn't anybody else now."

"That's—*dear* of you!" said Rand with a tender smile. "All right. I'll fix it the best way possible for us all. Then I've got to run over to the office for a few minutes to turn in some copy I wrote last night. They're depending on it. I promised I'd have it there or I wouldn't leave here just now, but I'll be back as soon as possible."

"Oh, you wrote all night!" reproached Dale. "You didn't get your rest! You mustn't get sick, you know."

He gave her a quick grateful smile.

"I'm all right," he said. "I'm tough! I'm used to going out on assignment, and losing my sleep for several nights in succession. Don't worry about me. Just you take care of yourself. You look rather all in your own self. Good-by!"

He gave her another quick handclasp and was gone. She turned back to the room again feeling what a tower of strength he was.

She went back and the nurse motioned her to go and lie down, but she could not sleep. She kept thinking how very strange it was that she was here with a little foundling baby she had never seen until yesterday, partners with a young man she had never known before till yesterday, and yet she felt that she knew him better than any man she had ever met before. Knew him and trusted him. What would her mother think about this whole situation?

Last night she had expected to spend this day in a fruitless search for a job, and she hadn't once thought of a job all day!

Then the baby roused and had another choking spell, and she was on the alert to help. This seemed a job that God had given her, and she had no thought for anything else now.

That night was a strenuous time. Rand came back while the doctor was there. He stayed and took one of the night watches while the nurse was sleeping, and the baby was desperately sick. The doctor stayed himself for a long time, watching the little feeble fluttering breath that came and went, the white little face that seemed to be turning to wax as they looked, the faint pulse. And when toward morning the demon of the disease seemed to be subdued for the time being, there was great relief in the little apartment. The baby seemed better that day, and Rand and Dale slipped away to the brief service at the undertaker's house. The poor little mother lay in her simple white robe with her baby's forget-me-nots in her thin white hands. A strange look of peace was on her very young white face, framed by its soft gold curls like a child's. The other flowers were about her feet.

"She must have been lovely!" said Dale, as they stood looking at her for a moment before the minister read precious words from the Bible and prayed a tender prayer.

It was soon over. The simple casket was handed into the care of the undertaker until such time as Rand could secure the right place in some quiet cemetery, where he meant to put a little white stone at her head, with the initials from the wedding ring inscribed upon it.

They went back to find the baby quietly sleeping. The tension that had been with them so long relaxed for a few hours, and they all got a little much needed rest.

But the disease was by no means conquered, and when the doctor came the next time he shook his head and frowned. The little heart was not acting right, and the fearful cough came back in full force. Anxiety stalked in and took its place. Death marched into the room and glanced around, and with a mocking smile stepped just outside the door again, but lingered about, not deigning to withdraw entirely, just lingering in the offing, a continual menace. It seemed as if this state of things were going on forever, and the two partners began to lose heart, and were deeply sad of countenance.

Then one day the nurse went to lie down for an hour and left Dale in charge.

But the baby looked so white, so delicate, as if a breath would blow him away, that Dale's heart was wrung, and after the nurse was gone she knelt beside the little crib, and prayed that God would do His best for the little one.

Rand, coming to the door very quietly, paused outside for an instant, and then softly turned the knob and opened the door. He stood there for an instant watching Dale, and then came tiptoe over and knelt beside her.

Quite quietly he knelt there, and in the low tone in which they had learned to converse near the little sick bed he spoke:

"Oh, Lord, I don't know whether I have any right to come and pray for this sweet little kid. I haven't been the right kind of Christian. I've forgotten Thee. I've lived for myself. I know I haven't been right. But Lord if You'll just have mercy on this poor little kid, and make him get well and grow up to be a good man, I'll try to serve You after this the way I ought to have done before. But Lord, if this isn't Your will, and there's any danger he may grow up to be bad, then please don't let him live. Do what You want to do! And forgive us for wanting this so much, if it isn't the right thing. But anyway Lord, do what You can for our two prayers. We're partners in this, and we both want him to live to be Your child!"

His hand stole out to Dale's in a warm clasp, and then gently he lifted her to her feet, and they smiled at one another.

A few moments after that, in the gray of the early dawning, the nurse came back as they stood there together watching the baby.

She stooped over and looked at the child, touched his little relaxed hand, his forehead.

"Why! He's *better!*" she said, astonished. "His flesh is moist for the first time. When did this happen?"

"Just now, I think," said Dale. "We were praying, and I think it happened then." She spoke with deep conviction, and the nurse looked at her amazed.

"Yes," said Rand, "I think God heard!"

The nurse turned toward him and showed her astonishment. A young man of Rand's evident good sense and fine strength talking like that! And as if he really believed it! She couldn't make it out. For Rand had made his statement like a conviction, as if he had just received a revelation, and were not afraid to let it be known.

The doctor, coming in a little later, looked with satisfaction at the tiny patient.

"He'll pull through now, I think," he said, after looking at the baby. "Man, I hated to come here this morning. I thought the little chap would be gone. I thought last night we had come to the end, but there's been a miracle wrought somehow. I'm sure I didn't do it. And I hated to see the little chap lose out after he's weathered so much."

"Yes," said Rand looking serious, "it was a miracle, I think!" and he stalked over to the window and stood looking out at the great flakes of snow that were falling thick and fast, shutting out the landscape as completely as if there had been a white curtain over the window.

"Yes, a miracle!" said Rand thoughtfully.

"Well, I think we're going to have a white Christmas this year. It certainly looks like it this morning!" said the doctor a little later, coming over to stand by the window where Rand was still watching the snow.

"It was a storm just like this the night the little fellow came," said Rand in a low stirred voice.

The doctor gave him a quick look, and glanced out the window and back to his face, with eyes full of concern, and wonder.

"You don't say!" he answered sympathetically. Then swinging around toward the baby, "Well, little chap, you've weathered it pretty well so far, arriving on a snowflake as it were. We must try and keep you here and make you grow into a good strong man!"

There was heartiness in the doctor's voice, but there was a grave look in his eyes, as if the matter still hung in the balance.

After a minute or two more of silence Rand turned and faced the doctor.

"Doctor, you're not sure about him yet, are you? You aren't perfectly certain that he is going to get well."

The doctor lifted honest eyes and spoke in a very low tone.

"Nothing in this life is certain, young man," he

said. "But it's a lot more likely, a lot more possible that he may recover, than it seemed to be last night! I should say if we can get him through the next two or three days, we could reasonably feel that he was on the highway to recovery. But you certainly have a right to be cheered this morning, for frankly the change seems nothing short of a miracle to me."

That morning Dale took a long nap, her heart more at rest than it had been since the baby was first taken sick, and when she came back into the big room where the baby lay she saw that Rand was kneeling again beside the crib, his head bowed. His whole attitude was one of humble surrender to a higher power, and when he heard her enter the room he rose and the light in his face was like the light from another world.

The nurse appeared on the scene almost at once, so they did not talk, except to ask her how she thought the baby looked now, and they took a careful joy from her encouragement.

That night Rand went away early. He said he had some work to do that he must finish tonight.

He was not far to reach if they should want him. But the nurse assured him that everything was going well, so he need not worry.

Dale took the first part of the night on watch, and about midnight the nurse came on, and Dale went to her rest, sinking into a sweet refreshing sleep as soon as her head touched the pillow. She had intended to do a lot of thinking that night, but sleep took her unawares.

She looked fresh and rested the next morning when Rand came in, a troubled look in his eyes.

"I've got to go on a journey," he said, looking anxiously toward the crib. "At least my editor wants me to, and I suppose I should, since I've just been promoted to larger things, and it behooves me to earn my wages of course. How is the boy? Do you think I should go? I won't stir a step no matter what they say if you think it will worry you to have me gone. I'm not so much good at nursing of course, but if I'm here there are always things I might do if there were need."

"I don't see why you shouldn't go," said Dale. "Of course you ought to. You mustn't lose your job when you've been spending so much money. And anyway it's time I did something in this partnership."

"You?" he smiled. "You're the most important member of the firm. But honestly, I don't need to go if you think I ought not."

"Why shouldn't you go? The doctor said last night we were almost out of the woods."

"Almost?" he said with a troubled look. "I don't like the implied possibility."

"Oh, but we'll be very careful of the little fellow, and you'll be surprised how well he'll look when you get back."

She tried to speak in a cheery voice, but her heart was failing her at the thought of his going. What if something should happen while he was gone, and she would be responsible! After all it was his baby—*he* had found it!

"How long would you be gone?" she asked with a desolate note in her voice.

"About four days at the lowest estimate, maybe five," he said, and his own voice sounded as if he were announcing a trip around the world. "It's some kind of a political conference, and the editor thinks I'm the only one on the paper fitted to cope with the subjects that will come up, and cover them as they should be covered. It's an honor of course, and at any other time I would be shouting with glee, but just now I can't bring myself to be glad over it. I don't want to leave until this boy is all out of the woods, and ordinarily safe."

"Oh, well, that of course is nonsense! Certainly you must go. Don't you think I'm worth anything at all? I can love that baby and care for him and be as anxious over him as you can, and aren't we partners? Can't you trust me just a little? Besides the nurse is inordinately wise and capable, and I'll promise to obey her and the doctor to the very letter."

He smiled tenderly down at her sweet earnest eyes.

"Of course," he said, "but I just don't like to leave you. However, I'll see what the doctor says. It may of course mean a lot to the kid afterward if I'm mak-

ing enough to finance him comfortably through his
life. And anyway four days isn't much, and we have
the telephone, and airplanes."

"Oh! Airplanes!" said Dale with a shadow of worry
in her eyes. "They still seem kind of awful to me."

Rand laughed.

"Some day I'll have to get time off and take you a
ride in one," he said with a mischievous grin.

Then when the doctor came and was consulted he
said at once,

"Why sure! Go! There's no reason in the world
why you should stay here. The little kid is holding
his own nicely. And besides, the little lady'll carry
on. Women do, you know. And sometimes make a
better job of it than the men do."

So in an hour Rand was gone, flying through the
sky, the sky that had sent down such billows of snow,
and might again at any time!

She didn't voice her fears. She didn't want him to
know she cared, was so fearful for him. She even tried
to persuade herself that it was because she dreaded
the responsibility without him. That she wasn't
really worried about him for his own sake. But her
face was sad as she went about the little apartment
and picked up the tiny garments that had been dis-
carded for fresh ones, and made the place look tidy
and pleasant. Though as she did it she marveled at
what a difference it made in a place, even a rented
apartment, when there was no man in it. Well, that

was ridiculous. For a girl who was independent and
had her living to earn pretty soon, she shouldn't go
around and get maudlin because there was no man
in the house. There was a dear baby, and he was
really getting better, and that ought to be enough for
any lonely heart. So she went by herself and thanked
God several times that He was answering prayer and
making the baby get well. And then she added that
earnest plea that he would care for Rand and bring
him safely back to them.

That afternoon the nurse insisted that she should
go out for a walk. She didn't want to go. She felt her
place was here where her responsibility lay, but at
last she yielded. She took her way to the post office,
and found two letters awaiting her in the General
Delivery. She left her apartment address, and hurried on to the bank, scarcely stopping to see who the
letters were from. One was from that agent who had
written her about her uncle's inheritance. Somehow
that seemed a thing of very little interest just now.
Of course if it amounted to anything it might help
her later if she found any chance to do anything for
the baby, but it wouldn't. It couldn't be enough to
make anything nice possible. Not any more than a
pretty garment, or a toy when he was old enough to
care for toys.

It was snowing again when she came out of the
bank and hurried back to the apartment. She looked
up into the wide lowering gray sky that was dotted

with whiteness, and thought of a plane flying high
above it all. She wondered if Rand had reached Chicago yet, and whether he had forgotten all about the
baby by this time. Of course men didn't carry burdens like that very long, not when they had business
cares upon them. And she had gathered that this was
a very important trip for him, and would have to do
with his future success in his chosen profession.

Back in the apartment she removed her snowy coat
and hat, carefully put on a dry dress, that no damp-
ness should come near the precious baby, and re-
manding the nurse to a nap went and sat down near
the sleeping baby to read her letters, but her eyes
were gazing far away into the snowy sky and seeing a
plane go venturing far above the world and the
storm.

Chapter 11

THE FIRST LETTER WAS FROM THE AGENT REGARD-
ing her inheritance, which it appeared was not an
inheritance at all, but money that had been put in
her name from time to time, during her girlhood. It
enclosed papers which she was to fill out and sign in
the presence of a competent witness, establishing her
identity. It suggested that she go to the bank through
which they had first made contact with her, and have
the papers made out in legal form. Then on her coming twenty-first birthday the money would be placed
in the bank to her account, and she would be at liberty to draw upon it. There was also enclosed a check
of several hundred dollars, which represented the
interest on her money for the last six months.

Dale sat stupefied and gazed at that magic little
piece of paper which the letter said belonged to her.
Gazed at it in wonder and couldn't make it seem
real.

Here she had been in dire distress for her daily
bread, mourning because she had so little to tide her
over till she found a job, grieving that she had no

possible means of taking care of this dear baby herself, if it should be in danger of being sent to an orphanage. And she had all this wealth!

For the instant her brain was too numbed to calculate what the whole sum of her capital was, but it seemed enormous to her. From nothing to plenty! That was how she had come! And it was the Lord's doing, that she knew! A direct answer to prayer. More than an answer to her prayer, for she had never asked for much, not even for plenty. "Just a little bit of money!" she had pleaded, and it was quite a while ago. Those days during the baby's illness had seemed so long that she had almost forgotten that she had asked for money. She had entirely forgotten that some money was coming some time. During these last few strenuous days her whole mind had been taken up with the baby and nothing else had seemed to matter.

How was it that a little human mite like that had so entered into her soul and drawn her love? Probably she was going to have another struggle by and by when—but no! This money would make it possible for her to take care of that baby now!

Still it wasn't her baby. It really belonged to Rand. He had found it. She couldn't just pick it up and carry it off without his wish of course. And it was going to be terribly hard to give it up. Tears welled into her eyes as she thought about it.

And because the nurse was going about in the

room, putting things to rights, getting the baby ready
for his evening meal and she didn't want the nurse
to see her tears, she stuffed the letter into its envelope
and took up the other one.

The writing looked strangely familiar as she studied it thoughtfully. Somehow it carried her back into
her school days. Why was that? Was that from Sam
Swayne? It must be. She remembered now that was
the way he used to curl his capital S.

It stirred her curiosity only slightly. She had left
Sam as far behind in her world as her little girlhood
days. He used to be a nice boy, nothing more, and he
got awfully annoying when he was always trying to
hold her hand. She had never had any inclination to
hold hands with any of the boys.

Sam was nice of course, well brought up and a
hard worker. He was active in the church and Sunday School, at least he was the one who passed around
the roll books for the classes, and always distributed
the singing books, and the Sunday School papers,
and sang in the young men's quartette. He hadn't a
very wonderful voice, but he sang accurately, and
could always be depended upon. He was never late
anywhere, and could always be relied on to serve well
on any committee.

She remembered now as keenly as when it happened, how Sam had come to her after her mother's
funeral, his new felt hat in his hand, set accurately
in the creases they had put in it in the store when he

bought it and twisting it around and around in his hands had told her that he had always liked her, and he thought it would be nice if they could get married and settle down together. He said he hadn't money enough yet to buy a house, but he had a good job, and he thought they could scrub along for a couple of years till he could save a down-payment and then she could pick out any house in reason that she'd like.

She had wanted to laugh, but she hadn't. She had felt sad for him. He looked so young and boyish, and her sorrow had made her feel so old then. He had told her she was too pretty to go out and work and that he'd like to take care of her the rest of his life, if she just wouldn't mind going easy at the start till he could get on a little.

She had smiled at him, and told him she was sorry, but she couldn't marry anyone now. Told him she didn't love him. That he was only a good friend, and she would always cherish him as a friend.

But he hadn't given up. He had told her very earnestly that he loved her a lot, and that she would get tired of working for herself and find out she'd like him to take care of her. He said when he got money enough for a down-payment for a house he meant to write to her and tell her to come on and select it.

So she turned to his letter with a curious wonder whether he had been true to his words since he had promised. Poor Sam! Hadn't he got over his infatuation yet? She would hate to have to go all over it again.

Then she turned to the letter and read:

Dear Dale:

It seems a long time since you went away, and it's been deadly lonesome without you. I guess you don't know how a fellow feels when he loves a girl and she turns him down and goes away off and he can't find out for the longest where she is! I think you might have been kind enough to send me your address.

But you know what I said before you left, how I loved you and wanted to marry you, and how I was going to let you know when I was able to get you a house.

So now here I am! Something really wonderful has happened. I've got a job that pays good wages, and I've found a house I can begin to buy right off. I've saved enough for the first down payment, and I want to get married right away. So if you can come home at once and see the house before we take it that would be nice. But anyhow I'm coming to you if you will write and tell me just where and what time of day I can best see you. I'd like to come this week if you can make it convenient, because I've got an option on the house, and it won't last long. Everybody else will be after it. It's a swell little house. So tell me where to come and when. I suppose you are working during the day, so I can come and meet you and take you out to dinner, and then we can go some place and talk it all over.

Yours as ever, Your true lover,
Sam.

Dale closed up the letter quickly and put it in its envelope. She looked over toward the nurse who was feeding the baby with spoonfuls of a prepared formula. She had a feeling that the nurse must have seen the effect of that letter in her face. She felt her cheeks were crimson. She was distressed. Poor Sam! Going as far as that! Picking out the house and getting together the money!

She hurried over to the little desk by the window and began to write rapidly.

Dear Sam:

I certainly was surprised to get your letter, and I'm so sorry that you have kept to your purpose, because Sam, I cannot marry you, ever. I do not love you with the kind of love people ought to have when they marry, and I never can. I admire you very much for your fine principles, and for your courage and bravery to go ahead and accomplish your purposes, but that is not love, and it is not the kind of feeling to base a marriage on.

You are just my good friend, Sam, and always will be that. I would like very much to see you sometime and have a nice little talk, but it can't be at present.

The job I have just now is helping to care for a sick person, and I cannot count on my hours at all, so it wouldn't do any good for you to try and come to see me, not at present. We'll just have to put that off till the right time comes. And Sam, I'd like to put it off until you have got over this idea of wanting to marry me, because you *never* can.

I would be so glad if you could find some other girl you could love, who would love you and make a happy home with you. I really want that for you, Sam. So please get to work and make it come true.

Your true friend,

Dale Hathaway.

Dale went out and mailed that letter at once. She
didn't want Sam coming down here to complicate mat-
ters. How queer to have a proposal of marriage right
in the midst of this strange situation she was in now.
She didn't want any wild ideas getting back to her
home town where they had known her all her life.
Mrs. Beck's remarks suddenly came to mind. There
was no telling what people might not think of her,
caring for a strange little baby, in a sort of partnership with a young man whom she had only known a
few days. Well, she couldn't help it of course. She
couldn't let the poor little soul die. She had to help.
She went sadly back to the apartment, feeling suddenly very much alone. It made all the difference in
the world to have Rand gone. His presence seemed
to make all things right, and maybe that was not as
it should be. Maybe she ought to get out of here before he returned and let him know that she could not
go on like this.

Then the memory of her inheritance came to her.
She had money now, and could take the baby if he
would let her have him. When he came back she
would talk to him about it. Of course if he felt badly
to give him up she mustn't—still, how would he take
care of a baby? Oh, of course he could hire a nurse.

That thought brought a desolate little sadness.
Then she hurried in to see if the baby was all right,
and as she came and stood above him while he was
being fed little sips of water, he seemed to look
straight at her as if he recognized her, and he swal-

lowed the water and then gurgled out a weak little "Ah!" as if he was trying to salute her.

"He knows you!" said the nurse looking up at Dale. "Can you beat that, at his age! And sick as he has been! He's a smart little kiddie though, to know you! Now isn't that sweet?"

The baby was licking his little lips and staring at her in a really concentrated stare. Dale felt a sudden pulling at her heartstrings to think the little thing knew her, recognized the difference between herself and the nurse. She gave him a sweet little smile that said she was glad he knew her, though she wasn't at all sure he did. Yet it did look that way.

And then the telephone rang, and her heart began to beat more wildly. Telephone! Who would call? The doctor?

She hurried to answer, and then she heard Rand's voice, eager, comforting, interested.

"Is that you, Dale?"

He had never called her Dale before, and while she didn't stop just now to analyze the fact, but put it away for happy thinking when this was over, it made her glad. She told herself quite primly that she shouldn't be so glad. Yet of course it was all right, for hadn't he been up in the awful sky, where all sorts of terrible possibilities were lurking? Yes, she was glad he was safe yet. He wasn't away from them in an unknown world. He was right there on the wire, talking in his old familiar voice, wanting to know—"Is that you, Dale?" and her heart leaped up in spite of her chiding.

So she tried to make her own voice sound quite matter-of-fact, "Yes, George!" but somehow she couldn't get rid of the lilt that crept in without her knowledge, and made the two words sound like a madrigal. The prosaic nurse heard it, and pricked up her ears.

"Yes, I thought those two—" she told herself, as she went on with her monotonous work.

"Are you all right, Dale?"

"Oh yes!" like an antiphonal chant. The joy of it seemed to throb over the wire, yet she only thought she was being quite quiet and subdued.

"Did you rest today?"

"Yes sir, a lot," she chanted gaily.

"Well, do you feel all right?"

"Why certainly," her laughter rang out like bells. "Why shouldn't I?"

"And the little guy, is he all right?"

"As right as you could expect. He's just enjoyed a nice drink of hot water, and the nurse says he recognized me. He said 'Ah!' He looked right at me and said 'Ah!'"

"No kidding?"

"No kidding!" said Dale happily.

"What does the nurse say about him?"

"Mr. Rand wants to know what you think of the baby tonight, nurse," said Dale lifting a formal glance toward the nurse.

"Why, I think he's doing finely," said the nurse. "This is the best day he's had since I've been here. I don't know how this snowy weather is going to affect him. It may bring back that hoarse cough, you know, but we'll take all precautions of course, and I'm hoping for the best."

Dale detailed the nurse's message.

"Well, do you need me?" was the next question.

"We miss you," said Dale trying to sound matter-of-fact, "but I think we're doing very well."

"When does the doctor come again? Find out what he thinks about whether I'm needed. I can work with more vigor when I know I'm on the path of duty and not missing something important I ought to be doing."

"The doctor doesn't come again till late this evening. He had an emergency operation tonight, but he means to drop in on us the last thing. He seemed to think the baby was going along all right. Did you have a good trip?"

"Oh yes, only I wished I was on the way home instead of on the way out."

"Oh, that's nice!" said Dale. Another lilt, quite distinct this time, and the nurse smiled vaguely to herself. It minded her of forgotten dreams far back in her own life.

"Well, you think I'm safe in staying a little longer?

And you'll promise to let me know if there is the slightest change?"

There were careful directions how to reach him, and then the conversation was over, but somehow the face of the earth had changed for Dale. All was right again. She took herself to task for feeling that way, and then decided there was no use. She was overtired and feeling the responsibility upon her. It was just nice to know he was keeping watch over them even from afar. And after all, Chicago wasn't so far away when one could talk with a friend so easily.

The next morning Dale went down to the little shop on the first floor of the apartment house and purchased some blue and white yarn and some needles, and began to knit little sweaters and socks. It somehow eased the tension and kept her from thinking. There seemed to be so many disturbing things to think about. There was the fact that she was getting too much interested in Rand. She was distinctly disappointed in herself. She hadn't thought she was like that. She had always scoffed at girls who got interested in young men just because they had performed some noble deed, or acted in a sane and pleasant manner. What was she, to get so excited because he had called her on the telephone? She was merely a helper of his, getting that baby well. The fact that she had a little money of her own now and could take care of that baby herself if there was need to, did not enter into the thing at all. She was just helping him out. He had called her his partner. They were in the business of saving that baby's life together. The whole thing was a business arrangement, like any partnership, and of course it was nice that she liked her partner. There was nothing wrong about that. But she had been getting too tired and too worried about various things, and she must stop feeling that every least little thing was a private burden of her own. She must stop thinking about what a fine man Rand was, and how pleasant it was to have someone to talk to in a friendly way.

Then she deliberately turned her thoughts toward poor Sam, whom she had sent firmly away, with no hope whatever of any future with her. Sam was young yet, and he would get over it of course, but what she couldn't understand was herself, and why she had ever thought of him as a rejected lover that she could on occasion take up at any time. Why, she wouldn't want to spend her life with Sam no matter how lonely she was. It was one thing to be nice pleasant friends, and quite another to be wholly given over to one who was not utterly beloved.

The next day dragged its slow length along. The baby was no worse, and when Rand called up and said he couldn't come back yet for two days at least, unless she felt it was imperative, she tried to speak cheerfully. The baby was still doing well, at least the doctor seemed to think he was, though Dale had felt he seemed extremely weak yet. Such a little frail thing to be so weak! She worried about it now and then in her secret heart, and then tried to pray and lay the burden in the hands of the Lord.

Chapter 12

BUT AN UNEXPECTED HAPPENING BROKE THE MO-
notony of the third day of Rand's absence. The
porter brought up a card for Miss Hathaway, and
when Dale looked at it and read Arliss Webster's
name she glanced up with a frown of annoyance.
Now what had he turned up for, she wondered. If
there was one person she did not want to see it was
Arliss Webster. Yet she must see him of course, or
give some reasonable excuse for not coming down.

She looked at the nurse who was preparing to get
the baby ready for the doctor who was due soon now.

"I have a caller. Can you spare me for a few minutes?" she said. "I'll get rid of him as soon as possible."

"Do you want to bring him up here?" she asked.

"Oh, no, I'll go down to the reception room."

"Go on, I shan't need any help," said the nurse.

So Dale went into her room and changed swiftly
into a simple brown dress, smoothed her hair and
went down.

Arliss Webster stood near the desk, looking about
for her, and as she stepped from the elevator he came

graciously forward to meet her as though he were conferring a great favor upon her. She tried to think in that minute what it was about him that always seemed so condescending.

He was a well-set-up man a trifle over forty, his cold fine eyes framed in imposing glasses that emphasized his importance, his heavy dark hair touched slightly with silver at the temples. He was noticeable anywhere he went.

"Just as lovely as ever!" he said with a slightly affected manner. "I was afraid you might have aged under your new rôle of hard worker, but you are as fresh as a rose. But excuse me, it isn't a new rôle, is it? You certainly worked hard when you were caring for your mother. I used to wish that I had the right to take you from that trying employment, and send you a good nurse who could have lifted all your burdens. If you had belonged to me that's what I would have done for you."

Dale felt her ire rising as he went on. As always, he was making her feel like a small naughty child who was to blame and whom he wanted to set right and take possession of. She lifted her delicate chin haughtily.

"Will you come to the reception room over here and sit down?" she said coolly. "I have but a few minutes to spare before going back to my job, and I'm sure we can talk more comfortably there and be without interruption."

Without waiting for his reply she led the way across the wide lobby to a small cosy room which was at that time empty, and offered him a comfortable chair.

"Well, this is unexpectedly pleasant," he said laying his hat on the table and looking around as he took the chair she offered. "Is this where you are residing at present?"

"This is where my job is at present," said Dale crisply.

The man stiffened.

"Oh, you are employed here?"

She nodded pleasantly as she sat down.

"In what capacity, may I ask?"

"Oh, I'm just helping to care for a sick person," she said lightly.

"Disgusting!" said the man with an expression of contempt on his aristocratic features. "To think that a member of a good old family should have been reduced to that!"

"Oh, I like it," said Dale. "But never mind me. Tell me the news of home. I don't often hear much about it any more!"

"Well, it's quite your own fault, you know, my dear. I gave you to understand before you went away that when you were tired of wandering and ready to come home and enjoy life you had only to send me word and I would be glad to rescue you from circumstances at once."

"Oh, but I'm not anxious to be rescued," laughed Dale with a light little imitation of a laugh that just fitted her caller's intellect. "I'm really having the time of my life just now. But tell me, is your sweet old aunt still living, and is she as sweet as ever?"

"My aunt? Oh, you mean Aunt Tabby McGrath? No, she passed away three months ago, more or less, and of course she's a great deal happier now. She had always had a hard life. But you know she wasn't really my aunt. That name was just given her out of courtesy by mother because she felt sorry for the poor old creature. And of course after mother passed away no one else had any further interest in her."

"Oh, but she was such a cheery person! I always used to hope that when I got as old as that I would be able to bear life as sweetly as she did!"

"Well, of course she bore her lot with patience. I've no fault to find with her, except that she was always in evidence. However, that's not news. You'll want to hear of the young people. You remember Mrs. McAllister? Well she has started a club for the young people, and really it's awfully popular. All your old friends. The Carloses, the Champneys, the Granbys, and the Dartleys are in it of course. They were your natural companions and friends if you hadn't been so hopelessly tied to your poor mother's couch. It is such a pity that she couldn't have seen what a mistake she was making in letting you sacrifice your young life in that way, when so easily a

nurse might have taken your place. A great pity that
you were cut off from your young friends, for that
was your rightful heritage."

"Oh, no!" said Dale sharply, "that was not my
rightful heritage! My rightful heritage is in Heaven,
and I had nothing whatever in common with the
girls of those families you have just mentioned. You
see, Mr. Webster, I didn't care for the things they
liked, and they didn't enjoy what I liked. How could
you possibly think we should have been together?"

"Ah, but you would have learned to like what they
liked if you had been allowed to be much with them,
and you could have been fitted to shine in any walk
in life you had chosen."

Dale smiled.

"Yes?" she said pleasantly. "Well, I don't really
care about that. Tell me about our church. Did the
minister get well, and is he still there?"

"No, he didn't get well, he became a hopeless invalid, so of course he was of no further use to the
church, and they had to pension him off and send
him away. We have quite a modern young preacher
now, very popular, and quite up to date in all his
ways. But you need to hear him once to find that out.
His sermons are charming, just poetry in prose. His
diction is so fine. And then he preaches on modern
themes, has a five minute résumé of the happenings
of the week before he begins, and then draws similes
from that in place of taking a regular text out of

scripture. It is really quite intriguing. People who
never came before are coming every Sunday, just to
find out what new thing he will do next. He has put
new life into the trite old service, this bringing things
down to where we really live, and not trying to take
us up into the clouds with dreams and fantasies from
the outworn scriptures, which have been preached
about so many centuries that they are quite threadbare. It is very refreshing. But my dear, I didn't come
all this way to hear you discuss the new preacher, or
Aunt Tabby. I came down to say that I am still of the
same mind as when you went away. I want to marry
you and make you mistress of my home. I have just
bought a most magnificent estate, and I know of no
girl anywhere who is so well fitted, after you have
had a little training which I shall delight to give you,
to be the mistress of my home. And so, my dear, I
have come down to offer you my hand and heart, and
to beg that you will come with me at once, today if
possible, and let us begin to prepare for a delightful
wedding, befitting our station in life. My idea is that
you shall take a small apartment in a fashionable
suburb where you will not have too much contact
with some of your former acquaintances, who will
not be desirable in your new life, and where you can
quietly get ready to shine socially. You will need
some instruction, you know, and I can secure the
right people to give that to you, and meanwhile
you can be choosing a proper trousseau, under the

guidance of one of the best couturiers our city affords. And I shall be glad to sit in on all your selections and offer my advice and approval."

He reached the point of a period and looked up, well pleased with the picture in words that he had worked out for her approval. Dale sat there aghast. Did he really think she cared for that sort of thing?

"I'm sorry to disappoint you, Mr. Webster," she said very kindly, "but I really wouldn't care for that sort of thing, you know. And I couldn't possibly marry you. I thought I told you once before that I do not approve of marrying a man I do not and could not love. I do not love you."

"Oh! *Love!*" he said with a smile of almost contempt. "We don't count that an essential to marriage in these days, do we? I am sure I am very fond of you or I should not have taken this long journey to tell you that I have decided you are the one I shall marry."

"But I do consider love essential to marriage, Mr. Webster. A marriage without love would be terrible!"

"Oh, well, a certain fondness, yes, I'll grant you that. But that is gained by time and living together. You get used to one another. It becomes a habit that one is loth to break. But what is commonly called love is made up largely of imagination, don't you think? And it is a great deal better to have a sane approach to one's nuptials, a common sense basis for union, that is not the outcome of a few wild moments of infatuation! Such a marriage is not liable to be wrecked on the rocks of divorce. Such a marriage goes calmly on to the end, riding above all storms and unpleasantness—"

"Stop!" said Dale, leaning forward in her chair and looking at him with flashing eyes. "I can't listen to another word like that! It is sacrilege against a holy institution that God ordained to be a symbol of Christ's own love for His church. It is blasphemy! Mr. Webster, I had a wonderful mother and father who loved one another with a tender sacred love that lasted through the years, even when there was suffering and trial and hard going. Their lives were made beautiful because of that tender love between them."

"Yes, but your father was never much of a worldly success. Can't you see how much better it would have been for your mother if she had married a man who was well-fixed in life, who could have given her comfort and luxury, instead of mere sentiment?"

"No!" said Dale rising from her chair and putting one foot down firmly. "No! My mother would never have chosen that. I would never want a life like that. And I won't have my mother and father's love for each other called 'sentiment.' Mr. Webster, I think we had better stop talking for I am getting very angry. Besides," and she glanced at her watch, "my time is up, and I must go back to my work."

She arose, her head held a bit haughtily.

"Now look here, Dale, that's perfect nonsense that you have to go this instant. I have come a long distance to see you and I don't intend to go back until I have said what I came to say."

"Oh!" said Dale wide-eyed, "haven't you said it all?"

The man flushed angrily.

"You certainly haven't improved in manners!" he snapped. He was not accustomed to being dismissed.

"Manners?" said Dale lifting her eyebrows. "I certainly did not intend to be rude, but you are insisting on talking about marriage, and I'm not willing to hear another word about it. I have no idea of getting married at present and when I do it certainly will not be to you! I hate to be rude about the way I say it, but it seems necessary in order to make you understand!"

"You really are quite insolent, you know," said Webster, "but I must own it's becoming to you. I never saw you look prettier, and if it's sentiment that you want I can be sentimental too if I try, but I thought you were too sensible for that sort of thing. I thought you were a practical type. But you certainly knew that I was exceedingly fond of you even before you went away from the old home. Call it love if you prefer. I felt that fondness was a little more refined way of putting it, but I'm willing to say I love you if you prefer that word. And I'm sure I shall be deeply devoted to you all my life! Now, sit down, please, for

I really have an important point to put before you that I have not mentioned yet."

"I prefer to stand. I really must go in just one minute," and her eyes were on her watch.

The man frowned. He was not used to being hurried.

"It's very annoying to have to say these things in a rush," he protested. "Things that have to do with our plans for a lifetime—"

"Excuse me, Mr. Webster," said Dale. "You and I have no possible plans that could have to do with a lifetime. Please get that definitely."

"My dear, you would not say that if you knew all that I intend to do for you! I—"

"Please don't keep calling me 'my dear'!" she protested. "I'm not your dear, now nor ever, and no amount of things you intend to do for me would change my feeling about that."

"Look here, Dale, don't be foolish. I came down here to arrange to take you back to look over the house I have just bought. I want to see if it suits you in every way. It is not too late yet to make some changes, and I want you to come with me no later than tomorrow to select wall papers and carpets, or rugs, and a number of things. Even if you do not feel that you can terminate your employment at a day's notice like this, you can surely get a day or two off, and I certainly feel that it is my due, after all I have offered you, that you should be open-minded enough

to come and look things over before you give me
such a final refusal. Now, will you grant me this request? Will you go with me tomorrow back to the
old home town and look over what I have been plan-
ning for you?"

Dale took a deep breath, and tried to put aside her
annoyance. Tried to answer in a calm quiet voice.

"That would be quite impossible, Mr. Webster. I
am in the midst of work that I could not possibly
leave for sometime, even for a day, not even if I
wanted to, which I don't. Now, I'm afraid you will
have to excuse me for I must go at once!"

Dale hurried away to the elevator, and the dignified caller, much bewildered at his sudden set-
back, started after her, but found when he got to the
elevator that its door had already been closed and it
was moving up out of sight. Dale's last glimpse of
him showed an angry and determined face gazing up
after her, and she gave a little shudder as the elevator
slid smoothly up away from him, for it came to her
what an awful thing it would be if she had to live her
life out under the domination of such a man as that!

Then she began to reflect on possibilities. From
what she knew of Arliss Webster he was not a man to
accept a rebuff easily. And if he should find out that
she was taking care of a little stray foundling baby,
for a young man whom she had known only a short
time, he would certainly raise an unpleasant disturb-
ance about it and bring all her mother's old friends
down upon her annoyingly. They would think they

had to do something about rescuing her, of course, for her mother's sake. She must certainly prevent such a thing. She felt sure that Arliss Webster would not drop the matter yet, but would pursue her. He was so inordinately fond of himself and his own plans, that he simply could not accept defeat. She should not have lost her temper. She should have been merely dignified. She must find some way to get rid of him definitely.

The baby was stirring uneasily, and giving little unhappy cries now and then when she got back. The nurse said he had been more or less restless ever since early that morning. She hadn't spoken of it before because she wanted to be sure, but she thought perhaps it would be as well to call up the doctor. The little fellow was running a tiny mite of temperature, and the doctor always wanted to know when that happened.

So she called the doctor, and he promised to run in as soon as he was free.

Then Dale, with all her anxieties back upon her, sat and worked with her soft wools, knitting tiny socks, and thinking about the baby. And when after an hour Arliss Webster called up and desired her to come down for a brief talk, she told him that the patient was not so well, and she could not leave until after the doctor came, perhaps not even then. Thereafter she sat and tried to work out a plan by which she could escape any further contact with Arliss Webster.

Chapter 13

THE AFTERNOON MAIL BROUGHT TWO LETTERS, one a note from Arliss Webster, begging Dale to say when he might see her for half an hour, as something very important had come up which he felt sure she would wish to talk over with him. The other was a brief communication from Dinsmore Ramsay.

It seemed so queer to her that just in these short few days she should hear so definitely and insistently from all three of her rejected suitors, when they hadn't even been in her mind for over a year, and never had been in her heart.

The letter from Dinsmore Ramsay brought a smile to her lips, it was so characteristic of him in every way, simply overflowing with his usual self-importance. In some ways he reminded her of Arliss Webster, although she knew Webster would be horrified to know that anyone could possibly liken him to a young insignificant underling in somebody's office.

Dear Dale:

A matter has just come to my knowledge which makes me think that you need my advice, and I of course stand eady to help you in any way possible.

I understand that you have inherited a tidy little for-
une, and am of course glad to know it. There is no one
would be so glad to see prosper as you. But at once I
an see where you will be in great danger from sharpers
who always stand ready, as soon as they hear of an inheritance, to bleed the poor inheritor to the death. So I
am writing you at once to beg that you will make no
investments at all until you see me. I am in a position to
know what is wise and what is unwise, and I would hate
to see you get caught by any of the modern fakes that
are lying innocently about to snare ready investors.

For your father's sake, to whom I was deeply attached,
during our close association, I of course should want
you to make no mistakes.

So I am taking the liberty of running down toward
the end of this week to have a little talk with you and
advise you about some fine investments that I am now
in a position to handle for you personally, and see that
you are not cheated.

I also want you to remember that I am still of the
same mind regarding you, and would like nothing better than to be in a permanent position to look after you
and carry all your burdens, and help you to decide all
perplexing questions. In short, my offer of marriage still
stands, and I assure you I still care as much as ever for
you.

> Yours with all my heart's love,
> > Dinsmore Ramsay.

When Dale finished reading this letter she put her
head back and laughed aloud, and the nurse looked
up in astonishment, but all the explanation Dale
made was to say:

"Aren't some people too funny for anything?"

And the nurse, after puzzling over this for a ful
minute said "Well, I guess maybe they are." But sh
went on wondering whether that letter could hav
been from Rand, or did Miss Dale have anothe
friend that was writing to her? And who was this per
son who kept calling up from down in the office t
know if he could see Miss Hathaway?

Dale made short work of answering that letter.
She wrote it at once.

Dear Dinsmore:

It was nice to get your letter, and of course I appreciate your kind offer of help for any time I might be in
need of advice or assistance in the way you mention.

But I can't think where you could have heard such an
unlikely rumor, that I have inherited a small fortune.
Dinny, that's ridiculous! There is no one belonging to
me who would ever leave me a fortune either large or
small, so you see your kind offer is superfluous. There
was a kind old half-uncle once who put something in the
bank for me to have when I come of age, but I'm sure
it was only a trifling amount, and I can't see how that
could possibly have been the foundation for such a tale
as you seem to have heard, and as I have never told any
of my friends about it, I can't see how you could have
heard any such tale.

I am sorry to spoil your plans, but I'm glad to be able
to save you the trouble and expense that you would in-
cur by coming to see me, which, although very pleasant
socially of course, would be utterly useless, for just now
I am engaged in helping to care for a sick person and

could not be spared to come away and talk with you.

Regarding your other suggestion, the question of marriage, I think I made you understand fully before I left home, that I could not marry you, and I have not changed my mind.

With all best wishes,

Sincerely,

Dale.

Dale dispatched the letter by air-mail, hoping to reach the young man before he should start on his way. And then she sat quietly by the window and watched the evening shadows come down and the brilliant lights of the city come up and drown out the darkness of the sky, till even the faraway stars looked dim in their glare. Red and green, blue and yellow, weird fantastic shapes and colors, jiggling and winking and blaring in and out, each one trying to offer a mightier attraction to the eye than the other. Christmas signs. What a travesty on Christmas! The birth of the Saviour of the world mixed up with advertisements of beer and toys! Christmas commercialized! She sighed over the way the world was going.

Yet Christmas had always been to her the crowning joy of the year. The time when human love and beauty reached up and touched Heaven, and earthly hates and passions were forgotten for a little while because of the long-ago birth of the Christ child.

The baby on the other side of the room fretted and turned restlessly again and she turned anxiously toward him.

"I think he's all right," said the nurse reassuringly.

"Isn't he getting hoarse again?" asked Dale with a note of anxiety in her voice.

"Oh, no, I don't think so. They have their ups and downs, you know, little things who have been as sick as he was. Anyway the doctor ought to be here pretty soon."

But the doctor didn't come, and the child continued to be restless, and Dale, sitting in the twilight tried to forget about her worry. Tried to think ahead. What kind of Christmases would this little child have as he grew older? Oh, if she had the chance how she would love to make Christmas a joyous time for him! But probably she wouldn't have the chance.

It wasn't thinkable that Rand would let him be put into an orphanage now, and yet, how did she know? He had been away from him these few days, and perhaps when he came back he would have thought it over and decided that it would be much better to put the baby in some permanent home rather than to keep him until he was fond of them and then tear him loose and put him into some other surroundings.

Oh, but she mustn't think these things. Rand wasn't like that. She hadn't known him long of course, but she was sure he wasn't like that! He was loving and kind, and even if he should happen to be engaged to marry someone either now or later, it seemed as if he would be one who would want this little child.

However, what an unprofitable line of meditation! This baby was God's child. God had sent it, and God would somehow care for it if it was to live and grow.

It was just the return of all these old acquaintances suddenly in this short time that made her down-hearted. And then it was so annoying to have Dinsmore Ramsay offer to assist her. How in the world did he ever get any such notion as that she had inherited a fortune? How ridiculous! Could it be possible that from the enquiries of those western lawyers who were trying to find her he had got that idea? Surely lawyers wouldn't tell anything, even about a small amount of money. But suppose they had and some reporter had overheard and thought he had got some news for his paper. How annoying if anything had been published about her in the home town paper!

But the more she thought about it the more she felt that something like that might have happened. For how else would Dinsmore Ramsay have got the idea? He was not original enough to have made it up out of whole cloth. And then, Arliss Webster! Had he heard it too?

For surely he wasn't in love with her, she was certain about that. But if he thought she was well off he might want to get hold of the money.

How perfectly absurd. Well, what difference did it make? She probably would never go back to the home town anyway, and it didn't matter what old acquaintances thought about it.

So she turned her thoughts to the baby, and went again to look at him as he slept uneasily in his crib, studying his delicate little face. Did she fancy it, or was it true that there seemed again to be gray shadows under the eyes, shadows that made the long golden lashes stand out with startling distinctness. Oh, she wished the doctor would come! She wished Rand would come back! Somehow she felt that if he were here now he would do something. But what was there to do? Anything that she ought to be doing?

Then the telephone rang.

She sprang to answer it lest it might waken the baby. The nurse had gone down to the drugstore to get something that was needed, and she was on duty alone. She hoped it might be the doctor. Oh, if he would only come!

But no, it was Arliss Webster again. She had been pretty sure he would have gone home by this time.

"Is that you, Dale? This is Arliss Webster. Well, I'm glad I've got you at last! That other nurse seemed only anxious to get rid of me. Didn't she tell you I had called?"

"She told me someone had called, but I guess she didn't remember the name. I thought you would be home by this time."

"Oh no," said the persistent voice. "I told you I came to take you home with me, and I intend to stick around till I get you, or at least till we can have some understanding. And this is perfectly absurd, you playing off your job this way against me. What's a job for a person in your circumstances? You have money enough without trying to earn more!"

"I don't know what you mean, Mr. Webster."

"Oh, yes, you know what I mean! A girl who has just inherited an immense fortune to be pretending you have to hang around and toady to an employer! I'm about fed up with that talk and if you don't come down at once and have a talk with me I'm going to your employer myself and tell him all about you!"

"Really, Mr. Webster!" said Dale, angry now with good cause. "You must be crazy! I can't imagine how you got this idea about a fortune, but it doesn't matter. It's not true, anyway. And I can't talk to you any more. The sound of the telephone is worrying my patient, and I shall have to say good-by. Please don't worry me any more!"

"Dale, listen, I'm sending you up some flowers. They'll be there within a few minutes, and I'm putting a note in the box which you will please answer at once. I shall wait here until I receive your reply."

Dale lowered her voice discreetly.

"Please, Mr. Webster, don't send any flowers to me. I would not be able to keep them in the room. They would not be good for the patient. And as I know nothing of a fortune, I would not care to discuss the matter with you or anyone else. But even if I had been left a fortune of millions of dollars I would not give up the job I have undertaken until I have done what I promised to do. So, if you will kindly go home and forget all this I shall be deeply grateful to you."

"But I have it on very good authority—" began the man's voice again.

"Sorry," said Dale. "I can't talk any longer now. Good-by," and she hung up, and found herself trembling from head to foot. She felt rather desperate. Was there no way to get rid of this presumptuous person? And what on earth could he mean by a fortune? Why didn't she ask him where he got the idea? But no, that would only encourage him to go on talking. If only the baby were able to be moved it would be nice if she could go somewhere else where he could not find her. But of course that was out of the question. And this place was ideal for the present needs. She must just ask the Lord to help in this matter, and then put it aside.

The baby stirred and moaned distressfully, and Dale put all other things out of her mind, and went to stay by the little crib and pray for that dear baby.

Oh, could it be that after all this anxiety and then the relief of knowing he was better, that the baby was failing after all, was going to have another attack of that terrible breathing, that awful choking? Oh, if Rand were only back!

She was relieved when the nurse came back. She couldn't trust her own judgment about things like pneumonia. She had had no experience.

But she could see by the serious look in the eyes of the nurse that she wasn't any too pleased with the way the baby looked, and the sound of his breathing.

The nurse went swiftly to work doing the things that had been done during the first of the baby's illness, and as Dale worked away helping as she had done before her own fears were confirmed. The baby was really worse!

Her heart sank, and she longed for Rand to arrive. It was almost his usual time for calling up. What should she say to him if he called? Suppose he wanted to know if he were needed? Oh, if that doctor would only come!

And then the doctor came.

"What's all this?" he said appearing on the scene so quietly that Dale was startled. He gave a quick glance around, saw what the nurse was doing, then another look at the baby.

"Yes, we'll need the oxygen again. Can you call Dr. Lane, my office? Tell him to get here with all speed!"

Dale felt as if all her strength were deserting her. And she mustn't fail now. The responsibility was on her. Rand wasn't here. She must do all she could.

She called the doctor's office and gave the directions the doctor wanted his assistant to have, and then she took a prescription down to the drugstore and left it to be filled.

As she came back to the elevator she glimpsed through the doorway Arliss Webster sitting at the writing desk just inside the little reception room, writing pages and pages. Were those presently to be sent up to her? Impulsively she stepped over to the doorway and spoke hurriedly.

"I wanted to ask you please not to call me up any more. I have a very sick person up there, and the telephone disturbs and annoys. We are in the midst of a serious crisis."

Arliss Webster looked up and beamed. He arose and came quickly toward her.

"I am so glad you are here!" he said eagerly. "I simply must have a few minutes' converse with you!"

"That's impossible!" said Dale. "I came out on an errand for the doctor, and he is waiting!"

"Well, let him wait! A few minutes more or less will make no difference. I must tell you that I really came here to be of use to you. I can help you immensely in your new responsibilities. I feel sure that when you know all you will be glad I can help—"

"There comes the elevator!" said Dale. "I must

go!" and she flew across the intervening space. Webster heard the gate clang shut, and there he stood with his half-finished letter in his hand, frowning across at the vanishing elevator. That elusive girl!

Then he frowned down at the letter he had been writing, and felt that it was useless to send that to her. Yet he would not go as long as he was convinced that there was a fortune in the offing. Why the girl wanted to pretend that she knew nothing about it, he didn't understand, for he had it from an old lawyer friend in the west quite straight. He had written him to try and find out where Dale was to be reached, and it is true that his information about the extent of the fortune was vague, but it was so worded as to seem at least a million, and he didn't intend to let any million get out of his hands that way. That girl *had* to marry him, if for no other reason than that she needed him to take charge of that money. She had no experience, and he was sure that if he could get sufficient time to talk with her he would be able to convince her fully that he was the husband who could help her combine happiness and business ability. So he finally settled down and added a long postscript to the letter already written, and sent it up by the porter. Then he betook himself to a comfortable hotel, and several kinds of drinks and decided to cease operations until the sick patient should have time either to die or recover from the present stress.

But when his letter came up to the door, Dale,

who answered the knock, recognized the writing and flung the letter in on her bed with a look of impatience. Would she never be free from him?

But her mind was too full of trouble now for anything as small as a mere importunate lover to trouble her, for the baby was really desperately sick again, and she was doing everything she could to help.

The doctor was staying all night. His face was grave. He had shed his coat and shoved up his sleeves. He was very alert, giving quick sharp directions to the nurse. Dale didn't attempt to ask any questions. She just did what they told her to do, and kept praying in her heart that God would hear.

Now and again she would remember that Rand had not called up that evening yet. She had no idea of the time. But she grew more and more anxious about it. What should she answer if he asked his usual question of whether he was needed? At last she mustered courage to ask the doctor.

"When Mr. Rand calls up do you think I should tell him to come?"

She was watching the doctor's face anxiously as she asked. Surely she could tell what he thought of the baby by what he said, by the way he looked.

"Oh," said the doctor, "why, he *did* call up. I answered the phone. He called while you were out getting the prescription filled. He wanted to know if he should come, but I told him no, I thought

everything was going to be all right. At least I promised to let him know if there were any worse develop-
ments. I told him I thought we had things pretty
well in hand, and that we had help enough for all
our need for tonight. I told him you were out and
that as soon as the oxygen came I thought everything
would be all right."

"But—is—it?" she asked breathlessly. "Isn't he
worse than he has been at all?"

"Well, no, I don't know that I ought to say that.
Some symptoms of course are a little more pronounced, but I think he is yielding to the treatment
very nicely. His pulse is decidedly steadier. And then
it isn't of course as if it were Mr. Rand's own child."

Dale's face grew troubled.

"Yes, I think it is," she said decidedly. "I promised
him that if there was any danger, any great change, I
would send at once for him."

"Oh, well, perhaps I should have told you at once.
But I was so busy over the little chap that I didn't
realize it would matter whether I told you at once.
But still, I think the case is somewhat different from
two hours ago. The baby is decidedly on the mend.
His pulse is steadier. I think the chances are very
good for him now. And it would be too bad to call
Mr. Rand up from a good sleep, perhaps, and have
him find out there was no real danger. I don't believe you should call him now."

Dale went and sat down. There was nothing for her to do just now, and she was terribly worried. Yet, if the doctor said no, she hardly liked to go against his advice.

Chapter 14

THE NIGHT WENT ON, AND THE DOCTOR AND NURSE worked steadily, and Dale stood by and did whatever she could, her anxiety sometimes increasing, as she heard the little voice crying out, gasping, and she looked at the strong steady face of the doctor.

"He is a sort of a symbol of God," she thought. And then her heart would turn to prayer again.

"Oh my Father, save the dear baby if it is Your will. But save him to grow up a good man and to serve Thee!"

Over and over she prayed, and her face was sweet with trust. The doctor noticed it once in an interval. He saw the weary lines, and he saw her drop her face in her hands and close her eyes.

"You are very tired," he said gently. "Why don't you go and lie down for a little while? We can get along nicely now without you."

She lifted her face, with a kind of shining in it, the shine of real trust, and he didn't understand it.

"Oh, no!" she said. "I'm not so tired! I couldn't lie down now, please."

"But you were so tired a minute ago you couldn't hold up your head. You had to close your eyes."

"No," she said simply with a shy smile, "I was just praying. I was asking God to make the baby get well if it was His will."

"Oh!" said the doctor, startled, abashed! This girl was different from any girl he knew. Then he added: "You know it's not such a great thing to grow up in this world and have to live a hard life, maybe full of sin and shame and trouble. Even if a kid has the best chances there are of help and environment he's liable to turn out a criminal perhaps, and this child— You don't know what he is, what he inherits. Or— do you? Is the child anything to you?"

"Oh, no! I don't know anything about him. I just happened to be there to help save his life!"

"H'm!" said the doctor studying her earnest young face. "Well, can't you see he may be better off dead?"

"Yes," said Dale quietly, "if he's not a child of God. But that was what I was praying about, that God would save him to be a good man, and serve Him. Not that He would save him anyway, just because we wanted it, but only if God saw it best."

"Oh!" said the doctor. "Well, that's a kind of prayer I'm not acquainted with. Wish I was. That's leaving it up to God. But if that's how it's to be, nurse, I guess you and I better get to work again and do our best. It might be God would want to be using us!"

The nurse stared for an instant, then veiled her surprise and went to work, with almost an awe upon her.

And the little soul whose life hung in the balance lay there and struggled for breath, and gradually began to be eased, at last falling into a sweet sleep, his breath coming with soft regularity, a relieved look on the pinched little face.

"Well," said the doctor at last, coming to stand before Dale, "I guess your baby's better. Your kind of praying seems to work. Maybe I'll get you to pray for me sometime. I need it, goodness knows. And after all this if that young man dares to grow up wrong just send for me and I'll settle him. I'll see that he understands he's under a very special dispensation, and he *has* to go right."

Then he turned to the nurse.

"Nurse, you'd better go get some breakfast, and bring this girl a cup of coffee. She looks pretty white. I'll be back in about two hours. I've got three or four pretty sick people to look after. But I don't anticipate any more trouble here at present. Just watch that pulse, and let me know at the hospital if it seems to change. And you two better get some sleep, one at a time of course."

Then he was gone and Dale was left with a glad heart. She felt he really believed the baby was better, and wasn't just talking to make talk.

She went to the little kitchenette and prepared a

quick breakfast for the nurse, toast and scrambled eggs and coffee with orange juice, while the nurse was picking up and making the room tidy.

"Now," she said softly to the nurse, "you've got to eat, and then you've got to go and take a nap. There's no use protesting, for I won't have it any other way! *You've got* to be in shape if another crisis arises. And I'm not the least bit tired. I haven't done a thing worth calling work all night."

"No," said the nurse dryly, "nothing but pray! If you ask me I'd say that was the biggest part of the work anybody did last night. To tell you the truth there were a couple of times when I thought that baby's life was gone, and it wasn't even worth praying for, and I guess it was you pulled him through!"

"No, it was God!" said Dale smiling with the glory look in her eyes. "God wanted him to live, I think, and so He let him get better."

"Well, you can say it anyway you please, but he's better, and I think you deserve to rest first."

"No," said Dale. "What you've said, that he's better, is enough to rest me all I need. And I really want to stay awake awhile just to realize it and thank God!"

"Well," said the nurse grimly, "have it your own way! You certainly are a different kind of a girl from any I know," and she sat down to her breakfast. When it was finished she went into her little room and lay down for a well earned rest.

When Dale had washed the few dishes, and felt
sure the nurse was asleep, she went over by the little
crib and knelt beside it, looking down into the sweet
baby face, so small, so innocent, so like a little white
flower, just resting there lightly on the pillow, her
heart going out in love to the little motherless child.
She prayed softly:

"Oh, dear Father in Heaven, I thank You for making the little dear better. And now—please—keep
everybody safe, and bless them." She *said* "everybody," but in her heart she meant George Rand.

George Rand, sailing high above the clouds on his
way back to the city was thinking about Dale.

Something in the doctor's voice last night when he
called up, and Dale wasn't there as usual to answer
him, made him feel uneasy. What had happened?
Was Dale sick that she didn't answer the phone, and
the doctor hadn't wanted to tell him? She had always
been there and answered immediately, before when
he had called. Of course it was an hour later than
usual on account of the committee meeting which
had lasted longer than expected, and had detained
him; but even so, it wasn't like her not to be there
till he had called.

Was he growing so sure of her that he had reck-
oned on her being too faithful? That was ridiculous,
for she had no call to be faithful to him of course.
Only he had come to feel that her interest was bound
up with his in that baby.

But he didn't know the girl very well. He had had only that brief experience with the freezing baby to judge by. She might be tired of her job. She hadn't ever expected when she came away from Mrs. Beck's gloomy abode that she would have to stay all these days alone carrying heavy responsibility. He had been so sure of her, but why did he think she, a stranger, would stand for everything? She might have heard of a job and had to take it. She might have paid the nurse something to carry on alone. She might have been called away to wherever she called home to attend some relative in severe illness. Why, there were a thousand things that might have kept her away from the telephone around the time he usually called. Well, he couldn't keep from trusting her until he had some reason not to trust her, and certainly just not being there at a certain time to answer him wasn't enough to mean a thing.

He scarcely knew why he had taken this plane in the night to get back instead of waiting till morning and getting a chance to sit in on that last session of an important committee. It was merely an uneasiness in his subconscious mind that had driven him to make this decision. After he had talked with the doctor he had a feeling that something was the matter. Either the baby was worse than the doctor had implied, or something had happened to Dale. And either was enough to drive him into quick action. So he had done some hasty telephoning, secured a reser-

vation on the next plane, excused himself from a few
obligations that had been thrust upon him, flung his
things into his suitcase and rushed off in a taxi to get
the plane. And here he was sailing through a brilliant night, looking down upon a far white world be-
neath him, and wondering why he had rushed home
in such a hurry after being assured that he was not
needed.

Well, here he was, and morning was on the way.
In the morning he would know whether he had been
foolish or not. But somehow he was glad he had
done it.

It didn't look much like the night of deep quiet
snow when he had come home and found that pitiful
tiny naked baby beating the icy air, and trying feebly
to call for help, there in the Beck vestibule. There
was nothing to remind him in the brilliant world
below of that night and the days and nights that had
followed before he had to come away and leave that
brave girl, and that poor little kid without his help;
but now as he closed his eyes and remembered, every
little detail of the whole happening came to him, and
swelled his heart with thoughts that thrilled him.
Even way back to the day he had picked up those
oranges for Dale, and carried them up to her room
for her. Dale, what a lovely name. Dale Hathaway!
He hadn't had much time to think about her since
he had been at that convention. He had only been
concerned in finding out the latest news, ferreting

out an obscure possibility, and writing it up to get it to his paper before other men got the same thing and beat him to it.

But now he had time to think, and the strangest things came to him. The way Dale had held out her arms for that little dirty sorrowful scrap of humanity, and gathered him close. The way she had sat beside the little tub, supporting him with her round bare arm, holding him in the curve of her elbow, washing him so gently, and patting him softly till he was dry, enfolding him in the warm dry blanket, and cuddling him close. The way she had bent over him and crooned to him. It had seemed to him like an ideal picture of womanhood, motherhood. And she was just a girl! A lovely little hardworked girl, evidently. He could see the little curl in the back of her neck as she bent over the baby. He could see the way she slipped the spoon in the baby's mouth, and stopped his pitiful weak cry with warmth and comfort. It all came back so vividly, and stirred the depths of his soul.

And then how she had lent herself to the recovery of the baby. He could see she was troubled about the situation, and yet she had not let herself hold back, even after Mrs. Beck's insulting words.

He went carefully over his own conduct. Had he always protected her in every way? Had he ever done anything that would make her feel embarrassed to be doing this work for him, or with him? He hoped not. Yet he knew there had been times when he would have loved to cry out and tell her how lovely she was!

He hadn't been keen after girls, like other fellows. His job had been for the present to look after his mother, and if there were to be girls in his life, *a* girl, he had felt they would come later. He had sometimes admired Pat Ragan, the keen girl reporter for The Blade, and even Madge Barron, with her red hair and her comically smart speeches, but they both were special friends of other men among his associates, and he hadn't either the time or the taste to go to some of their rowdy parties. He had never really got intimate with any of them, a joke now and then, good friendliness, but that was all. He had thought that when his mother came she would make a home, then there would be a place to bring friends like that when he found some he liked especially.

He sighed as he thought about it now, speeding along among the clouds, looking down on a moonlit world all in white, with now and then a city spattered with Christmas lights.

Suddenly it came to him how he would like to tell his mother about Dale. He could think of the questions she would ask, and how he would answer them. He would have so liked to take Dale home to see his mother, if there was any home, and mother hadn't gone away to live with God.

He closed his eyes and tried to rest, but the picture

of the girl and the little child kept coming to his mind, as something sweet to which he was going back. Would they both be there and be the same?

It seemed to him that he had been away from them for months. He wondered now why he had consented to go. Of course it was something that his chief had asked, and his chief had just been promoting him, and had honored him by asking him to take this assignment. He couldn't in conscience refuse, especially as he felt that upon this man's interest hung the needed money he must have if he took care of that child.

Was he going to be allowed to take care of him, to count him his? He had learned at the police headquarters the possibilities of adoption, its rules and regulations. A certain time must elapse to search for possible relatives. Well, there seemed no likelihood that any relatives would interfere in a matter like that. But if they did not and he got control of the child, how was he going to care for it? Hire a nurse perhaps, an oldish woman, and set up a sort of disjointed household?

It was too deep and too troublesome a question to answer now, going through the white night to find those two who had been in his heart ever since he had gone away. It was something that would just have to work out step by step as he came to it.

Thinking back over the days when the baby was so sick and he and the girl worked side by side to save that little breath of a life, he wondered the more at himself that he had consented to leave it all until he was sure that the baby was safely through with that fight with death. He wished he hadn't left the girl to fight it alone. Yet she wasn't alone of course with the doctor and nurse, both the best of their kind.

And then as he watched the moon pale and the dawn come softly over the rim of the world, and he knew that he was nearing his goal, he began to be strangely excited.

Would it all be the same when he got there? Would the girl be glad to see him? Would the baby be all right?

And if the baby were all right, what were they going to do next? There was just one thing of which he was sure, and that was that he did not intend to let that little baby boy go into any kind of an institution to be perhaps bullied around by bigger, tougher boys, not while he was little and frail anyway, and not able to hold his own. No, that baby was his job. It had been dropped at his very feet, and it had been given back to him in answer to his prayer, and it was his job to look after the little chap, if God suffered him to live. He would teach him to grow up a good man, and not be sorry that he had been saved from death.

And there in the sky between the dying night and the dawning day George Rand felt himself to be in the presence of the Most High God, and most amazingly, he suddenly knew that God loved him, personally, and was waiting for him to consent to fellowship with Him. He was conscious that the only thing between them was his own sin, and the greatest of all that sin loomed now as indifference to God! But he also knew, for his mother had done her best to teach him, that all that sin of his that stood between him and his God, was already laid on the person of Another. For the first time, though he had known it before, George Rand saw Jesus Christ, the Son of God, hanging there on a cross, nailed there by his, George Rand's, own sin.

Humbly, with broken heart, he made his wordless confession to God. Then with dawning peace in his heart he sat and thought it all over. Why had he never had this personal dealing with God before? It was not till God had taken everything else from him, and sent that little freezing child to make him see what he needed, that he had been willing to pay attention.

So, in the early darkness, coming swiftly toward the landing field, he prayed.

And at the very end, as the swift-winged airship began to slide down the air to the landing field, he added to his prayer:

"And, oh, Lord, bless her—!"

Chapter 15

THE DAWN HAD BROKEN AS THE PLANE LANDED, and Rand took a taxi and drove the familiar way down through the streets he knew so well.

The sun was coming up in a great glorious crimson ball to take the place of the many colored neon lights that had illumined the night. Those were now but dull garlands of pastel shades, paling more and more as the sun grew brighter, and creating a garish effect of summer and daytime stepping in where evergreen and holly should have sway.

But Rand's heart was glad as he looked about on the glistering snow, which glowed almost blood red where the sun was touching it full. The scene seemed to fill him with wonder and delight.

It was quite a journey from the flying field to the apartment house where he had left Dale and the baby, and he was all impatience until as he drew nearer, he was filled with fear and a great dismay.

What if the baby should be worse? What if it would be gone?

He thought of the little white dead mother and

the small headstone with the mysterious letters on it. Only God knew what they stood for. He shrank from the thought that perhaps the baby might have to be laid away beside her.

"Oh, God!" his heart cried out. "Oh, my own new God! You heard me once. Hear me again! Do Thy will for us all, Thy best will, and blessing, Lord!"

And then they were at the apartment house, that seemed as plain and real as it had before he left. He looked up its simple surface to the windows of the seventh story, and wondered, were they there? How foolish he was! And how strange and shy he felt, as if somehow it were all a dream that he was trying to act out. He had never thought of himself as a fool before. He had always thought himself sane and cool, and here he was actually trembling at the thought of going up in the elevator and knocking at that door. He might even have to sit down in the hallway and get cool before he went to face what was before him. Face what? A baby? Was that it? He knew better than that. He knew it was a girl he had to face. A wonderful girl!

At least he thought she was wonderful! He *hoped* she was wonderful! But he was afraid after this interval of hard work that he would come back to find out she had been just an ordinary girl like any girl he met every day. And he didn't want her to turn out that way.

He owned to himself that he had carried her in his

mind as an ideal, a dream girl. To discover that she was made of clay would be a desperate let down.

The thrill of her voice over the telephone was still in his soul. It had seemed like having some own folks again to have her talk about the baby to him, as if they had a common interest.

Well, he must pull himself up and get out of this fool state of mind or he wouldn't be worth a cent. And probably there would be a lot of questions to decide. The trouble with him was he had over-worked, sitting up till all hours to finish his writing. Getting it off by air mail. Half breaking his neck to cover all the extras that had been suggested. He knew they expected him to stay longer and do several special features while he was out there, articles that were of general interest, but needed a special han-dling, and he had done it all, in between the im-portant features he had gone out there to cover. He had worked a great deal harder than he had to, just so that he might come home as soon as the conven-tion was over instead of taking the two or three extra days his chief had suggested.

And then this hunch that something was the mat-ter! Maybe the baby was dead or dying! It wasn't like him to get that kind of hunches! He had been working too steadily, and lost too much sleep. That was a fact. But then he had often done that. It was something more than hard work. It was this business of the girl and the baby that had got him.

Well, here he was! The elevator door clanged
open and he stepped out. Now! Now in a moment
more he would know!

He walked down the hall to the door and gave his
special little finger-tip tap, and almost instantly he
heard Dale's soft footsteps. He wondered how it was
that he was so sure it was Dale and not the heavier-
footed nurse.

Then the lock turned, and Dale was standing
there.

He gave one breathless look and then he saw the
stars in her eyes. Stars of gladness! He had been
afraid to believe that she would be glad!

She had come to the door, thinking it was the
boy from the drugstore with something the nurse
had ordered. Dale was wearing just an ordinary pleasant look. When she saw who was standing there the
glory of a great gladness came into her face and made
it radiant. She put out both her hands in a lovely
welcoming gesture. Oh, she hadn't meant at all to
look glad like that, just pleasantly glad when he
came. But she didn't know what joy was in her face,
what eagerness was in her eyes. And Rand's heart
rose up with an answering gladness, and put it into
his eyes.

He dropped the suitcase he was carrying, and took
both her hands in one of his, and his other arm went
about her, and drew her close. And then he stooped
and laid his lips reverently on hers, and drew her

close to his heart. Such tenderness, such gentleness, such preciousness! They stood so for several dear seconds, his lips at her lips, her eyelids, and whispering softly in her ear.

They forgot that the door was wide open, and his suitcase was dumped on the floor in the hall, forgot the nurse who might appear at any minute now. They even for a minute forgot the baby who had brought them together and might wake up any time and demand attention.

"My dearest, I love you!" whispered Rand softly, and kissed her again, and her eyes lifted to his and gave their sweet answer in like words.

Then suddenly the elevator shot up, far down the hall, and the gates clanged open, letting someone out. Footsteps came down the hall. All at once the two became conscious of the world about them.

Rand's arms came down from that sweet enfolding, and he came to instant attention. He grabbed his suitcase from the hall, and disappeared into the room, vanishing into the little kitchenette, from which stronghold he peered out cautiously.

"Is that that ubiquitous nurse?" he asked in a scared comical whisper.

But Dale with very rosy cheeks was twinkling her eyes at him, her mouth all made up in a cute little quirk of mirth, as she backed into the room and shut the door softly, locking it with a definite little noise.

Then Rand came out of hiding and went over to

her again, laying a hand on each of her shoulders, looking down deep into her eyes, and then drawing her very close again in his arms.

"I'm telling you that I love you with all my heart, my sweet," he said, and his voice was throbbing with tenderness. "Do you mind, little Dale? Do you mind if I love you? Dear heart! This is the greatest thing that ever came to me. Are you listening, Dale? I want to ask you when you will marry me. Where is that nurse? Is she liable to come in on us any time?"

"She's gone to get some sleep. She was up all night. I just heard her snoring," said Dale with a twinkle. "Oh, George, it's so wonderful that you've come back! Somehow it didn't seem as if you ever would! And then when I thought you didn't telephone last night I began to think you had forgotten us. I began to think you were just a figment of my imagination."

"You did?" he said astonished. "You darling! Why, that's just the way I felt. I couldn't believe there was such a girl as you, darling. You will marry me, won't you dear? Tell me, and set my heart at rest. I've just been so lonely and so discouraged!"

"But George, you don't know me at all. You've only seen me a few times!"

"I've seen you all I need to see you to know you are the one I want to marry!" said George stubbornly. "But of course if you feel that way about me, why, we'll wait till you're ready. But Dale, you kissed me as if you loved me—! I'm not good enough for such a sweet girl as you are, but I'll make it up by loving you the more!"

"I do love you," said Dale shyly. "But I really know you, you know. Didn't I watch you save that dear baby's life? Didn't I see how gentle you were? Didn't I know how you took care of us both, and got the very best there was for us, just two strange little foundlings, and you took us out of Mrs. Beck's terrible house, and put us in this beautiful apartment, and got us a doctor and a nurse, and you stuck by and helped—"

"Yes, but you forget, I loved you both! And you were taking care of the little baby that God let me find—"

Then all at once from the other side of the room came another little voice:

"A-hhh! Goooo! Ahh! Ahhh?"

They both looked up in wonder and then with delight. The baby was talking to them in a sweet little voice, as if he were giving his blessing. As if he had heard what they said and approved it. As if he wanted to get into the conversation too.

George pulled Dale to her feet, and with his arm around her and one of her hands in his they walked over to the crib.

"How about it, fella? Do you approve my choice?"

The baby looked at Rand as if he understood, looked at him almost as if he recognized him.

"A-hhh! O-ooo! A-hggoo!" said the baby, ending

PARTNERS

with a little cheerful crow, like a well baby. And then he drew one corner of his mouth into the shadowy semblance of a smile.

"Why, he's smiling at you, George! He's never done that before! He's never talked like that before!"

"Yes, well, fella, I'm glad you bucked up and smiled for your daddy. You knew your daddy when he came, didn't you?"

"Ahh-ooo-ahhh!" answered the baby looking earnestly at Rand.

"And so you approve the lady I've selected to be your mommie, do you?"

The baby looked at him solemnly.

"A-h-h-h! O-o-o-o-ah!" said the baby, and suddenly gave a little lift to his small feet, tossing them up and ending with a cheery crow, and a regular smile this time, with the dimples clearly showing.

"Well, say, fella, you're a regular guy, aren't you?" said Rand, filled with delight. "Has he been doing these stunts right along?"

"Oh, no," said Dale sadly. "He's been very sick. For two days we were frightened. Even the nurse looked grave, and sent for the doctor. I think the doctor himself was worried. Didn't he tell you? That was last night when he answered the phone."

"All he told me was that he had to hurry away to an operation and he would call me back when it was over. He said the baby was fine!"

"Well, he didn't go to any operation. He stayed

here all night. I know he was worried!"

"Well, I had a hunch! And I'm glad I followed it out this time. But I was mighty uncomfortable until I decided to come home."

"Well, I was very unhappy, too," said Dale in a small voice. "I thought maybe you had stopped caring for him, and I began to try to plan a way that I could perhaps take care of him."

Rand drew her closer to him, and looked down keenly into her eyes.

"Then you really want him?" he asked searchingly. "You won't feel he's a burden you have to have just because I want him?"

"I really *want* him!" said Dale. "I *love* him."

"And you won't feel after a time that I ran him in on you and spoiled our home and our life?"

"How could I feel that way? Why, George, he's the one that brought us together. He's the angel God sent to introduce us!"

"You dear!" said George, drawing her closer, and setting a slow reverent kiss on her brow.

Then they could hear the nurse stirring about in her room now, and Dale ran lightly over by the baby, while Rand put on his most dignified air and stood looking out the window at the white white world, but enchantment was shining in the eyes of both.

"Oh, has Mr. Rand got back? That's nice," said the nurse, coming in with the air of being ready for work. "Why, I thought you said you were going to stay another day or two."

"Well, you see I got a hunch the baby was worse," said Rand with a sheepish smile, "so I just finished up my work as fast as I could and flew back."

"Now can you beat that!" marveled the nurse. "He *was* worse again, pretty bad for a few hours, and I didn't know but we'd have to send for you, but we got the doctor and he brought him around in fine shape. But to think you'd feel that across a lot of miles! You must be sensitive to thought transference, aren't you?"

Rand grinned slyly across at Dale.

"Perhaps I am," he said amusedly. "I never realized it before. But it must have been something like that."

Dale turned away quickly to hide her smile.

"Well, how's my baby this morning? Is he awake yet?" asked the nurse going over to the crib.

"Oh, yes," said Dale. "He's been talking to us. You ought to hear him. It sounded as if he was really trying to say things."

They all circled around the crib, and the baby was greatly intrigued. He looked up and fixed his big blue eyes on Rand, and remarked quite casually, just as if he knew he was being the center of admiration, "A-hhh! O-ooo-ah!"

"Well," said the nurse in a tone of deep satisfaction, "he's better, and no mistake now! He never did that before, did he?"

"No," said Dale, smiling. "It seemed as if he recognized Mr. Rand. He gave several little sort of crows to him, and he really smiled and showed his dimples."

"Well, I'm sure he's better. We must tell the doctor when he comes. It's a good indication when they begin to take notice."

She went over to the crib and laid her hand lightly on the little forehead.

"His skin feels better, too. Yes, little boy, you'll be well enough to enjoy Christmas. Just one week off today, isn't it? That's time enough to get a pretty good start. Only we'll have to be very careful that he doesn't get another set-back. Well, now, young man, I suppose you're ready for your breakfast, aren't you?"

"Ah*hhh!*" said the baby quite insistently, and they all laughed.

The nurse hurried away for the bottle, and Rand slipped up beside Dale and put his arm about her.

Dale thrilled to his presence, and her cheeks grew rosy.

"Sweetheart!" he whispered, and then they heard the nurse coming back.

"We're going down to get some breakfast, and then out to take a little walk," said Rand to the nurse. "Will that be all right? You won't need us right away, will you?"

"Oh, no, I shan't need you. This young man will

sleep a little while after he gets his breakfast, and when he wakes up he'll be having a bit of a bath. No, I shan't need you."

So with radiant faces, and eyes full of a great joy the two went off together, and the nurse sat down with the morning paper in a chair beside her, prepared to feed the baby and take a little easy time before she had to get the room "redd up" as she called it, and prepare for the baby's bath, which was still a most careful operation.

The room was very warm and quiet, the food was just to the baby's taste, the nurse was sitting close by. He could see the top of her head as he rolled his eyes dreamily that way, and the little place where the gray hair parted on her pink forehead. She represented comfort and relief from annoying hunger, or cold, or weariness. She was a comfortable thought even as she sat there crackling that paper now and then, and startling him as he drowsed happily off, almost asleep. It was perhaps after all a pleasant world to which he had come, through so much tribulation, although it had been so terribly cold at first. Perhaps it was only a bad dream, that coldness. That cold white stuff that he put his bare little claw into. That world where there was a glaring light above and nobody to help, and then suddenly big strong arms lifted him and bore him away.

Where were those two who had been there to do such nice pleasant things for him? That sweet-faced girl that crooned to him and put him into nice warm water! The big man near by who fed him nice hot sweet water. And then that bottle the girl gave him!

"Mm-mmm-mmmm!" They knew what to do for a fellow when he had that gone, empty pain in his tummy! They knew how to smile and talk sweet talk, and call him nice names, and make him feel as if somebody loved him again!

His eyelids drooped, and he swallowed soulfully. He rolled his eyes a little, and glimpsed the nurse in the offing, and felt drowsy and comfortable and good. Then he dropped off into a sweet oblivion and never knew when the nipple slipped from his repleted lips, and the bottle rolled down against the willow side of the crib. The nurse pulled the blanket softly up around his shoulders and took the bottle away, and he was asleep!

But the nurse dropped down with a sigh and finished the paper, and then drowsed off herself, with her head back against the soft upholstery of the chair, and really slept until someone knocked at the door sharply, and a youthful voice called out:

"Telegram!"

Chapter 16

A KIND OF STRANGE EMBARRASSMENT CAME UPON Dale and Rand as they went out into the hall and took the elevator downstairs. A sudden sense of their new relation. A breathlessness at the thought, the memory of the sweetness of their lips upon one another's. The thought of being close and dear and knowing that each cared for the other.

Somehow it didn't seem real yet. Somehow Dale felt as if she must have dreamed it, or if it were true Rand must have merely yielded to an impulse, and that surely he must be sorry. A feeling as if she must give him a chance to escape from what he had done.

He watched her furtively as they went down, noting the sweet outline of her face, the purity of brow and lip and chin, the delicacy of feature, the little curl at the back of her neck which had often lingered in his memory and intrigued his thoughts.

Was it really true, he thought, that she was his? Hadn't he taken advantage of her somehow to have dared to take her in his arms?

Then suddenly she turned and looked up to him

with her shy smile, and a glory of joy came into his face. He reached out quickly and caught her hand that lay near his own, and thrilled at the touch!

He dared to grasp the hand close, and looked defiantly toward the imperturbable back of the elevator boy who was attending strictly to business and wasn't seeing them at all. And was it fancy that her fingers curled about his and almost nestled there, shy, almost fearful little fingers?

She stepped demurely out of the elevator, with shy glance upward for his guidance as to where they should go.

"I know a nice new place to eat," he said gravely, lingering an instant in the lobby. "Or, are you in a hurry? We can go to the restaurant here, but I would like to show you another place."

"Lovely!" said Dale. "That will be nice. I don't think there is any especial hurry. The nurse has had a nice long sleep and she didn't seem to need us."

He led her out and took a taxi, and soon they were in a pleasant quiet restaurant where the waiters came and went silently, and there were restful walls of tapestry, groups of palms and ferns, and an air of intimacy and privacy.

"Now," he said, "you are going to have a good breakfast. You look as white as a sheet, and I don't believe you've been eating enough to keep a flea alive."

She laughed happily. It seemed so new and alto-

gether lovely to have anyone care what she did, or
whether she ate.

"Why, I think I've been eating all right," she said
thoughtfully. "You see, there were two or three days
when there wasn't much time to eat. And then we
were too anxious to feel like eating. At least I was. I
felt as if I had the whole responsibility on me, though
I suppose the nurse thought she really had it. But
I couldn't help feeling as if it were mine, although
I didn't always know what to do when the baby was
so desperately ill. And it seemed to me that if anything happened to that dear baby before you came
back I should just die! I never thought I could love
a little stranger baby that way. It was a beautiful
surprise to me to find a thrill like that in my heart.
But sometimes I got to thinking about him, and
wondering, if he did get well, how I could ever bear
to part with him. I somehow felt that you loved him
that way too, and you wouldn't want to give him up
to me even if I could find a way to take care of him."

Rand was watching her keenly, tenderly, his eyes
lighting at her words. It seemed he could see her
lovely spirit in her eyes.

"You are dear!" he said in a low voice, an expres-
sive look in his fine eyes. "You are more beautiful of
spirit than I had even hoped, and that was a great
deal! Now, dearest, I don't want to be insistent, nor
to rush you into something you do not feel ready
for, but I wish you could feel your way clear for us

to be married right away. Sometimes it seems as if I could not wait to have you with me all the time."

Her face kindled wistfully.

"Oh, I know, I feel that way too, for you are wonderful, and I've been so lonely. But I tell you, you don't really know me. You might be greatly disappointed after you got to know me better. My mother used to say that if people were not in such a rush there wouldn't be so many divorces. I couldn't bear to think you would grow weary of me."

Rand's face grew almost stern.

"That isn't possible!" he said. "I have an indelible picture in my heart of you with a little freezing child in your arms, and your face filled with a loving motherhood that I can never forget. You are the only girl I have ever seen who has stirred my heart, the only one I ever thought I wanted as my lifelong companion, and *I* feel, whatever you may feel about it, that we have been brought together in such an unusual way that it is a sign God meant us to belong to one another. Yet, of course, if you do not feel that way, it wouldn't be right for me to urge you. I don't want you to make any mistakes, and spoil your beautiful life."

Her face suddenly sparkled with eagerness.

"Oh, I don't feel that I would ever be making a mistake to join my life to yours. Not on *my* part. For—" her eyes dropped down for an instant and then lifted and looked at him steadily, the gorgeous color rising in her cheeks.

"For you see," she went on, keeping her eyes upon his, with all her lovely soul in evidence, "I knew several days ago that you were the only man in the world I could ever marry, and that I loved you with all my heart. But I couldn't ever think you could possibly feel that way about me."

There was wistfulness in her eyes and voice, and his glance met hers without wavering.

"And why not?" he asked in that low husky voice of his that demanded the truth. "Why couldn't you think I could care for you that way? I'm quite sure that others must have loved you, and perhaps told you so. Why was I so void of understanding?"

Her face grew rosy once more, the tell-tale blood flushing her cheeks, her eyes owning to the truth.

"Tell me!" he demanded. "Isn't it so? You have had other lovers, haven't you? And you have loved them, perhaps? Maybe still love someone?" His eyes were compelling hers.

"No!" she said sharply. "No, I have never loved them."

"But there have been other men who have loved you. Please tell me. Let us get them off the carpet, out of our way. So that if possible they shall no longer stand between us!"

"Oh, they could *never* stand between us," said Dale breathlessly, "because, you see, I never cared for them, never even *thought* I did. It was all so silly.

One was only a boy in high school. A nice enough boy, but I never enjoyed being with him. He was sort of a bore. Another was a young man in my father's business. He thought he knew everything and condescended to me. He wanted to advise me, and adjust me to his way of thinking. I came away from my home town partly to get away from him."

"And the third one?" His eyes were still steadily on hers.

Dale laughed.

"The third one isn't a lover at all. He is just an awful nuisance! He must be twice my age, and he thinks it is foolish to talk about love. He says that is a very poor foundation for marriage. He has just made up his mind that I would be a good wife after he gets me what he calls 'molded' or 'trained.' He lives in a fine house, and seems to have a lot of money, and he wants me for a 'hostess.' He has even traced me to this place, and written, and been to call, and I cannot get rid of him. I almost wished I could run away and hide somewhere. But I wouldn't call any of them lovers, would you?"

Rand's face broke into subdued joy.

"Perhaps not, unless maybe the high school boy, but he'll get over it. As for the man from your father's office, I think I could soon show him where to get off. But the rich old guy who wants to train you, I'd like to wallop him!"

"I wish you would," said Dale with a twinkle. "If

he turns up again I'll send for you. His name is Arliss Webster."

"Well, if Artless comes around again I'll be right there on the job. Now, is that all?"

"That's all," smiled Dale.

"So! Having disposed of my three rivals let us go on to other more cheerful topics. When will you marry me?"

"Oh!" said Dale a great joy growing in her face. "Oh, do you think we should consider that, now, before the baby is perfectly well?"

"Why not? Don't you think we could better take care of him if we were together? I don't want any more Mrs. Becks nosing around in our affairs, and saying things about you, do you?"

"Oh, no!" said Dale catching her breath. "But— that's not a reason for getting married, is it?"

Rand sobered.

"It's *a* reason," he said, "perhaps not *the* reason, for I still belong to the company of those who consider the sentimental side of marriage important, and I agree with you that Love is the great important reason for marriage. And so I am putting it up to you. Do you love me enough to want to marry me, or do you not?"

"I do!" said Dale solemnly as if it were a sacrament. "My dear mother taught me that was the important thing when I was only a very little girl. She impressed it upon me that I must never marry a man that I did not love with my whole heart. She made it second to only one other thing."

"Yes?" said Rand, lifting his head quickly, and eyeing her with a startled look. "What was that?"

"That was that I must never marry a man who had not accepted my Christ as his own personal Saviour, and was living for Him and putting Him first."

The room was very still. There were few others in the restaurant and those far away. Dale sat very quietly, with her eyes downcast as if a thing of great moment were in the balance.

Rand was looking at her with awe. Tenderly he spoke with great humility.

"Well," he said, "two days ago I could not have qualified in that respect I'm afraid. But I had a talk with God last night, and I told Him I was His."

Slowly she looked up with a dear trembling faith in her eyes.

"I was sure about it the night we prayed together," she said. Her voice was so soft that it was hardly audible, but Rand reached out his hand gently and enfolded hers in it.

"Dear," he said, "that's true! I didn't know what was happening in me that night, but I guess God was already working on me, even then."

The shining look that passed from one to the other and back again was one that the angels must have rejoiced to see.

"And now," he said at last, as they rose from the table, "what shall we do about this marriage? Do you feel you must wait and think it over further?"

"No," said Dale quickly, "I'm sure it's right. I know it's the most happy thing that could happen to me, and I'm ready to carry it out whenever you think is the best time."

They walked quietly, thoughtfully out of that restaurant, and as they paused in the doorway for Dale to put on her coat, Rand said gently:

"Well, what would you think of our going over to the court house and getting a license? Then it would be ready in case we wanted it soon. That doesn't commit us to an immediate marriage, of course. We can talk it over later."

So they went and got the license, and came away with a new look on their faces, a new feeling of the tie that bound them to one another.

As they went back to the apartment house Rand looked at his watch.

"It's later than I thought," he said, startled. "We'd better hurry up and relieve the nurse. But by and by perhaps there will be an opportunity for us to get together and make a few immediate plans. Think it over, dear heart, and let me know just what you want."

She flashed him a beautiful look, and his own in answer was like a benediction.

So they went back to the apartment. But when they opened the door and slipped in, tiptoeing as they glimpsed the baby asleep in his crib, they found a most perturbed nurse, going around the room, silently, it is true, but excitedly, and tears flowing down her cheeks!

She faced about and began to tell them, handing out the telegram she had just received and motioning them to come into the tiny kitchen alcove.

"It's my dear old mother!" she said, mopping her red face with the corner of her apron. "She's been in an automobile accident with my brother and his wife, and she's broken her hip and one arm and a rib. She wants me to come to her right away, and I've got to go! Much as I wanted to see you through this case I've got to go!" And then she gave way to a deluge of tears. "She's the only thing I've got left in this world that's all my own, and I've got to go. I was meaning to retire next year and make her have a happy time for the rest of her years, but now this has come, and I'm not sure if she can ever pull through!"

The nurse dissolved in bitter tears again.

"Why, of course you must go!" said Rand. "What can we do to help you? Where is your mother? Does she live in this city?"

"She lives away out west, Wisconsin it is. There isn't any through train till six o'clock. I won't get there till tomorrow morning, and she's going to be operated on this morning, maybe right now in a few minutes!"

"Well, that's tough luck. But, what do you say we

try to speak to her on the phone now, if she hasn't been taken out to the operating room yet? Or, if it's too late for that, at least you might be able to get through a message they could give her as soon as she's out of ether, or even before she goes under. Give me the names and addresses and I'll try to put the call through for you."

"Oh, thank you! You're good! I never thought of that. Perhaps there might be time to talk to her yet. They have a phone in every room at that hospital where she is. I nursed there for my first two years. I know it like a book!"

Quietly Rand took the addresses she gave, and went to work to connect with that far hospital. The capable nurse stood by with bated breath and watched, listened, suggested, her tears and her eagerness held in abeyance while she waited.

At last they got the connection, and the word came through. No, the patient had not gone down to the operating room yet. Yes, she was conscious and could understand. Yes, she wanted her daughter to come to her, and the attendant nurse reported that a great relief and joy had come to the mother's face when she knew that her daughter would start west that night. Her message was, "You are not to worry. I'll be all right!"

Then the light of hope and restored strength came back to the nurse's face.

"Oh, that's so good to know she's cheerful!" she

said, mopping away her tears. "Now, I can take heart and do what I have to do."

"Well, what have you to do before you start? Can't we help you?" asked Rand.

"Why, no, I guess that won't be necessary. I've just to stop over at my boarding place and pick up my things. They're already pretty well packed. I always leave them so that I could get them in a few minutes any time. If I leave here about three this afternoon I think that would be time enough. You'll have things you two will have to do if I'm going away. I'll stick by you as long as I can. You'll need to hunt another nurse, I suppose, for it isn't likely I can come back for a long time. I'll be wanting to give mother all my attention, at least until she is entirely well and able to walk again, if that is possible."

"Of course," said Rand. "You mustn't think of us now. But if there is really nothing important for you to do right away, it might be well for us to run out and do a few little things we ought to do before you leave us and we can't get away together."

His eyes sought Dale's for consent, and she joined in at once.

"Yes!" she said, "I think that would be a good idea. If we go right away we might be able to get everything done in time for you to get a good lunch before you go. Or, suppose I call down to the restaurant and have them send you up a tray at half past twelve? How would that do? Then you can eat in quiet and be ready to go as soon as we can get back."

"All right. That will be nice," said the nurse with relief in her voice. "Then I'll have time to get the baby's bottles ready for the rest of the day, and write out the directions the doctor gave me. I suppose I ought to let the doctor know I'm going. Would you want me to ask about another nurse?"

"Well, suppose you wait till we get back," said Rand thoughtfully. "Miss Hathaway and I want to talk that matter over of course. And isn't the doctor coming around today? Wouldn't it be well for us to be here when he comes? What time does he usually arrive?"

"Yes, he's coming, and he usually gets here around one-thirty or two."

"We'll try to be back. If we're not you tell him you're going, and ask his advice, and we'll call him up as soon as we get back," said Rand.

"All right," said the nurse. "You're very kind, I'm sure. Of course you know it's rather out of order for me to leave this way without notice, but you know you can't always—"

"Of course!" smiled Dale. "It's quite all right. We'll miss you a lot, but we wouldn't have you stay away from your mother for a minute, and we're glad you can go to her."

"Well, you're *good!*" said the nurse vehemently,

wiping a furtive tear from her eye. "I've seen a good
many professing Christians, but I never saw one I
believed in as much as I do in you two. I'm only
sorry I've got to leave you, but I'll be better all my
life from having known you, and that's the *truth!*
I'd give a good deal if that baby was all well, and not
such a care to you, before I leave. But you'll get on.
And anyway, I think he's pretty well over his trouble,
and he'll begin to chirk up and really grow in a few
days now. His cheeks are rounder now than when I
came, and that's a great deal for him to show that,
sick as he's been. But of course he's been getting his
good feedings right along. Well, I'll get your bottles
all ready, and I'll write out the formulas for you,
and his schedule. I guess you know pretty well what
it is, but it's just as well to have it in black and white
if you should happen to have any question about
anything. Now, you go, and don't hurry too much
about getting back. I really could get my packing
done if I didn't get to the boarding house till four,
I guess. There isn't so much for me to do."

Dale smiled.

"We'll be back!" she promised happily. "Come,
George, let's go. I'll be ready in just a minute," and
she hurried into her room, and was out again very
quickly ready to go.

Chapter 17

"DO YOU SUPPOSE YOU CAN GET HOLD OF OUR minister right away?" asked Dale as they stood waiting for the elevator to come.

Rand flashed her a gorgeous look.

"You are willing then?" he asked tenderly. "You are willing to have it right away?"

"Why yes, of course," said Dale happily. "There isn't any question, is there? It's sort of as if God ordered it this way, isn't it? We asked to be shown what was right, and of course when the nurse had to go it put the whole thing in a very different light. It was either now or wait, perhaps a long time. I can't quite see how we can do our very best for the baby unless we both work at it sometimes. Or get another nurse, and I don't see that that is necessary any longer, unless the doctor says we must."

Rand twinkled at her.

"Do I understand, Miss Hathaway, that you think it is sufficient reason for getting married, just that we may save the price of a nurse?"

She looked up in dismay, and caught his merry laughter.

"You are just kidding me," she said, laughing herself with her cheeks flaming rosily. "You knew I only meant it was a good reason for doing it *quickly!* That is, if we were going to do it *anyway!* But—" There was mock dismay suddenly in her voice, "perhaps you have changed your mind and don't *want* to marry me! Is that it?"

Rand reached down and caught her hand, squeezing her fingers softly, and gazing down at her with a wonderful look.

"You little witch!" he said. "Now it's you who are kidding me!" And then the elevator shot up to their level, the door slammed open and they stepped in.

He studied her tenderly all the way downstairs, and smiled at her lifted eyes.

"How soon can you be ready?" he asked quietly, in a casual voice. He might have been asking about some everyday matter.

"Ready?" she said, and then *"Oh!"* in great dismay. "I forgot that a bride should have gala attire. I meant to get the right kind of a dress and come to you in bridal array. But it would take time to do that, and I haven't anything that would be any more suitable than what I have on."

"That looks good enough to me," said Rand with a dear grin, giving her garments a friendly glance. "I can't see that clothes could make any difference. It's *you* I'll be marrying, not your garments. I'd rather have you now, as you are, than wait even a half hour for you to doll up. You know it doesn't really matter what you wear. The main thing is that we shall belong to one another."

"Yes, that was my idea of course, but now I remember that you were the one who thought it important that the little boy's mother should have proper garments for her burial. You felt it would be nice for him to know afterward that she was suitably garbed. Won't this be something too that we ought to remember in the right way? Shouldn't I go into a store now and get something nice, and put it on before I go to the minister's?"

"Look here, lady, that's not a parallel case. You're not on the same level as that little unknown dead mother. You'll be my wife and it will be your face I'll remember, not your clothes, you know. And besides, if you feel sensitive about it, lady, you can go at your leisure and buy a nice wedding dress and put it carefully away in moth balls and perfumery and label it 'Wedding Dress.' Then when we have anniversaries you can get it out and wear it, and really enjoy it. But just now it does seem as if we're rather hurried, doesn't it?"

She gave a gay little laugh.

"That's what I must have thought, I guess. I was just aiming to get the ceremony part over so that we would have a right to go on and take care of the baby as we saw necessary without any Mrs. Beck having anything to say!"

"That's the spirit!" said Rand happily. "We'll attend to all the doodads you want after we get that little kid on his way to health, but just now we're concerned only with forms and ceremonies before God, and critical gossips, aren't we?"

"That's it," said Dale. "Oh, it's going to be wonderful that you will understand!"

Another glowing look carried them out into the bright sunlight on the snow, into the crisp frosty air.

"I hope I'll always understand," said Rand in the tone wherewith one utters a sweet vow. "Now, shall we drop into this drugstore while I telephone?"

So Rand stepped into a telephone booth, and Dale realized that she held in her hand a letter, and brought her attention to it.

It was from the bank asking her to step in that day and take over the money that had been deposited in her name, and she came to herself sufficiently to gasp over the amount. $12,758.50. The figures danced before her eyes and meant nothing to her. If she had been made to say at that moment just what that amount was she might have answered, "Twelve dollars and seventy-five cents," so utterly confused was her mind, so entirely filled with other matters. Money which had been the chief concern of her weary days so long had withdrawn from its important position, into the background. Money wasn't as important as she had so long thought it was.

She folded the letter absent-mindedly and put it in her purse, registering only that she must stop at the bank and get that money settled. Perhaps she might want to use it sometime soon, and it had better be fixed right away. Then she turned brightly toward Rand as he came shining from the telephone booth.

"He's there!" he said eagerly. "He says it's all right for us to come at once. Did you really mean that you were wanting to go at once? You don't have to do anything first?"

"No! Oh—! Why, perhaps I ought to stop at the bank for a minute! It's right on the way. But if you think it would be better later it can wait, I guess. I had a letter from them asking me to step in. It's about a deposit that was made by my old uncle years ago— I don't suppose it's very important."

"Well, it won't be difficult to stop a minute or two and get it out of the way," said Rand. "But if it's a question of money don't worry about money. I've got enough to see us through."

She smiled happily and they got into the taxi and went to the bank.

"What is this business at the bank?" he asked as they settled down in the taxi. "Anything you need my help in?"

"No, I guess not. Well, that is, I don't really know. I got a letter from a lawyer out west saying an old uncle of mine had put a small sum of money in the bank for me the day I was born, which was to be handed over to me when I came of age. I think I have that letter in my purse. Yes, here it is. There were some papers of identification I had to sign."

She handed the letter over to Rand.

He read it swiftly, and then looked up.

"How much is this money?" he asked.

"Oh, why, I forget. The bank letter came this morning. Here it is. I was so busy thinking about getting married that I really didn't take in how much it was."

He looked at the letter, and then back to her eyes again.

"You've been holding out on me," he charged. "You're a wealthy lady and I thought I was marrying someone rather poor. Don't you think that was taking an unfair advantage of me? Now, maybe I oughtn't to marry you. You maybe could do a lot better than to marry me."

"Oh!" she gasped. "What do you mean? I don't care for money! I'll give it all to you. I'd rather throw it away than not to have you!"

"Do you mean that, sweetheart?"

"Why, of course," she said sweetly nestling her hand in his.

"Then that's all right!" he comforted her. "We'll put your money away safely, then when you find something you want that costs more money than I have, we'll get it for you."

"Oh, no, not for me! How about the baby? Can't we use it for the baby?"

"Well, that's a thought. Keep it to send him to college? But we mustn't let him know it or he'll get his head turned sure. Look here, when is this twenty-first birthday of yours? Can't we put this thing off a little? We don't have to go to the bank today, do we?"

"Why no, I guess not maybe, or *do* we? What day of the month is this? The sixteenth. Why it's *today*! *This* is my birthday! Isn't that funny? I forgot all about it. You know I've been trying ever since mother went to Heaven to forget when my birthday came because it was so lonesome all alone."

"Well, it's not going to be lonesome for you any more, sweetheart, if I can help it!" said Rand holding her hand tightly and smiling into her eyes.

"You can!" said Dale softly. "Oh, yes, you can!"

"That's good!" said Rand. "And thank the Lord we'll soon be in a position to talk a little about all this without the danger of the world listening in on us. Yes, driver, this is the place! Right here, First National. Do you want me to go in with you, Dale?"

"Of course," she said gladly, realizing how wonderful it was going to be to have someone always belonging again.

The business transacted and all papers duly signed, Dale introduced Rand to John Ward, the friendly teller. Ward acknowledged the introduction pleasantly, with a sudden keen look at Rand, and then a smile.

"There's been another friend of yours in here this morning asking for you, Miss Hathaway," said the teller. "A Mr. Arliss Webster. He seemed to know you would be coming in here today, and said he especially wanted to see you. He waited some time for you, and when he went out said he would be back again. I think he said he was your fiancé, though he looked rather older than you are. Perhaps I was mistaken." He gave another keen look at Rand with a puzzled expression on his brow.

Suddenly Dale laughed a clear little sweet laugh like a chime of jubilant bells.

"No, Mr. Ward, he's not my fiancé, because Mr. Rand is that. You must have misunderstood him."

Ward's brow cleared.

"Oh, doubtless!" he said as if the matter was explained. "He must have said he was expecting you with your fiancé." He gave a congratulatory bow toward Rand.

Rand thanked him and grinned.

"Oh, was that 'Artless'?" he twinkled, looking at Dale. "Perhaps we'd better beat it then! It's getting late, you know."

"Yes," said Dale, sweetly smiling. "If he comes in again, Mr. Ward, you might tell him that we were in a hurry and couldn't wait. Thank you!" and they hurried away.

Back in the taxi they kept as much out of sight as possible, giggling together over their escape.

"You don't suppose Artless is going to keep this

up indefinitely after we're married, do you, sweetheart? I might have to wallop him after all if he gets
troublesome."

Then they arrived at the plain little chapel where
they found the minister waiting for them, and Arliss
Webster was forgotten.

It was plain enough as a chapel, in its simple archi-
tecture, but it was not entirely cheerless, for the
young people of the congregation had been garland-
ing the walls with evergreens for the coming Christmas celebration, and resinous hemlock trees stood
about the pulpit in all their unadorned simplicity
of loveliness. The minister, whose name was Harvey
Blessing, had got his wise young wife to arrange
Christmas roses, crimson and white in a crystal bowl
on the pulpit.

So as Dale walked up the aisle in her plain little
brown wool dress, and stood with her hand resting
on Rand's arm, she was in a veritable bower of green,
and the air was filled with the spicy pine odor
touched with rare perfume of deep winter roses. It
seemed a heavenly place, and she could not but
think that her dear mother, if she could look down
from her heavenly Home, must be glad for her that
day.

The service was simple and beautiful, and it
seemed to the two who stood there entering into
the sacred relation, that the Lord Himself stood there
beside them, making covenant with them as they as-

sented to the vows.

"I never came so near to God before," said Rand solemnly as they came away, with the words of the marriage benediction still ringing in their ears.

They brought the Christmas roses with them for the minister and his sweet-faced wife would not have it otherwise, and so after all, in spite of their hurry, the bride was not without a bouquet.

"This has been a great day to remember!" said Rand. "Our wedding day! Our wonderful wedding day! A birthday bride carrying Christmas roses! We couldn't have done better if we had taken weeks to prepare, could we, sweetheart? And if I was too untaught and dumb to remember to provide a bride's bouquet myself, my bride was not without roses, and there are still days to come, and years to come, I hope, when I may give her my own roses to prove to her how I love her, and how glad I am that she is mine. Just you wait till we have a little more time, my Dale, and we'll have all the frills and doodads of a regular wedding!"

"This was a regular wedding, George," she said softly. "I will not have you spoil it by saying it was not."

"Even if we do have to ride away from the church in a yellow taxicab?" grinned Rand.

"Yes, even a yellow taxicab. I love it all!"

Very quietly they entered the hallway of the apartment house and took their way in the elevator up to the apartment.

"Look!" Dale said to the astonished nurse who hadn't expected them back for an hour yet. "We have been to our own wedding, and it was lovely! I have brought back my bouquet for you to see! And we are going to have the wedding breakfast in a few minutes. It will be served up here, and you and the doctor are both invited!"

The nurse stood entranced, divided between her tears and her love of the romantic.

"Oh, you children, you!" she said, with great delight. "I just thought it was going to end that way, but I didn't expect it so soon."

"Well, you see you sort of rushed the performance a little. But my dear, it isn't the end, it's just our *beginning!*"

"Bless you, children!" the nurse said fervently, and then suddenly her face became anxious. "But what about the blessed wee baby?" she asked earnestly. "Is he to be shunted off on some orphanage?"

"Not on your life!" said Rand solemnly. "He is the little fella who brought us together. He's going to be the light and joy of our home!"

"It really was for his sake," said Dale coyly, "that we got married in such a hurry."

"Oh yes?" said the nurse with quite an effect of the street lingo in her voice. "Tell that to somebody who hasn't lived with you both for some days. I saw it coming, I tell you, and I hoped it would be. And now what's to come of those three men that wrote letters, and sent roses, and demanded to be hangers on, I should like to know?"

"If they dare come around again I'm going to wallop them all!" said Rand solemnly.

"Good!" said the nurse. "I hope I can be present when it happens. That *old* one! I saw him one day, and I did my best to make him understand the lady was busy!"

"Well, *we'd* better get busy!" said Rand. "The doctor's due about now, and I have to see if that wedding breakfast is ready. I ordered it before we started."

"I'll get the tables ready," said Dale. "Two of those small tables together will do, don't you think?"

"Sure!" said Rand. "And how's the little fella? Is he going to eat with us? He doesn't sleep *all* the time, does he?"

"Ahhhh! Oooooo!" came a soft cooing sound from the crib.

"There he is, right on the dot!" said Rand. "Young fella! This is a celebration, and it's all your fault, so you've got to be a good boy and not get sick again."

He stood for an instant looking down at the child, and the baby looked up and smiled. A real smile it was, and Dale stole up with Rand's arm about her to see, and then called the hungry-eyed nurse to see the baby smile.

It was like a little family, the three people gathered about the little child, and the nurse watched everything wistfully, for was she not having to go away and leave the baby just as she was beginning to love him, just as she was loving the whole family!

Then suddenly Rand hurried down to see if his orders were being carried out, and while he was gone Dale and the nurse created a charming table with the Christmas roses in the center.

Rand came back with the doctor, and then the waiters arrived with the dishes and trays, the nurse finished feeding the baby, and the guests sat down to the table and enjoyed the feast.

And after the turkey and mince pie and ice cream had been enjoyed, and the doctor had gone over the baby and pronounced him in fine shape, then suddenly it was time for the nurse to go. Rand sent for a taxi, gathered up her belongings, accompanied her to her boarding place, and left her, promising to return there and see her to her train.

The doctor had stayed with Dale to give her a few last directions about the baby and before he left Rand arrived back. The doctor looked at the two with a broad genial smile.

"I don't just know how to tell you two what I think of you," he said. "I thought you were rare people before, but after today's response to the trying situation I put you on top of all the young men and women I know."

"Well, now, that's nice!" said Rand. "I can't just understand how we attained all that excellence, but I appreciate your applause. But, may I enquire just what you suppose *any*body would do in a situation like that? Would you have expected us to lock the nurse in and refuse to let her go?"

The doctor grinned.

"There are plenty of people I know who would have stormed around and deducted some of her pay, or maybe held her to finish out her week at least. I've seen many of that kind in my experience. But then of course, the very fact that you're taking care of this little foundling child this way, treating it exactly as if it were your own, sets you in a class by yourself."

"Oh no!" said Rand. "I don't believe there are any *Christian* people who wouldn't do that, not many, anyway."

"*Christians!* Oh, well, I don't know so much about them, but I've seen a lot of *so-called* ones that would have excuses galore for getting out of a thing like this. Why, man, this is a life work you've undertaken!"

"I trust so!" said Rand solemnly, with a kind of radiance in his face. "We want it to be that!"

"Oh, *yes!*" said Dale lifting a glory-look to the doctor.

The doctor stood there looking at them with growing wonder in his eyes, and something almost like reverence mingled with his admiration.

It grew almost embarrassing to them, the look he gave them, until Rand in a matter-of-fact tone said: "Doctor, if this little chap continues to improve at the rate he's doing now, how long do you think it will be before we dare move? I'd like to get my family into a more convenient home before Christmas if it's at all possible, but of course we don't want to run any risks."

The doctor came down to practical things at once. "Oh! *Move?*" he said sharply. "How far do you want to take him? Out of the city?"

"Oh, no," said Rand, "just into a larger, sunnier apartment. There's a place around on the next avenue in the Curtiss building where I have found an apartment that is much more suited to our needs for the rest of the winter. My wife hasn't seen it yet, but I'm sure she will prefer it. It's much more conveniently arranged, and the service is better."

"H'm!" said the doctor frowning and looking down at the sleeping baby. "Well, I suppose he might be moved that far in two or three days now. We'll see how things go tomorrow or next day. If he doesn't have any more set-backs he ought to be able to weather it pretty soon. How about a nurse? Are you going to get along without one for a while?"

"Yes," said Dale smiling. "I can perfectly well take care of him now."

"Not altogether!" said Rand firmly. "There will

be times when we'll both have to go out at the same time of course, and eventually we'll have to have someone, but I thought we could take our time. We've been waiting to see if you knew of the right nurse. Or should we continue to have a regular nurse now for a few weeks? We want to do the right thing of course."

"Well," said the doctor thoughtfully, "I do know two or three good nurses who might be right for you, but they're out on cases just now. If you could get along for another week, perhaps even only four or five days, I think I could find you just the right one."

"Oh, we can!" said Dale. "I'm sure we can. And by that time we'll likely know just what it is we want, anyway. We haven't really had a chance to get adjusted to things yet, because we've left everything to Nurse Hatfield, especially while the baby was so very sick."

"Well, Hatfield's all right of course. Sorry she had to leave you this way."

"Yes, we'll miss her," said Dale, "but we couldn't think of wanting her to stay away from her poor mother. We'll be all right."

"Yes, I guess you will," said the doctor looking at her with unqualified admiration. "You would have made a good nurse yourself, you know."

He went away and then at last they turned to one another with a look of utter joy on their faces.

Chapter 18

THE BABY WAS VERY GOOD THAT NIGHT. He seemed to like the gentle hands that handled him, the pleasant way his food was administered. And when he was replete he gave a tentative kick or two, feebly, as if just to test his power, and dropped off to sleep again.

"Do babies always sleep so much?" asked Rand as he saw the eyelids droop slowly down on the cheeks.

"I don't know," said Dale, "there are a great many things I don't know about babies."

"For a person who doesn't know, you've managed to do pretty well, I'll say. You've taken over the nurse's job like a professional. Say, has it struck you that the little fella is filling out a lot? I'd hardly recognize him for the same little mite that I found in Lady Beck's entrance hall, would you?"

"No, I don't believe I would," said Dale happily. "And his hair is definitely curly. My! I like that! He'll be lovely, I'm sure he will."

"Well, if he is I'm sure I'll get jealous," grinned Rand.

"You dear!" whispered Dale softly, putting her lips against his hair, and nestling close.

Rand enfolded her in his arms and drew her down beside him in the big chair.

"Say, isn't this wonderful!" said Rand. "Just ourselves, and no nurse around! To have you all to myself at last! It seems somehow as if it couldn't possibly be true that I am yours and you are mine!"

"And to think that just a few short days ago we didn't know each other at all!" said Dale. "Just picked up a lot of oranges together for a minute or two, and then scarcely saw each other again for several weeks."

"Well," said Rand bringing her cheek down to rest on his, "I had you in the back of my mind ever since. That's right, I did! You had golden lights in your eyes, and a special little curl in the whiteness of your neck that stayed with me, and lured me. That's right, you did! I noticed it the first time I saw you. Where is that curl? Ah! There it is. Turn around here and let me touch it. I always wanted to curl it around my finger. How soft it is. It feels just as I thought it would. I shall play with that curl a great deal, beloved. Shall you mind? Because I like you a lot, and I like that little curl."

"Well, and you had red lights in your hair and a dear grin on your nice lips," said Dale. "It made me like you at once. I felt safer somehow, and more content, because you belonged in that house, though I didn't suppose I would ever have any closer acquaintance with you than picking up those oranges. But do you know when I really fell hopelessly in love with you, so it was impossible to get you out of my mind?"

"No, when?" he asked with bated breath.

Dale's voice was very low and solemn as she answered:

"It was the night that you knelt down and prayed for the baby. The night I saw that reverent look on your face, and that holy light in your eyes. Then I knew you could stand the test that my mother had told me about. You might not ever care for me of course, but I knew you belonged to God, and it filled my heart with peace."

"That's what makes you so different from other girls," he said tenderly, awed by her thought of him. "You care about things of that sort, and most other girls don't. I don't think I've ever known a girl before who did, except my mother. And she wasn't a girl of course. Have you always cared?"

"Yes, in the back of my mind I have. I didn't always work at it much," she laughed shamedly. "You see, after mother died and things got pretty fierce I began to think God didn't care about me any more, and I didn't always go to church. I got away from God. I only prayed half-heartedly, and I didn't read my Bible much, at least only very hurriedly, not enough to really take in what I read. It's very easy to do that when you get your heart filled with worry."

"I guess it would be. Probably that's very much what was the matter with me. I joined the church when I was fourteen, but it never meant much to me. It was only a form, a ceremony, which gave one respectability and a certain amount of prestige with God. That's about all. Mother was sweet. I know she was a true Christian herself, but I think she considered that I was safe because I had at last joined the church. I remember that the day I united with the church it meant a lot to her, and I remember being a bit surprised that she felt so, because really it hadn't meant so much to me. Not as much as when I entered high school. But we always went to church of course, while I was at home. It was when I came up here to my job that I stopped going, and I haven't thought much about it since until God sent that baby and you to startle me into knowing what I was doing. I guess you have to keep in practice in religion as well as in anything else."

"Yes," said Dale thoughtfully, "I remember hearing a preacher say once that one of the necessities of the Christian life was that the Christian should walk 'in the light.' I remember the verse he quoted: 'If we walk in the light, as He is in the light, we have fellowship one with another, and the blood of Jesus Christ His Son cleanseth us from all sin.' I think it was that verse that was somewhat responsible for my finding our minister and the little chapel. I was very blue one night, and I realized that I had got away from the path my mother taught me, so I started out to find some Christian fellowship, and God led me to the chapel. How surprised I would have been if I had been told that very soon after I would be married in that same chapel. I found Christian fellowship that night, and went home with a lighter heart to bear the loneliness. I realized at least to a certain extent, that I had been starving my spirit by staying away from Christian fellowship, and the message of God."

"It seems," said Rand seriously, "that there are a great many things *I* have to learn. I can see it is going to make a big difference in my life. It was a great thing God did for me when I had been so indifferent to Him, sending you two into my life. I wouldn't think I would have been worth it to Him. He took a lot of trouble for me, and I've got to bear that in mind all my life, and walk softly before Him. Isn't that a phrase from the Bible? I seem to remember hearing it somewhere. I know when I heard it read in church I always used to think of the times when I had sneaked off to go skating without permission, and had to sneak in again and get my wet stockings and shoes changed, and came in clean and innocent looking to 'walk softly' before my mother so she wouldn't know I had gone off without telling her. But now I can see a different thought. It has more the idea of trying to please, doesn't it, because of all He has done for us? But say, oughtn't we to be getting settled for the night so this little chap won't be disturbed?"

It was the next morning just before Rand left for the office that they spoke about the new apartment.

"I suppose we could get along here all right for a while, and not worry about moving until the baby is well beyond any question," said Dale. "Wouldn't that be better? We are fairly comfortable here."

"We *could*," said Rand, thoughtfully, "but I believe he would get well quicker over there, and it would be a hundred percent easier for you. The rooms are large and have lots of sunshine, and there is a tiny laundry besides the bathroom. The kitchen is larger, too. There's a sunny alcove for the baby where he wouldn't hear every noise and be disturbed while he is sleeping, although goodness knows he seems to be able to sleep through anything. But I'd like you to see it as soon as we can manage to get out together, for I think you'd like it, and I don't want to run any risk of losing it. It seems to me the right place for the present and the price is right too."

"Oh, well," laughed Dale, "we don't need to worry about price just now, as long as my miraculous fortune lasts. That's probably what it was sent for."

"Is *that so?*" laughed Rand. "Think again! I'm the

man of this house, not my wife, and it is my fortune that pays for where we live, and not your private money!"

"But I thought we were partners," said Dale with wistfulness in her eyes. "It's just my dowry that I brought with me. Isn't that what you call it? My share of the general fund?"

"Well, of course we're partners, but there are some things a man ought to look out for, and besides, if we're partners, we've got to agree on what the monies under our control shall be spent for, haven't we?"

"Yes," said Dale smiling back. "All right, go ahead and get the most expensive mansion you can find. I'm satisfied!"

He grinned back.

"That's all right, Dale, I don't want to be extravagant, even if we have got more money in the offing than we ever expected to have. I've been saving too many years and going without things to get a home for my mother to want to blow it all in now. You needn't worry about me. I'll be amenable to reason when we get you and the kid fixed in comfort. Now, is there anything else before I go? Sometime you and I have got to get out and do a little Christmas shopping. So if the doctor knows of a safe nurse who could look after the kid for a couple of hours now and then, tell him to send her."

"Christmas shopping!" said Dale laughing. "I

guess we could skip that this year, couldn't we? We've got enough else to do. And the baby is far too young to expect it."

"No *ma'am!* I'm not going to have that kid remember that the first Christmas we didn't provide him any presents or a tree or anything! You wouldn't want that, would you?"

"Don't be silly!" said Dale with twinkling eyes. "We'll get up a Christmas he will like, without shopping for it. Don't be in such a hurry to rush the season."

"Okay!" said Rand, coming back to kiss her again before he finally took his leave.

"Something to come home to!" he murmured, looking down into her eyes. "This is going to be great!"

It was a busy happy morning for Dale. The baby was awake and smiling, actually smiling, and he greeted her with a genuine crow, louder and sweeter than any he had yet given.

"You darling!" she said as she stood over him for an instant looking down.

Then he crowed again and beat a quick little tattoo with both small fists. But she noticed with joy that the fists were no longer actually scrawny. They were not exactly chubby yet, but they were shapely and graceful, and it was noticeable that he was much stronger, and more energetic than he had been the day before.

She prepared for the baby's bath and breakfast
much as if it had been a birthday party she was
expecting, and as she went about assembling bath
tub, towels, wash cloths, soap and lovely smelling
powder she chirruped to the baby, till he entered
into the spirit of the thing himself and began to
crow back to her, and flap his little hands in joy. It
was as if he knew that he had passed from the hands
of the hospital nurse into the loving hands of a
mother.

It was beautiful to her to hold him on the blanket
on her lap. It minded her of the days when she was
playing dolls. She exulted in each tiny gain in flesh,
and touched the roseleaf skin delicately. It seemed
as if the baby enjoyed it too and looked up to her
face and cooed and gurgled at her, and once again he
smiled, just a little wavering smile. His two dimples
flashed out and disappeared and gave his face a
lovely expression, with a dawning beauty of form
that filled her with delight.

When the doctor came she had him snug in his
crib, fed and happy, gurgling softly to himself, while
she went swiftly around the room gathering up the
towels and soap, and putting things to rights.

"Well, I should say you're doing very well," announced the doctor as he stood looking down at
the fragile little child. "He looks as if he really might
grow up to be a solid bit of humanity after all."

Then he asked keen questions, and finally sat

back as if entirely satisfied.

"Well, I've found a woman I think may be a help to you, if you want her. She's been a practical nurse in her time, and I used to say I'd rather have her than any modern trained nurse. She really has a knack with her, and she loves babies. She isn't very strong, can't lift heavy patients any more, and has to take it a little easy. By rights she ought to be in her daughter's home being taken care of, but her son-in-law is rather a wild number and doesn't want her around, and she's too proud to stay around and be a burden, so she's looking for a quiet place where she can be of use and earn at least her board. I think she'd be all right. At least you could try her out for a few days and see what you think. I know she's a good faithful woman, and you can depend on whatever she says. She knows a lot about nursing, and you'd find she'd be glad to take hold in the kitchen too. She can cook a tasty meal when she tries."

"Why, that sounds wonderful!" said Dale. "Where can we see her?"

"Oh, I'll send her over this evening if that will be convenient for you. She's calling me up around seven. She's coming off the case of an old lady who broke her arm, tonight, and I happen to know she's no place to go, so it will be all right if you want her to begin at once."

"Thank you so much, doctor. That sounds good. We'll be looking for her. It will be a great help. You think it would be safe to leave the baby with her in a day or two when he has had a chance to get used to her?"

"Oh, yes, there's nothing she couldn't manage. She's brought up seven children of her own, besides a lot more of other people's children. The only thing is she's a bit lame herself, and won't make much of a showing if you want to doll her up and send her out in the park with the baby next summer."

"Oh, we wouldn't want that!" laughed Dale.

"I thought you were too sensible for that," twinkled the doctor. "She's Scotch and I think you'll like her."

"I feel sure we will," said Dale. "It's going to be very convenient to have someone to stay with the child when I have to run out on errands, you know."

"I thought you'd find that out. Well, I'll be going on. You won't be needing me here very much longer. I guess that kid'll be able to be taken out, with care, by the end of this week, if you don't go more than a block. But put some protection over his face, a light wool veil or something. Good afternoon! I'll be sending Mrs. Morton around this evening. Her name is Sarah."

When Rand came home the sound of his step along the hall thrilled Dale with a strange new delight. This was being married! To have someone in whom you delighted come back to you at night. It was wonderful! And to think that only a few short weeks ago she was in Mrs. Beck's rooming house, glooming sorrowfully by herself, thinking there was nobody in the world who cared whether she existed. Well, of course there had been Dinsmore, and Sam, and that poor old fool Arliss. But somehow they had never counted with her. She couldn't ever have been glad to have any one of them coming back.

She was at the door before George could get his key into the lock. She met him with a happy face lifted for his kiss. He drew her quickly inside, shut the door and gathered her into his arms. Wonderful refuge! Oh, it was good to have her husband come home!

He dropped his hat on the table by the door and plunged his hand deep in his pocket.

"I've got something for you," he said eagerly, like a boy with a new toy.

He tossed her a tiny white box.

"Open it," he said, and stood beside her watching her face.

"Oh, but it isn't Christmas yet," she said. "Don't you want me to put it away and save it until Christmas?"

"No!" he said with a grin. "It isn't a Christmas present. There's something that comes ahead of that. Open it!"

With trembling eager fingers she opened the box and found inside another box wrapped in tissue paper, a little box of white velvet with a bit of a pearl knob to touch the spring that opened it, and there inside sparkled two rings. One a simple circlet of platinum, the wedding ring; and the other a gorgeous sparkling diamond set in platinum also.

"Oh! My *dear!*" she murmured, her voice full of wonder. "And you said you were not going to be extravagant!"

"It's not extravagant to buy a wedding ring!"

"But such a glorious wedding ring! It's fit for a princess!" said Dale drawing in her breath, her eyes shining like two stars.

"It *is* for a little princess!" he said, and drew her close into his arms. "Now, put them on, the wedding ring first, and then the diamond."

Dale looked at them in wonder, then she handed the little velvet box over to Rand.

"You must put them on me, you know!"

"Oh, is that the way of it? Why sure, I'll love to do that. Now put out your hand! Is this the finger? One, two, three! Now, first I must kiss the finger!"

He laid a tender kiss in the rosy palm of her hand, and then touched with a butterfly kiss each finger tip, and then the rings. With a little ceremony of his own he slipped the rings on, with tender words of love, and then folded her close again and laid his lips upon hers.

"A-h-h-h!" interrupted the baby.

Rand looked up and grinned.

"Now sir, that'll be about all from *you* just now!"

he ordered firmly. "This may be something *you* brought about, but you needn't think that gives you the right to horn in on every minute, and we want just a few minutes to ourselves, if you don't mind."

"O-o-o-o!" said the baby calmly.

"Do they fit?" asked the lover, gathering his laughing bride back into his arms, "I had to snitch one of your gloves to get the size. The man said it was next to the smallest size."

"Is that where my other glove went," said Dale. "I thought I had lost it, and it was still a good glove!"

"Well, here it is, but I think you'd better put that pair of gloves away in moth balls, because that is sort of sacred, having performed the ceremony of getting the size for your wedding ring. My, how good that smells. Is it something you are cooking? Can you really cook?"

"It's just a kettle of soup," said Dale. "I thought maybe we could eat our dinner up here tonight if you don't mind."

"I should say I don't mind! Why, that will be heavenly!"

"No, not heavenly," said Dale. "It's only a very common kind of vegetable soup!"

"That's great! I love vegetable soup. Can the little guy have some too?"

"No, not yet. He has had his own little soup, and is quite content with it. Shall we sit down? It's all ready. And there's a woman coming to interview us afterward."

"A *woman!* What kind of a woman? *You're* the only woman *I* want."

"It's a woman the doctor is sending. She's a Scotch woman. Sit down and eat your supper and I'll tell you all about it."

"Now, lady, don't you go getting dictatorial on me! I've been through a great deal of excitement the last few days, and it might give me heart failure. I want to take these things one at a time, with great deliberation, and be sure I don't get a shock!"

So they sat down to delicious soup such as Dale's mother used to make, and had sweet converse.

"Do you mean she is going to stay tonight?" asked Rand. "It might be a good thing. If the little fella goes to sleep early we might run over to that apartment and look at it, couldn't we? That is if we like her looks and can trust her. He doesn't usually wake up at this time of night, does he?"

"No. Well—perhaps," said Dale. "You don't think it might frighten him to see a strange face, do you?"

"Oh, we'll turn the small light on, and he wouldn't notice she was strange."

"He'll know the touch of her hand is strange," said Dale with conviction.

"Well, we'll just trust he won't wake up, and anyway we won't be gone but about ten or fifteen minutes in all."

"We'll see when she comes," said Dale. "If you don't like her looks don't say anything about it, but if you like her, just ask if I can go. And if I don't like her looks I'll say no, I can't go tonight."

"Okay! You give me the high sign."

A few minutes later there was a tap at the door and when Rand opened it Sarah Morton entered.

She was thin and stooped and sad looking, with gray straggling hair that had never seen a permanent, nor tried to wave itself. But she had a sweet faded mouth that seemed trying to smile and very tired brown eyes that had a true light in them. She wasn't young any more. Not even as young as Nurse Hatfield.

"The dochter said you wanted to see me," she said shyly, a dreary wistfulness in her glance and voice.

"Yes," said Dale, liking her at once. "He thought you might be able to help us out for a few days till we know just what we are going to do, and look after the baby when we have to go out. Perhaps do a few other things. Would it be possible for you to do that? We've had a nurse ever since the baby was taken sick, but she was called away to her own sick mother, and it makes it awkward for us because we are moving to another apartment pretty soon and we both have to be out at the same time occasionally, until we get settled. The doctor thought you might be willing to come and try it."

"Yes?" said Sarah Morton wistfully. "You'll he
ben hevin' Nurse Hatfield, hev ye no'?"

"Yes," said Dale, cautiously, wondering why she
asked.

"She's a guid nurse!" said the woman unquali-
fiedly. "I'll like tae coom efter her. I ken her ways."

"Well, that sounds good," said Rand, barging into
the conversation.

Dale flashed a covert smile at him and went on.

"Then suppose you come and look at the only
room we have for you, and see if you are willing to
try us out for a few days till we know just what we
are going to do."

Sarah Morton followed Dale willingly to the little
room which had been occupied by Nurse Hatfield
and as the two women returned to the big room
Rand heard the woman say:

"I'd like it fine tae bide here. Right noo I cud
bide. I've got my suitcase wi' me. But, cud I get
awa' fer a coople of oors on Christmas? I'd like tae
tak a bit package tae my wee grandson, up in the
coontry. I'd na bide lang."

"Why, of course," said Dale. "We would want to
be here ourselves most of the day, perhaps all day.
We certainly could if it was necessary."

The woman's face bloomed with relief.

"Then tha's a'richt!" she said happily.

"We could give you the day if you wanted it,"
said Dale.

"Thank ye kindly, Mrs. Rond, but that'll no be necessary. I wad na be wulcome tae bide at my son-in-law's hoose. They'll be hevin a gay pairty. But I juist yearn tae see the bit laddie fer a wee whiles."

"Well, I'm sure we'll be able to arrange that," said Dale. "And now would you like to see the baby? He's asleep of course, and he doesn't usually waken easily this time of night."

They went softly over to the screen that sheltered the crib, and the little woman stood for a moment and looked. The expression of her face was sweet and tender.

"Ah! The puir wee laddie!" she breathed as she came back to the other end of the room, and Rand watching her decided that she was all right.

"By the way, would it be all right with you, Mrs. Morton, if we were to go out for fifteen or twenty minutes right away? There's an errand we have that is rather necessary tonight."

The woman's face brightened.

"It surely wull," said Sarah Morton. "I'll juist be layin' off me coat an' bunnit, an' sit right doon o'er here. The wee laddie willna ken ye're gane."

Dale had her hat and coat on by the time the woman came back and she and Rand started out together.

"Let's hurry," said Dale. "It somehow seems kind of dreadful to leave him with an utter stranger like that."

"But then, after all, you must remember that we were utter strangers to him not so many days ago. And besides, we have the doctor's word for it that she is all right, and that's more than the kid had for us."

He grinned at her lovingly as they got into the elevator, and her eyes assented, but still she felt that they must hurry as fast as possible.

It was wonderful to be walking along arm in arm with Rand, that strong hand so possessively under her elbow, her feet keeping step with his firm stride. The crisp keen air struck their faces, and Dale gave a little shiver.

"You aren't warm enough, Dale," said Rand. "You need a thicker coat!"

"Oh, I'm all right! My thicker coat got so shabby I had to abandon it. But I'll be getting some new things pretty soon when I have time."

"Indeed you will, lady. And now, here's where we turn!"

"Oh, how lovely! That park draped in snow wreaths! And see the Christmas lights! Isn't it beautiful? And that church with the great spike of a steeple. It is beautiful as a temple with minarets!"

"Do you know, I thought you'd like that. I thought the little chap might like it too when he goes out to ride."

"I think it is wonderful for you who have never had anything much to do with children, to have

hought of all those things," said Dale. "Oh! And is
his the building? It's very attractive."

Then suddenly from across the park where the
tall steeple shot up among trees that gave it such a
lovely setting, there chimed out the melody of Christmas bells.

> It came upon the midnight clear
> That glorious song of old,
> Of angels bending near the earth
> To touch their harps of gold.

"Oh, I'm so glad for that!" said Dale drawing in a
quick breath of pleasure. "I shall love to hear those
bells ring."

"Yes, I thought maybe you would," said Rand laying a warm hand over hers and pressing her fingers
lightly.

Then they went in, up the elevator, and entered
the other apartment. Such a charming place!

There was a big living room, a well-planned
kitchen in small compass with a breakfast alcove, and
three other rooms which might or might not be bedrooms. But two of them were bright with windows,
showing now the brilliant lighting of the street and
the park. One room had a big bay window and was
especially attractive for the baby's nursery. Two
bathrooms. It seemed ideally planned for their little
family.

"You like it?" asked Rand, watching her glowing
face. "Then that settles it. I got an option on it to-

day. Now, let's go back. We can be getting together
a few furnishings day by day. You're sure you're
satisfied?"

"Oh, yes," said Dale. "More than satisfied. It seems
too good to be true!"

"Then I'll phone him tonight that we're taking
it," he said in a decisive tone.

They found Sarah Morton reading the evening
paper that Rand had left lying on the table, and
ready enough to go to her rest.

The baby hadn't stirred.

"I don't believe I'll have to disturb you tonight,"
said Dale. "I'm rather used now to looking after him,
and I want you to get a good sleep tonight. Good
night!"

Sarah Morton went thankfully to her small room,
and the little new family prepared for its second
night together.

But when they wakened in the morning there was
a cheery smell of coffee on the air, and a hint of
bacon cooking, showing that Sarah Morton was anxious to prove her willing ability to satisfy.

"Seems as though she might be going to be worth
her salt," said Rand cheerfully as he brushed his hair
before the mirror and flung on his coat. "And say,
lady, how does the thought of your new apartment
look to you in the light of day?"

"Lovely!" said Dale. "I'm looking forward to it.

George, the baby looks wonderful this morning. See! His cheeks are a little pink, and his forehead is cool and nice! He didn't waken once in the night. I believe he's going to get well! I've been afraid to say so before, but I feel somehow assured this morning. Come and look at him, George. There is something so ethereal about him, and yet it is a look of health, not too angelic. I think he's going to be a beautiful baby!"

"Of course!" said George. "Look who found him! Look who saved his life and took care of him! Is it any wonder he'd be beautiful after that?"

"Look what a great God we have!" breathed Dale softly. "And it's going to be just wonderful to have him have a father like you! A father who loves God! Just suppose Mrs. Beck had had to bring him up! What would he have been like?"

"She wouldn't!" said Rand. "She'd have put him out on the doorstep. He might have been brought up in Heaven, but not on earth. Bless his little heart. We must take great care to bring him up to know the Lord. Dale, I'm going to start in this Christmas Day telling him all about it! I'll tell him the story of the angels and the shepherds and the wise men, and the Christ who came and lived and died for him! I'll begin right away and I'll keep it up day after day. He's not going to be able to say he never heard the truth."

"George, how perfectly absurd! As if a baby like that could understand words!" said Dale with a tender smile.

"Well, he may not be able to understand words," said Rand stubbornly, "but he's learning them all the time, and somehow he finds out what things mean. You never know how soon they begin to understand. Why he understands already what a bottle of milk is! I'll warrant he had some vague idea when I found him that he was cold and needed comfort and warmth. He knew then he needed saving. What's the reason we can't implant the idea in his little mind that he needs saving from other things? He'll understand sin soon enough. Just watch him as the days go by and see how quick he wants to have his own way. I've seen it in babies on the trolley cars, stiffening their little backs and flinging themselves fairly out of their mother's arms, and howling their heads off. They know they're doing wrong. And they need the idea of salvation implanted in them. You can't tell how early that idea will be implanted and take. Do you know how many words a child has in his vocabulary at two years old? How do you know how many they have at one year, only they don't know how to voice them? I tell you I'm going to see that that little guy hears about his Saviour right along, all the days, till he gets old enough to want to take Him for his own."

Dale's eyes were dewy with agreement as she

looked at her husband.

"We'll begin now, so it can't ever be too late to begin."

"George, do you know I think that's really rather wonderful," she said. "Perhaps there is something in it. Anyway I'll help you all I can. We'll see our little boy gets to know all about the Lord who died for him. Isn't it queer how much trouble we take to teach babies how to eat, and walk and get along with other people, and we think they're too young to know about salvation? Well, we'll begin at once, and he'll never remember just when it was he first heard about the love of God to him."

So they went out to eat Sarah Morton's nice appetizing breakfast, and then to get ready for moving and for Christmas day.

Chapter 19

IT WAS THE SATURDAY BEFORE CHRISTMAS AND Rand had been in consultation with his editor about some important articles that the editor wanted Rand to handle. They had talked it all over thoroughly and Rand felt that he knew his editor better than ever before, and liked him a lot. He felt his new line of work was to be tremendously interesting. This had come just after he handed in the last article of the series about the western conference he had attended, and his heart was happy over work well done. He told himself that it was knowing Dale, and having the baby that had inspired him for the work. He had lost the feeling that there was no longer anyone on earth who cared especially whether he did well or not. So they concluded their decisions, and Rand got up to leave, with a cheery "Merry Christmas!"

"The same to you, Rand!" said the editor cordially, putting out his hand and giving the younger man a hearty hand-shake. "I like your work, and I feel we are going to get along well together in this new field. And oh, by the way, have you got your

Christmas invitation yet? The boys weren't quite sure they had the right address, and told me to ask you."

"Invitation?" said Rand wonderingly. "What invitation?"

"Why the paper is giving a Christmas dinner to the unmarried workers on our staff, men and girls, you know, and they are anxious to be sure that you come. It's to be at the Bellevue, and it's sure to be something pretty nice. I think you'll have a lot of fun. Sorry I can't qualify myself for an invitation, only my family seem to think they can't spare me on Christmas day."

Rand answered with a merry grin.

"Thank you so much for the invitation, Mr. Bigelow," said Rand, "but I'm afraid I wouldn't qualify either. You see I'm married too, and it's the baby's first Christmas. I really couldn't be away, you know."

"What! You married, Rand! Why, I supposed you were a confirmed bachelor living in a desolate boarding house. Well, you certainly have been quiet about it! Why, if I'd known that, you'd have had a wedding present and a good deal larger raise. You know we always look after our married men. I'll have to see about that! Here, just wait a minute—"

The editor seized a slip of paper and scribbled something on it, handing it over to Rand.

"There! Take that down to the desk and cash it in with your other check. A baby, too! And his first

Christmas! Of course! Well, Merry Christmas, and a Happy New Year to you all!"

"Thank you, Mr. Bigelow, and very many Happy New Years to you and all of yours. Good night!" With a light step and a lighter heart Rand went gaily down to the cash desk and then home to Dale and the baby.

Dale met him with a happy face.

"The doctor says we can take him over tonight," she said breathlessly. "He says it had better be tonight while the weather is good. He thinks there's going to be a big snow tomorrow perhaps, and he wouldn't want to risk his going out in that, not so soon. So if we are anxious to be moved for Christmas we'd better go tonight!"

"Hurrah!" said Rand. "Isn't that great! What say, little fella? Ready to move on? But—are you sure the furniture has come yet, Dale?"

"Oh, yes," said Dale smiling. "It came about ten this morning. I went over and told the man where to put everything and it all looks wonderful! I'm glad we got the walnut set for our room. It's beautiful, and the beds just fit. There's plenty of room. And the chairs look so pretty in the living room. The leaf table came too and it fits perfectly into the little corner where you said it would when it's not in use. I'm glad you got it. The chairs are very nice. I don't see why you thought you couldn't buy them without me. In fact I think perhaps you're almost extravagant when you go shopping alone. Because we really don't need to be so very grand when we first start out, you know."

"Well, I believe in getting good things when we get them, because I hope we'll be using them a long time, and we don't want to begin to dislike them before they are half worn out! But say! You don't need to worry about money just now. My editor came across when he found out I was married."

"Oh, tell me about it!" she said eagerly. "How did he know? Did you go and tell him?"

"Not I!" said Rand decidedly. "I didn't think it was any of his business. But I finally had to own up because he was inviting me to a bachelor dinner, girls and men, and I couldn't see staying away from you on Christmas night, so I told him. And then what did he do but raise my pay! It's a regular salary now, instead of just so much a column, you know!"

"Isn't that grand!" said Dale. "Well, I guess I won't scold you this time for buying such a handsome table and chairs. You got *six*, didn't you? I thought you said four would be enough."

"Well, I thought we might need that many if we had guests sometime, and perhaps we couldn't match them."

"Yes, I suppose that's wise. But say! If we're going to take that baby over we'd better go at once, hadn't we? I'm all packed up." She pointed to a pile of baggage over by the door. "And how about the crib?

Oughtn't it to go first? He can't lie in it until it is thoroughly warmed, you know. I had Sarah go over this morning and dust the furniture and make up the beds. Wasn't it nice the sheets and blankets came yesterday? I sent down to the store and got a big clothes basket, and had the hall boy carry them over. The baby can lie on our bed till his own gets warm."

"Fine!" said Rand, stooping to touch his lips to Dale's. "You're a real little housewife, aren't you? Well, I'll call up that man who promised to come with his truck. I only hope he doesn't say his working hours are over. However, I guess we can find somebody who wants to earn a dollar or two more."

He went eagerly off to the telephone, and soon was back.

"He's just come in for supper, and says he will come right away. Is this everything? We can't keep him waiting."

"Yes. Be careful of that basket. It has the baby's bottles packed in it. And that other basket has the saucepan for heating the milk. Now, I'll get his coat and bonnet on!"

"Well the truck will be here in a minute. Is this everything? Are you sure? Hasn't Sarah Morton got some things?"

"No, she took them over this morning. She took something every time she went over. She's a treasure, George!"

"Well, that's great! Now, young fella, do you realize we're going to move?"

"A-h-h-h!" said the baby, giving one of his little steps in the air with his small blue booties.

"So, you like the idea, do you?"

"O-o-o-o!"

"Well, that's good you approve! Now, all set?"

"Wait just a minute till I get his veil."

"All right! Here comes the man to get the things!" as a knock sounded. "By the way, Dale, I suppose we ought to lay in a supply of food for Christmas Day when Sarah is gone."

"Oh, that's all attended to," said Dale. "I went out this morning and got a lot of necessities, and they are over in the electric refrigerator. I found there is a very nice caterer only three blocks away and I've ordered our Christmas dinner served in our apartment. We haven't any dishes, you know, except what we got for the baby, and we don't want to buy dishes in a hurry. We haven't kitchen cooking things either. And if we want more than we can get here, on Sunday, we can have our dinner sent in then too. Do you think that was extravagant? I thought there would be so much to do getting settled, and with Sarah away."

"Extravagant? No! I think that is just the right thing to do. It's going to be fun, isn't it? Ah, there's the porter!"

He gave the directions about the baggage and then they started, Rand carrying the baby again, the crib

denuded from its blankets by Sarah, traveling down
by the baggage elevator.

The baby seemed to enjoy it all hugely. He cooed
softly to himself, and his bright eyes searched the
beloved faces that hung over him anxiously. Then
he gave a little crow of wonder, a sort of question
when the taxi stopped at the other apartment house
and Rand carried him out. He seemed to search the
sky over his head, and the walls and doorway he
entered into, and study with wonder the elevator that
took him up; to scan the walls of his new home and
chuckle with glee when the veil was taken away and
he was laid carefully on another bed. Gradually he
was unfolded from the chrysalis of soft woolly things,
one at a time, and presently he drowsed into a sweet
little nap, well guarded by pillows on every side.
Cautiously closing the door against sound the rest of
the family went into action.

"You and I ought to go out together a few minutes," said Rand. "The little fellow's got to have a
tree and a few doodads."

"Certainly!" said Dale. "He won't know the difference of course, but we can tell him about them
next year or the year after."

"Why, sure," said Rand. "And we'll get some
dinner, too, while we're out. I don't want much but
a bowl of soup and some coffee. Then Sarah can go
down to the restaurant and get herself something."

They bought a lovely tree and had it sent up to

the apartment. They bought some balls of red and silver and blue, and some tinsel. They bought a few strings of lights. And then they went to a toy store and got a lovely bright rattle all little jingly silver bells, with a light handle that the baby could hold pretty soon. Dale found a beautiful dancing dolly, on a music box with a stick that could be rolled in the hands to make it play a gay tune and whirl the dolly around, her bright pointed skirt flying wildly in time with the tune. Rand was so charmed with it that Dale said she was buying it for him. And then all the traditional things like candy canes, and Santa Claus stockings, and stars they bought to put on the tree.

"George," said Dale, "we're not buying these things for the baby, we're buying them because *we* are big children ourselves, and want to go back to our childhood again. The baby's only an excuse."

"Well," grinned George, "call it that if you like. I'm having fun, aren't you?"

"Yes," giggled Dale, and bought three lovely tan camels, and a handful of little woolly sheep.

"Get an angel or two, sweetheart," he said watching her amusedly. "They all belong. Let's have all the trimmings. And I know where I can get a lovely electric star. We need to teach the baby the shape of a star right at the beginning of his life. He'll likely be able to understand a star before anything else."

When they got back to the apartment they looked

like Santa Claus himself, with all their packages, and Rand went right to work putting up the tree, stringing the lights around it, hanging the balls and bright things they had bought, even the camels and sheep, and then the great star.

Joyously they worked like two children, with Sarah Morton standing by and helping, running errands for tacks and wire and tissue paper, cutting a few little tricks herself from memories of her childhood.

Then when it was finished they stood and looked around the room.

"It still looks bare in spite of that big tree," said Rand. "We'll have to get to work after Christmas and get the rest of the things we need. We should have a rug, a nice bright one, soft and warm for the baby to creep about on. And I have a grand bookcase full of books in storage. It belonged to my father and I've never had any place to put it since mother died and we gave up the old home. I think it will about fit on that bare wall over there. Do you like the idea? It has sliding glass doors, and reaches up about as high as a mantelpiece, or perhaps a little higher."

"That will be just the thing," said Dale. "And I have my piano! I forgot all about that. It's a good one. Father bought it for me the year before he died, and it's the one thing of all our goods that mother wouldn't let them sell. She said I would want it some day. A friend of mother's is keeping it for me.

She's an invalid and lives alone, and had a room where she could put it, so it hasn't been used for several years. I can get it any time I want to."

"That's great!" said Rand. "It will be nice to have something out of your childhood. I wish it were here tonight. I'd like some music right now."

Then as if in answer to the thought, suddenly the bells in the steeple sprang into action, clear and sweet across the lovely park, and they drew near to the window and looked out across the fairy scene, as the bells chimed on:

> Joy to the world the Lord is come,
>   Let earth receive her King,
> Let every heart prepare Him room
>   And heaven and nature sing.

It seemed some wondrous charmed spell that it flung over the many colored park and the brilliant city in the distance, and they listened with thrilling hearts to the old old story as song after song rang out, songs that they had known all their lives, and yet whose beauty they had never felt before.

> Oh, come, all ye faithful, joyfully triumphant,
>   To Bethlehem hasten now with glad accord;

"But I haven't been faithful—" said Rand sorrowfully. "Oh, why, I wonder? I had a Christian father and mother."

"Yes, and so had I," said Dale with a hint of tears in her voice. "But I haven't been faithful either."

Rand leaned over and pulled her to her feet.

"Come, let's go to Bethlehem together, and start all over again," he said, and he slipped his arm about her and drew her down to her knees beside him. And there in the quiet of their new living room, with the baby asleep in the bedroom, and Sarah Morton asleep in the little room beyond the kitchen, they reconsecrated themselves together to their Lord, asking for help to bring up the little child He had sent to their door.

Then they rose and stood with their arms about one another, looking at the fairy loveliness of the scene before them, while the last notes of "Silent Night" were pealing out their midnight music. Suddenly they knew there was a soft blur of whiteness coming down, sprinkling the sky, and dimming the lights, and Rand said softly:

"It is snowing again, dearest. Snowing just as it did that awful night the little boy came to us. How thankful we ought to be that we got here before it came! It might have been days before we could have moved him, and look here now how cosy we are! And he is safe and getting strong. You don't think he could have got any harm from being brought here, do you?"

"No indeed!" said Dale. "Not a breath of cold air got to him, and he is sleeping like a little lamb. Don't you think God will show us how to take care of him?

We don't know anything but He seems to have been arranging things for us."

"Yes, of course," said Rand. "We know as much perhaps as most earthly parents do at the start, don't we? They all have to learn step by step. If we just go day by day asking His guidance I guess we'll make the grade somehow."

"Of course we will!" said Dale, and her heart was singing softly,

"All is calm, all is bright—"

And so singing together they went away to their rest. One glance they took as they left the window. Many of the colored lights were out, and the great white stone steeple that looked like lace in the daytime had disappeared into the white feather blending that the sky was sending down to make its own Christmas decorations.

Steadily, softly, noiselessly it drifted down through the night, dressing all the trees in cleanest white again, touching roof and turret and pinnacle, and leaving them unsullied once more, as if to make a world befitting the coming festival, the birthday of a King.

And when the morning broke once more, and the sun arose and took command, the snow as quietly ceased as it had begun, and there was the world, deep in snow, and glistening as the rosy light came more and more upon it and made a glory out of the softly dropping flakes that had so incredibly soon covered up the world and made it new.

> Christians awake, salute the happy morn,
> Whereon the Saviour of the world was born;

rang out the bells on the snow-muted air, and Dale and Rand lay listening and thinking their sweet thoughts. Christmas was going to mean more to them than it ever had before.

"How about going to church today?" said Rand. "I wonder what the weather is like?"

He sprang up and went to the window.

"That would be wonderful!" said Dale. "And I don't care what the weather is like. I have galoshes, and I love to be out in weather. Let's go anyway. It isn't far, and I think we should. Worshiping in the sweet place where we were married would be lovely!"

"Well, it has stopped snowing," announced Rand. "The snowplows and shovels are hard at work on the sidewalks. I guess it won't be so bad even if it snows some more."

So they eagerly prepared for church, and after seeing the baby serenely settled with his bottle, and cheerfully accepting the aid of Sarah Morton as if she had always belonged, they started out, amid sweet carols from the bells.

The sermon that morning made very clear that the coming of the Lord had been for the definite pur-

pose of taking sin upon His sinless Self, that those
who accepted Him as their personal Saviour might
go free from the burden and penalty of their sin.

"I don't think I ever quite understood it when I
was a boy," said Rand thoughtfully, as after a pleasant greeting from the young minister they started
back to their apartment. "Most of the ministers I
ever heard left it all so vague and kind of indefinite
that it seemed only a form that one must go through,
like making out papers for taxes or something of that
sort. It never entered my head that I hadn't done
everything I ought to when I stood up before people
and 'joined church'! I thought that was all that was
required, and I had sort of bought a ticket to Heaven.
But now I see that there has to be a definite decision
of your very innermost soul to accept what Christ
has done for you, or His work is of no effect for you
personally. I'm glad we went to church this morning. That wasn't a Santa Claus sermon, it was a
Christ message."

"Yes," said Dale, "it was very clear. I feel as if this
was a very happy Christmas, and a wonderful beginning for our life together. A real Christmas beginning."

Chapter 20

They had a pleasant dinner down at the restaurant, and then hurried back to the apartment, finding the baby just wakened from a nice long sleep and smiling at their coming. That was a definite thing now, that he could really smile, and show actual dimples.

Rand, still thoughtful, stood looking down at him.

"Well, now, boy," he said, "it's about time you and I had a talk. Could I hold him in my lap, Dale, or would that be too much of an experiment?"

"Why of course you can hold him," said Dale, coming smiling to his assistance. "Here, let me fix him in your arms!"

She gathered him up with a little blue blanket about him and Rand sat down and held the little fellow carefully, as if he were china and might break.

The baby lay there and stared up at him, fixedly, earnestly, and then suddenly broke into a real, happy smile.

"Why he likes me, Dale! Just look at that. He almost acts as if he knew me!"

"Yes, of course," said Dale happily, "why wouldn't he know you? See! He looks as if he was remembering back to that time in the Beck front hall when his overcoat came off beside a bank of snow, and you picked him up and carried him to comfort. Certainly he remembers you! He's getting it across to himself that you are the head of this little family he's come to live with, and he likes it."

And then suddenly Rand bent his head and touched his lips lightly to the little forehead.

"Yes!" he said, and there was a sound of tears in his voice, and a look like moisture in his eyes. So much so that Dale stooped over and kissed her man on the forehead, and then brushed her lips lightly over the baby's hand.

"And now, boy," said Rand soberly when he could get the huskiness out of his voice, "I've got something to tell you. It's a story, a really truly story. Will you listen to me?"

"A-h-h-h-g-g-g-o-o-o!" said the baby quite distinctly.

Dale laughed softly and turned away to hide the quick happy tears that had sprung to her own eyes.

"That's right!" said Rand. "I'm glad to know you're listening, son. Now, this story, son, that I'm going to tell you is very important. It's about the most important thing in this life, and I want you to remember it. I'm going to tell you again and again, over and over, but this is the first time, and it's the beginning of it all. Now, listen! Long ago there was a baby born. A Christmas Baby! His name was Jesus, and he was born in a manger, where the cows eat their hay, because there wasn't any palace or mansion ready for Him, just a manger! And God set a big bright star over the stable where the manger was, to let the world know God's Son was born. It was a star something like that one up there on the wall. See? And everybody wondered about the star that night. God had told the world He was going to send His Son sometime, but nobody thought He would be born in a stable with just a manger for his crib, so they didn't recognize Him. Not even when that great big oversize star came out to show where He was, they didn't know. They just wondered.

"Only there were some wise men who had read about the baby that was coming some day, and the star that was coming to point the way. And away off in a desert somewhere they saw the star and followed it, and finally found the little baby and worshiped Him. They prayed to Him. Sometimes, pretty soon when you can talk, we'll teach you how to pray to Him too. You have a great deal to thank Him for when you get old enough to understand, and we're going to teach you all about it. But now, today, it's important for you to know about this baby that was born, and about the wise men who came on camels to see Him, and about the shepherds on the hillside taking care of their little woolly lambs. You see some

of the shepherds had heard there was a baby coming,
and one night when they sat by the fire on the hillside
under the starlight, with little stars sprinkled all
around the big sky, they saw a great big light, and
while they were wondering a bright angel came stepping down gold stairs in the sky, and they were very
much afraid, but the angel told them not to be afraid
for he was bringing some happy news for everybody,
because Jesus, the Saviour, the little Christ, was born
right then that night, over in the little town of Bethlehem, and if they wanted to see Him they could go
right over there now and they would find Him lying
in a manger, in a stable, with just little plain clothes
on, the kind all babies wear. Just like the little
clothes Mommie Dale put on you. And then all of a
sudden there were a whole lot of angels came stepping down the sky, singing out just the way those
pretty bells sing out, 'Glory to God in the highest,
and on earth peace, good will to men!' You must ask
Mommie to teach you that some day so you can say
it for me. Perhaps not next Christmas, but very likely
the next. And so when the angels went away the
shepherds began to talk. They said, 'C'mon, fellas,
let's go over there and see if this thing that God has
sent us word about has really happened.' So they
went, and they found it all true. There was the little
Jesus lying in a manger in the nice soft straw, and
there was His Mommie Mary right beside Him, just
like your Mommie Dale is right here beside us now,

and there was Joseph waiting on them and taking care of them. And so those shepherds were so happy their little Christ, King Jesus had really come at last that they kneeled down and worshiped Him. And oh, how they loved Him! They wished they had a lot of nice presents to bring Him, but they didn't have anything to bring, so they gave Him their own selves, and then because they couldn't do anything else for Him they went out back to the pasture and their sheep, but they told everybody they met about the Christ having been born. And that's what you and I and everybody who knows and loves the little Lord Jesus must do. They must go out and tell everybody they meet that the Christ Saviour has come, and why He came, because we all have sinned. He came to be a sacrifice for our sins, so that everybody could be forgiven who would believe on Him.

"And now, son, we'll just say a little verse together, you and I and Mommie Dale too if she wants to. It is called John 3: 16. I learned it this morning, and so can you if you try. We'll say it three times and then we'll take a walk across the room and look at the pretty balls on the tree, and hear the bells ring 'Glory,' and then it will be time for your bottle. Now say it: 'For God so loved the world, that He gave His only begotten Son, that whosoever believeth in Him should not perish, but have everlasting life.' "

The baby blinked, gave a faint smile and gurgled sweetly. Dale wondered if the angels were listening to this extraordinary talk to a tiny child. Could it

be possible that there was anything in what George
had said, that you couldn't begin too young? Certainly a wee baby like that could not understand,
and yet, he was gathering a vocabulary. Even scien-
tists admitted that very young children began at once
to store up words in their minds. Well, it was a sweet
thing to hear George talk to the baby. Of course it
could do no harm, and might perhaps lay a foundation, if only with the name of Jesus, the word Saviour.

They went to church again that night, for Sarah
in view of the holiday she was promised on the morrow was only too willing to stay quietly with the
baby. And on the way home they encountered more
than one group of carolers singing in the streets.
When they were at last getting to their rest they
heard sweet voices singing down below their window:
"Christ the Saviour is born."

Then as the midnight hour struck, wild and sweet
the bells began to repeat the old sweet carol:

> When marshalled on the nightly plain,
>   The glittering host bestud the sky,
> One star alone of all the train,
>   Can fix the sinner's wandering eye.
> Hark! hark! to God the chorus breaks
>   From every host, from every gem;
> But one alone the Saviour 'speaks—
>   It is the star of Bethlehem.

Dale as she drifted off to sleep wondered if there
ever had been such a dear Christmas Eve as this, and
then began remembering back to the days when she

was a little girl and stars and trees and lovely dolls
and other presents bulked large in her little-girl
mind, and her mother's kiss was sweet on her lips,
her father's loving voice in her ears. Yes, there had
been dear Christmases before. But perhaps it was
that there had been a long interval of darkness and
sadness, and great loneliness, and now life seemed
to have blended the sweet old things with the new,
and Christmas was still Christmas, dear and sweet,
and brighter than any other day of the year, yet with
a meaning for eternity that other days did not have,
and never could have, perhaps, unless it was Easter.

Then suddenly Rand, whom she had thought
asleep, spoke out of the darkness:

"Dale, are you asleep?"

"Oh, no, just dreaming of the marvelous day.
What is it?"

"Dale, did you notice the little poem in the sermon
tonight?"

"Yes, wasn't it lovely? I wanted to write it down,
but didn't have a pencil. I wonder if we could remember it."

"Well, I know the last two lines," said Rand. "I
remembered them because they seemed to fit my
case. 'I only know the manger-child has brought new
life to me.' "

"Oh," said Dale. "Wait! I thought I'd remember
that first line. I tried to memorize it as he repeated it.
'I know not how—' it began. Yes, that's it.

> 'I know not how that Bethlehem's Babe
> Could in the Godhead be;
> I only know the manger-child
> Has brought new life to me.' "

"That's it, Dale. I'm glad you remembered it. I somehow wanted to go on record with you tonight, our first Christmas Eve together, that the manger-child really *has* brought new life to me. And I guess that is why our little fellow was sent to us. To bring me all the way to God, and help me to understand."

"Oh, George, dear, isn't He wonderful?" said Dale softly, reaching over and slipping her hand into his.

"And now," said Rand after another few minutes, "What are we going to call that kid? We've got to have a name for the adoption papers next week, you know. It seems as if it ought to be something significant. Don't you think so?"

"Oh, yes!" she breathed. "It seems as if there isn't any name good enough for him!"

"Well, what would you think of Ransom? It means 'redeemed,' you know. The only trouble is, it's my redemption, not his."

"Oh, but you're mistaken," cried Dale. "It would mean the baby's redemption too. Don't you see? For suppose he had lain in Mrs. Beck's hall till she called the police, or had been sent to a Home where they didn't know the Lord, and they let him grow up wild without knowing God. Suppose he had never found anybody who loved him or knew the Lord? It

was the baby's redemption, for now as long as the
Lord lets him stay with us, he'll be taught every day
about Him. We'll have to study the Bible and help
him to grow up knowing the truth. And it will be in
commemoration of the night he was saved, from
physical death, and spiritual, too."

"Yes," said Rand. "I thought of that too, only I
didn't know how to say it. I only wish we knew if the
little white mother in the cemetery knew God."

"Well, we've nothing to do with that of course.
God knows, and some day He will tell us, and explain it all, how everything happened, and we'll be
glad that it brought redemption and a new life to us
as well as to the little beloved child. Yes, I like the
name Ransom. It goes well with ours too. Ransom
Rand! That sounds very good. And when he goes to
school they'll call him Rannie."

"Yes," said Rand. "Until he gets in high school
and then they'll call him 'Rand' of course, and won't
know what it's all about. But we'll be sure that he
understands, himself, that his name means redemption, and the redemption of more than one! We'll
try to teach him that he owes it to the One who was
born on Christmas Day to save him, that he should
dedicate his life to saving others. He can write like
his foster father, or he can be in business as his play
mother was, or he can do any of the things that God
puts in the way of doing, but he must always remem-

ber that first and before everything else he must always be telling others about the wonderful Saviour, the baby Jesus, who was born to redeem him and others. He must always bear about in his mind the real meaning of his name, Ransom. Redemption! Isn't that good, Dale?"

"Yes, that is good!" said Dale. "There couldn't be a better name for the little boy he is. Oh, George, it is so wonderful that you who haven't been sure about your salvation till just these last few days, should know how to talk this way. I suppose it's because you're a writer and know how to say things."

"Think again, sweetheart! I had a mother who knew God well, and a father who, I believe, really loved Him, and they talked before me. I had a background of that sort. I don't remember how early they began to talk before me. My trouble was that I liked the world and wouldn't give in till God gave me trouble and disappointment for teachers. But I guess it doesn't just have to be that way. It's because we choose the way of trouble ourselves rather than to give up our own way."

They talked a long time, till dawn began to creep up the sky-way, and then softly below the open window a carol began to rise:

> This is the winter morn,
> Our Saviour Christ was born,
> Who left the realms of endless day

To take our sins away!
Have ye no carol for the Lord,
To tell His love, His love abroad?

"Dale, we'll have to make our lives a carol. Can't we?" said Rand as he turned on his pillow and prepared for sleep.

"We can," said Dale solemnly, "and we will, please God!"